FOLLOW
ME TO
THE EDGE

ALSO BY TARIQ ASHKANANI

Welcome to Cooper

FOLLOW
ME TO
THE EDGE

TARIQ
ASHKANANI

THOMAS & MERCER

Text copyright © 2022 by Tariq Ashkanani
All rights reserved.

Published by Thomas & Mercer, Seattle

www.apub.com

Amazon, the Amazon logo, and Thomas & Mercer are trademarks of Amazon. com, Inc., or its affiliates.

ISBN-13: 9781542031325
ISBN-10: 154203132X

Cover design by Ghost Design

Printed in the United States of America

For Sami

May 1993

The blood wasn't going to come off easily. It had long since dried.

The water was cold, which didn't help. Empty soap dispensers, too. It made Joe think of high-school bathrooms. Kids who used the mirrors to wipe their fingers dry; who wouldn't bother washing their hands after a piss even if there *was* soap.

That had been all Joe could think about on the ride over here. Getting clean. Sitting in the back of a cruiser, gliding along that straight, narrow highway in the dark. At some point it had started to rain. Heavy enough to dull the sounds of the road, to have the wipers on full. Joe had watched the droplets race along his window, his bloodied hands in his lap. They'd trembled all the way back to Cooper.

The icy water came off his skin rust-tinged. Progress of a kind, he supposed. He scratched at his fingers, digging at the clumps that had collected between his knuckles. The blood had splashed across his chest and down his legs. It was in his shoes.

The mirror in the bathroom was cracked. Shattered glass that sent a thousand of him back. Pale-faced, and with the right side of his blond hair matted with red. He must have run his hand through it. Afterward, maybe, while they'd waited by the side of the road. As the air cooled and the dusk settled. Together, the dead and the dying, and Joe, and the boy. And now his chest shook, and his hair was slick with another man's blood.

The detective at the door cleared his throat. Tossed him a towel. Joe took it, dried himself. When he was done the white material was red, and the detective pointed at the laundry hamper in the corner.

The guy had been his shadow ever since they'd picked Joe up at the scene. Three hours in a little room with nothing but a plastic cup and a growing urge to piss. Said his name was Fields. Said it like him and Joe had never met before, only they had. A bunch of times. Detectives never did pay much attention to lowly patrol officers.

Joe had told his story four times now, to four different people. People who nodded sympathetically and scribbled notes; people who got him coffees and offered him cigarettes. Offered him reassurances. That it had been a clean shooting, that Ballistics would back up his story. They'd taken his gun anyway.

"One of our own," they kept saying. They meant Frank. His partner. The guy who had just taken a faceful of buckshot during a routine traffic stop. Joe hadn't even thought; he'd just pulled his Smith and Wesson and returned fire.

"Come on," Fields said, pushing open the restroom door. "Weather's bad. I'll give you a ride home."

But Joe didn't want to go home. Didn't want to try to sleep; he knew what he'd see when he closed his eyes. Hell, he could see it with them open: the red Buick, pulled over to the highway's dusty shoulder ahead of them, its hazards flashing. The gleam of silver as Frank tossed the dime to decide who would approach. Frank's laugh as it landed. *Your lucky day*—his last words.

No, Joe wasn't going home.

◆ ◆ ◆

2

He got a ride to the hospital instead.

The waiting room was filled with the usual Friday-night clientele. Guys in football jerseys, chanting, leering at a woman passed out in the corner. Bar fights and drunken falls. Overdoses, people covered in vomit, holding their broken arms, holding each other. Joe pushed past a couple of hookers who catcalled him, calling him "baby" and "sugar." They were flying, their faces busted. A drunk clutched a bloody towel in his hands and lay across three seats, crying quietly. Joe spotted a single nurse trying to keep order. She brandished a clipboard like it was a shield.

Joe reached the edge of the throng and didn't stop. Through double doors and into a long corridor. Someone called after him—that nurse, maybe—but he kept going. His shoes squeaked on the linoleum floor. He was jumpy, his heart staccato. Every cry from a patient's bed was that kid howling from the back seat of the Buick. Every door slam was buckshot. Maybe he'd been wrong to come here.

He knew where he was going. He barely glanced at the signs, the muscle memory still fresh. Half a childhood spent here with his brother, then five years as a Cooper cop to fill in any gaps. He'd gotten to know the hospital all too well.

He dodged an orderly with a cart, barreled through another set of double doors and up two flights of stairs.

Emergency surgery. Cathy was sat outside in the waiting room, this one smaller but no less crowded. She'd been crying, her eyes red and puffy. No makeup; dressed in the first things that had come to hand. When she saw him, her face crumpled. He let her sob into his shoulder.

"Oh, Joe," she said. "They won't tell me what's going on with him."

And so they sat together in the corner of the room. Together, among the dead and the dying. Cathy slept on his shoulder and Joe slept too, and maybe he saw the red Buick and maybe he didn't.

They were woken by the doctor. An older man with white in his beard and tired eyes. Buckshot had caused Frank's brain to swell. He was in a coma.

They hoped it would only last until morning. But then morning came and Frank still slept. A day passed, and then another, and then a week went by and Frank went on sleeping. Cathy watched over him, every night by his bed. In a chair, her back breaking.

She couldn't sleep. Frank had stolen it from her.

Around them, the town moved on. People went to work, they ate takeout food and watched shitty movies, they got drunk and argued and cried and fucked, and through it all, Frank slept. He slept through the rain, the worst rain Joe had ever seen. Across the Midwest it pushed rivers so far over their banks, the flooded fields resembled not just lakes but inland seas. Cathy said it was a sign, said it was her husband hanging on, fighting to stay with her. Joe smiled and kept his opinions to himself.

Five months passed. Joe's shooting was ruled justified. The sergeant who gave him his gun back told him to go speak to someone if he ever felt emotional. Said it with a laugh. Closest that prick had ever come to shooting someone was at the local arcade. Probably liked to twirl the plastic handgun around his finger after blowing some zombie's head off.

Maybe what had happened to Frank was a catalyst. Maybe Joe had just gotten tired of sitting in a prowl car ten hours of the day. He finished his exams and got his detective's badge, and then on a warm day in October, when the rains finally stopped, three members of the Richardson family were bludgeoned to death in their beds. Three of them, and one just a baby.

Chapter One

The reservoir at the edge of Cowan's land had always held special memories for Joe. A bored kid growing up in a town like Cooper, most of those memories were sexual—like skinny-dipping on his sixteenth birthday with Holly Williams from the grade above. He'd lost his virginity to her about a quarter mile into the nearby forest not too long after. For years it had been impossible not to think about her whenever he drove past.

But now he was older. Now it was eight-fifteen in the morning and a man was dead on the banks of the reservoir. Now Joe knew that whenever he thought of this place, he would think of this.

Course, right now, Joe was mainly thinking about the weather. About how it was still so damned hot, even though it was the end of October. All spring and into the summer—crazy, biblical-scale flooding. And now the switch had been flipped. If Joe had been a praying person, he'd have figured it was God, turning the oven on high and skipping town.

The dirt slope down to the reservoir was baked, each step kicking up dust that settled on his newly polished black shoes. Already he could feel sweat breaking out on his forehead and under his arms. The sun had barely been up an hour; the air still hot from the day before.

The man had died right at the water's edge. Died sprawled on his back, his legs dangling in the lake. The water here was black, and it had traveled upward along his grey sweatpants in dark tendrils. Inky roots snaking up from the depths. Like a dead body wasn't unnerving enough.

Yellow tape was strung up around the scene. A young officer stood next to it, about as far away from the victim as he could get. Some folks just couldn't handle death. Joe knew this, had seen it in other officers time and time again. In their expressions, in their reluctance to engage. He'd seen it in their sick days and their shift trades, and every time he did he wondered why they chose to work in a place like Cooper.

A second man was crouched over the body. Rolled-up sleeves and purple gloves, a flash of light and a camera's whine.

"Morning, Bob," Joe said.

Bob swiveled round, his eyes crinkling against the sun. He smiled warmly and stood up. "Morning. Dispatch said Fields was on today."

"Fields went on a bit of a bender last night, asked me to trade shifts."

"Lucky Fields. Come to meet my new friend here?"

"We've not been properly introduced."

"Ah, well, that's because I don't know his name yet."

Joe nodded, peering closer at the body. There was a thin trickle of blood, now dried, leading down the left side of the man's chest from the edge of the knife protruding from it. A line of red running across his off-white T-shirt.

"What can you tell me?" Joe asked.

"Well, in my considered professional judgment, he died from a stab wound," Bob said. Then added, "Look, I got here a whole ten minutes before you did."

"And in those ten minutes, did you happen to work out how long he's been here for?"

"Rigor is pretty well set in, so I'd say sometime in the last four hours, maybe eight. Difficult to tell in this heat, though. Speeds up the process."

"There isn't much blood for a stab wound."

Bob shrugged, stretching a little, letting the camera swing on its strap around his neck. "Judging by the trauma site, I'd say he probably died from a pneumothorax. But I'll need to get a proper look at him."

Joe wiped at his brow. "Get him back to the station as soon as you can," he said. "Sun's going to cook him."

"Lucky I skipped breakfast this morning."

"Whose vehicle is that?"

Bob's gaze followed where Joe was looking. A rusted, maroon SUV sat a little farther along the bank of the reservoir. Beyond it stood another officer. He was talking to a woman.

"Vehicle belong to her, you think?" Joe asked.

"I don't know."

"Know who she is?"

"First witness on the scene. Out camping with her boyfriend, came across the body this morning. They had to drive a mile and a half into town to find a working payphone."

"Alright. Finish the victim. I'll check in with you later."

Joe moved away toward the yellow tape and the nervous young officer. His uniform looked near-enough brand-new, his collar buttoned tight around his neck. His name badge read *Gennero*.

"What can you tell me about that SUV?" Joe asked him.

"It was here when we arrived, detective."

"You boys run the plate?"

"Not yet."

"Uh-huh. Where's your cruiser parked? Up the path there?"

"Yessir."

"Good. I want you to run the plate back at the station, alright? Find me the owner."

"Oh, I can pull the owner's name from my car."

"I know you can. But I don't just want their name. I want their picture. Can't do that in your car. Run the plate back at the station and see if it belongs to our John Doe here. If it's a woman's, find out if she's married. Might be her husband, or her brother. Find me our victim's name."

The officer nodded vigorously. Happy to help; happier still to get away from the reservoir.

Joe turned and started walking back the way he'd come. Into the brush and up the slope toward his car. Already he was lost in the cool shade, climbing the dry verge back to the main road. Truth be told, he couldn't blame Officer Gennero for being jumpy around this place. Joe's memories of the lake were special, sure, but special didn't always mean good. Didn't always mean nice. He wasn't exactly shocked to have found a dead man washed up on its shore.

Something about this place had always given Joe the creeps. Since he was a kid, a nervousness rooted deep in the back of his mind. The way the morning light sank into the dark water, maybe. Like the lake was feeding off it, off everything around it.

There were times he forgot all about his sixteenth birthday. Forgot about the way his hands had shaken as he undid his belt, his eyes glued to the image of Holly Williams shedding her clothes, casually, like it was no big thing. Her pale skin made paler by the moonlight as she sank slowly beneath the surface. There were times he forgot he'd ever swam in that lake, and there were times he wished he'd never emerged.

Chapter Two

Joe checked his watch as he pulled up outside the school. It was just before nine. He'd nearly missed it.

Across the street, he watched as parents ran along the sidewalk and darted over the crosswalk. Clutching their kids by the hands and arms. One of them carrying his little girl out in front of him like she was an offering, racing to get her through the gates before they closed.

For a long moment Joe thought he *had* missed it. Not that it mattered much; today wasn't his first morning here, and likely wouldn't be his last, either.

It wasn't like he came every day—he wasn't obsessive.

He glanced down at the notebook lying on the passenger seat. Told himself he should've locked it away in the glove compartment. A man sitting outside a school with a notebook, watching the children arrive. He knew how it looked.

The radio played the morning news. The ongoing fallout of the Mississippi bursting its banks, what they were now calling the "Great Flood." A congressman shouting about Black Hawk Down, about American soldiers being dragged through the streets of Somalia. Repeated clips of President Clinton ordering a full withdrawal of American troops.

Across the street, he spotted her. Sarah Miller. A tall woman with shoulder-length blonde hair. Today it was tied up in a bun; messy, like she'd been in a rush. She was doing that crouch-run that parents do when they're trying to get their kid to hurry the fuck up. Behind her was a young boy in dark pants and a white shirt. His backpack was too big for him; his head was down as he walked. His name was Ethan.

Joe leaned closer to the window and wiped at his forehead. The morning heat was ridiculous. His car was old, a black Pontiac that was starting to rust. The AC barely worked—and besides, he knew the clatter of his idling engine would draw attention. He cracked the window. Let the warm air and the excited shouts of the school-yard roll over him.

He watched as Sarah and Ethan skirted the gate and bounded up the steps toward the main door. An older, plumper lady was manning the entrance, and she gave them a smile and a shake of her head. Ruffled the boy's hair as he went by. Joe felt himself shiver; he'd always hated people doing that to him.

Afterward, Sarah slumped off, visibly relieved. Joe didn't need to see what car she was headed to. A yellow Ford, license plate 2-D6875, with a dented front passenger door. She'd be heading to the grocery store, or the laundromat, or back home to her house next to the church. He watched her drive past him, his fingers toying with the key in the ignition.

His radio crackled. Dispatch, Officer Gennero trying to reach him. He picked up the receiver, squeezed the Talk button.

"Finch."

"Uh, detective?"

Christ. "Gennero, you run that plate?"

"Well, yeah, that's the thing . . ."

Joe sighed and rolled his neck. The Ford was still waiting at the intersection. Her turn signal flashing. "I don't have all day, officer."

"The captain wants to see you back at the station."

"What?"

Ahead of him, the light changed. The Ford moved off. Joe tracked it as it turned away and then it was out of sight.

"The car?" Gennero said. "It belonged to the victim."

"Yeah? What's his name?"

Joe started his car and pulled out. Spun a U-turn, toward the station. Away from the Ford.

"Victim's name is David Richardson," Gennero said. "Married, with one kid and a grandson. Lives on Memorial Park. It's out past—"

"Out past the sawmill. I know where it is. Have you sent a unit to check on the family?"

"Yessir. I went around there myself."

"And?"

There was a pause. Joe somehow knew what was coming next.

"They're dead, sir. They're all dead."

Chapter Three

The Richardsons lived out on Cooper's edge. That blurred line where the town began to fade into the cornfields. Where the narrow spaces opened and the light came in; where the birdsong replaced the police sirens.

That was the idea, at least. And not just for the Richardsons, but for each of the families living out here. Memorial Park: twelve little houses and a road that was already halfway to dirt, snaking away past the homesteads and into the rolling farmland beyond. Rows of corn, golden brown and stretching high above Joe's head. A dusty sweetness and the low drone of a combine. Harvest time.

Each house here was a statement—an attempt to leave behind Cooper's rotten core. They thought life out here would be better. Safer. The squadron of cars parked outside said otherwise.

The biggest mistake the Richardson family had made was thinking that a little distance was all that mattered. As though horror couldn't travel. Couldn't hop in the back of a dusty pickup. Couldn't get on its own two feet and just walk down the goddamn street if it had to. Horror was a man standing over your bed as you slept and it didn't matter one bit where you lived.

Joe parked his Pontiac down the road. It was nearly lunchtime and the vultures were circling; the concerned neighbors, the eager press, the rubberneckers. A dead family would keep them fed for weeks. He spotted Daniel Gonzalez, the reporter, short and fat with a camera in hand, pushing his way into the crowd. Nobody would gorge himself more than Gonzalez.

Officer Gennero hadn't said what the house number was. Joe had wondered about it the whole drive over. A one-in-twelve chance. Now, staring at the people pressed together on the neighboring lawns, he felt his stomach tighten.

Six Memorial Park. His childhood home.

Twenty years he'd spent avoiding this street; avoiding the shit it stirred inside him.

He told himself it wasn't his house anymore. Glimpsed the front door through the crowd. Half-open, swarming with men in white suits. The Richardsons had painted it red.

The temperature had continued to climb steadily all morning. Even with the AC turned to full, the heat in Joe's car was oppressive. He slipped his suit jacket off, used the lining to mop at his face. He rolled his shirtsleeves up past the elbow and adjusted his sunglasses. Popped open the door and climbed out into the dense, humid air.

People glanced at him as he approached. Maybe drawn to the glint of the morning sun on the badge clipped to his belt. Most turned away, but a handful of them started whispering to each other. "That's Joe Finch," he heard a woman murmur. "Alison's boy."

He flinched a little at hearing his mother's name, at being reduced simply to being *her boy.* Like he was eleven years old and helpless all over again. He glared at the lady as he passed by. She shrank back a little, her face reddening.

One man held his gaze. An older guy, with thinning grey hair and a white collar around his neck. First time Joe had ever seen a priest at a crime scene. The man gave a slight nod, then the crowd shifted and he was gone.

Moving through them, Joe saw Gonzalez waiting for him on the other side. The reporter was grinning, his wide face slick with sweat.

"Morning, detective," he called out.

"Gonzalez."

"Welcome home, Joe. Would you care to make a comment?"

"Not at this time."

"Six Memorial Park claims another family. Is it true they murdered the baby as well?"

Joe felt the kickback in his throat. Shot Gonzalez an angry look. The reporter barely flinched.

"Out of the way," Joe said.

He pushed past, motioning to the boy manning the tape. Stepped under to the sound of a camera flash. His own Hollywood moment.

Ahead of him lay the front yard and a handful of forensic guys in overalls. They milled about in silence, as though out of some sort of respect. Zoom in and there was that red door, standing open like it was inviting you in. A darkness inside; the curtains drawn but something more. He could feel it, even standing on the street in the hot sun he could feel it—a physical presence. It made him edgy, made him quiet. Made him want to get the hell away from it.

"Detective!"

Joe turned, saw a man in a Stetson ambling across the lawn toward him, hand half-raised in greeting. He was tall and slim, with thick stubble across his cheeks and a cigarette dangling from the side of his mouth. *Christ.*

"Brian Ackerman," Joe said as he approached.

"Joe Finch," Ackerman said, holding out his hand.

Joe shook it. "Mind if I ask what the hell you're doing here?"

"Captain hasn't spoken with you?" Ackerman frowned, pulling the brim of his hat down lower to block out the sun.

"Not yet," Joe said, "but I can probably guess what he's going to say." He sighed and stretched out his neck, ran his gaze over the house. Truthfully it wasn't a surprise. He was still fresh—Cooper's newest detective by nearly a decade. A dead man was one thing; a dead family was above his pay grade. What really rankled was who they'd given the case to.

Everybody on the force knew Brian Ackerman. A weirdo who lived out on the local trailer park. A burnt-out wreck of a detective who dressed like a cowboy and who'd transferred from some Texas shithole about six weeks back. Cooper only had a handful of detectives, but still, there was a certain sting in losing the case to someone like him.

"Look, it's nothing personal," Ackerman said.

"Yeah, I get it," Joe muttered, turning to leave. "It's all yours."

"No, it's ours."

Joe looked back. "What?"

"Captain said we're to work it together."

"I don't work with partners," Joe said, his face set. "It's nothing personal."

Ackerman shrugged. The guy had a good couple inches on Joe, and he hunched forward as he rolled the remains of his cigarette between two fingers. Blew smoke out slow and mashed the stub into a little metal tin he pulled from his pocket.

"Hey, I get it," he said. "This morning, it was your case. I didn't wake up and see the news and decide I wanted in. I just got the call, same as you."

"I didn't get a call," Joe said. "I took a shift and picked up a case. Now I'm being told I have to share it."

"For what it's worth? I prefer my own company as well. Been riding solo ever since I got here and it's suited me just fine. And look, you want to leave? Go for it. But there's a dead family in that house and whoever did it is still out there. You telling me you don't want to catch this guy?"

Joe grimaced. Ackerman was right. Personally, professionally—it wouldn't be right if he just walked away. Besides, out of the corner of his eye he could see Daniel Gonzalez, standing at the edge of the throng with his camera raised. Two arguing detectives would make a great front-page splash.

He forced a smile. "Partners it is."

Ackerman nodded. "Good man. Come on, let's go inside." He took off his hat and wiped at his brow, then started toward the house. Joe fell into step beside him. "Victims are all upstairs. It's mainly bedrooms and—"

"Three bedrooms, two bathrooms. One en suite. Small office downstairs and a pull-down ladder to the attic."

Ackerman paused. "Oh. You speak to Forensics already?"

"Didn't need to. You been inside yet?"

"Yeah."

"How is it?"

"Well, they were bludgeoned to death as they slept," Ackerman said, staring into the shadowy front doorway ahead of them. "So just about as bad as you'd expect."

For a moment, Joe saw it in his face. That little piece of the Richardson house that Ackerman had taken out with him. Joe recognized it, knew it was now his turn to go inside and take a little for himself.

He had started to say something when his pager went off. He frowned, digging in his pocket for it. Glanced at the numbers on the screen—Zoe's—before silencing the beep.

Ackerman's gaze was on the pager. "You need to get that?"

"No." Joe jammed it back into his pocket.

"You sure?"

"It's no one important."

His new partner nodded and motioned toward the front door. "After you," he said.

16

Chapter Four

That uncomfortable feeling persisted as they prepared to step inside. It wasn't wrong, what they were doing. It just seemed that way.

The last time Joe had passed through that doorway, he'd been eleven years old. It had been a warm day then, too. His father walking alongside him, his large hand on Joe's shoulder. The fingers trembling a little. No real weight to it, no reassuring squeeze. A gesture of affection that was more accidental than anything else. Even so, it was probably the closest he'd ever gotten to showing it.

Joe could still recall the gathered neighbors watching as he and his dad approached their car. The kids on their bikes, the mothers with their Tupperware containers and bottles of homemade iced tea. As if his father would forget to make him dinner, or more likely had never known how. Joe had waited in the passenger seat as his dad dutifully collected everything and stuck it on the floor of the back seat, mumbling his thanks.

The biggest mistake Joe had made that day was to look back. Back at the house as they pulled away. The sudden force of all those people staring at him, it made his stomach cramp. Like all the pity and all the shame in the world was concentrated outside his home.

He'd trained his gaze on the front door. Knew if he looked anywhere else, he'd find someone's stare. He'd see their sympathy, their regret—or worse, their relief. Relief that it wasn't their family this had happened to. Relief that he and his dad were moving away. *Keep the Tupperware! What's a dollar ninety-five to watch you leave?*

Joe hadn't wanted to see that. Not one bit. He'd thought about closing his eyes, only then people might think he was crying, and he didn't want *that* even more.

So he'd watched the front door as it receded behind them, until they left the street behind. And then he did cry—quietly, his head down. His father kept both hands on the wheel and said nothing. Could be he didn't know what to say. Could be he never even noticed.

And now Joe was back here, staring at that front door once again. He stood next to Ackerman and prepared himself. Together, they pulled on pairs of thin blue gloves and snapped plastic over their shoes, and the feeling of unease got worse. Joe tried to push it aside, add it to the ever-growing pile of shit he didn't want to think about.

They moved slowly through the still house. The first floor was quiet; muffled footsteps and the occasional camera's whine from upstairs. Cream carpets and striped wallpaper. A row of cherubs on the mantelpiece; cut-glass, cheap. No drawers lying emptied or upturned. No missing TV. Everything in its place and nothing as it should be.

The house was different in many ways, and yet it was so dreadfully familiar. The changes were all surface level, the real heart of the building left untouched. It seemed to build in Joe's chest with each step he took. The past coming back for him. Seeping from the walls, pressing itself against him. Snatches of his brother's laughter echoing through the empty rooms.

"Everything alright?" Ackerman asked.

He'd stopped in his tracks without even realizing it. Ackerman was watching him closely. Concern on his face. For Joe, for himself at being burdened with an anxious partner.

Joe cleared his throat. "Full disclosure, I've been here before."

"Oh yeah?"

"Yeah. I grew up here."

"You grew up in Memorial Park?"

"This house. I grew up in this house."

Ackerman fell silent. "Well," he said at last, "that's a hell of a coincidence."

"You don't know the half of it."

"What's the other half?"

"I don't really feel like getting into it. I'm sure one of the boys will fill you in at the station."

"You good?"

"I'm fine."

"Because you look—"

"I'm *fine,* Brian. Let's keep moving."

Ackerman scratched at his stubble, watched him for a moment longer. The air in here was sticky and thick. Joe could feel sweat building on the back of his shirt.

Finally, Ackerman turned and continued upstairs. Joe scowled and followed after.

The fourth step creaked loudly underfoot, same as it'd always done. Joe imagined someone climbing these in the dead of night. He tried going slow, tried rolling his plastic soles. The same tricks he'd used as a boy. Same level of success, too. Maybe the Richardsons were heavy sleepers.

Near the landing, Joe spotted the first sign. Ackerman pointed to it as they got close. Blood. Smeared across the wall at chest height, crimson on cream. Off the killer's shoulder, maybe. A carelessness as he left.

Joe could hear people moving around up here. A man in white drifted across the hallway ahead of them. That same uncomfortable feeling came back strong, like fresh vomit.

Ackerman took the first door on the left, pausing to look back.

"This was the girl, Emily's, bedroom," he said. "Seventeen years old."

"Used to be mine," Joe said quietly. He suddenly felt a little embarrassed, for reasons he wasn't quite sure of. He took a breath and stepped inside.

Emily Richardson was still in bed. Still lying on top of her sheets; it had been hot last night. Even with the windows open, the heat had hung around.

Her face was caved in. Nose broken, eye sockets purple and swollen. Her mouth hung slack. Fractured jaw most likely. Joe spotted a number of her teeth scattered around her. He forced himself to keep his gaze moving.

From the small window he could see the backyard and the start of the corn. The view was the only thing that hadn't changed about the room. A small desk now sat in the corner, a bunch of sci-fi posters on the walls. Movies Joe had heard of but never seen. *Blade Runner. Alien. 2001.* Bloodstains too. Impact splatter across the headboard. He tracked the droplets upward. There was red on the ceiling.

But perhaps the worst thing in the room was the little crib by the window. Joe stared at it, not quite able to bring himself to walk over.

"How old was the kid?" he asked.

Ackerman said, "Jacob. Four months."

"Jesus."

Joe breathed out slow and took one last look at Emily Richardson. Her hands were up by her head, both of them clenched into tight fists. He stepped closer. Tufts of hair were wrapped between her fingers.

"She didn't go fast," Ackerman said quietly, and it took Joe a sickening moment to realize what he meant.

Despite her massive head trauma, Emily hadn't died immediately. From the looks of things, she'd been aware of what was happening around her. Of what was happening to her son in his crib. Lying there, barely able to move, she'd torn out clumps of her hair.

Emily's mother, Marcy Richardson, lay in a crumpled heap on the floor of the master bedroom. Halfway between the large bed and the door.

Joe stood in the hallway and stared down at her. Had she been running from someone? Or had she heard the noises from Emily's bedroom and gone to investigate?

Her face was turned inward, buried in the crook of her arm like she'd tried to protect it. He could see the start of a deep welt across the exposed cheek. The blow that dropped her, maybe. Once she'd fallen, it didn't look like she'd gotten up again. The back of Marcy's skull had been beaten so severely that the bone had cracked. Her head was pulped, her dark hair matted with blood.

The brutality of the attacks was plain to see. A frenzied assault that seemed at odds with David Richardson's single knife wound. And yet there was something methodical about it all. The way the killer had caught each of them in their bedrooms; the lack of an obvious motive. This wasn't a robbery gone wrong. This was a planned attack.

"Do we know what was used?" Joe asked.

"Tire iron," Ackerman said. "Killer dumped it next to Marcy Richardson."

"Guessing it wasn't his then. Anyone check David Richardson's vehicle by the lake?"

"Forensics still working it. You think it came from the car?"

"Maybe. If it was parked in the driveway, the killer could have popped the trunk and taken it in with him."

"Then what?" Ackerman said. "He bludgeons Richardson's wife, daughter, and grandson—what, while Richardson watches? Then drives him across town in the guy's own car?"

"I'm just thinking out loud here."

"And then he stabs Richardson to death when they get out there?"

Joe shrugged.

Ackerman just looked at him for a long moment, then said, "Come on, there's more," and gestured toward one of the forensics guys heading out of Emily's room. The man was carrying a bundle of objects zipped into little plastic evidence bags, and Ackerman reached out to take one. "We found one of these on each of the bodies," he said, holding it up. "Whoever killed them must have put them there."

Joe stared at the clear bag. Inside was a small, stuffed bear. A child's toy. He took it off his partner and ran a gloved finger over it. A pair of glassy eyes stared back.

"What does this mean?" Joe asked, but Ackerman just shrugged.

Afterward, they retreated down the stairs and into the kitchen. A small mound lay on the floor, a white sheet pulled over it.

"The family dog," Ackerman said, looking at it. "A Labrador, I think."

There was no blood anywhere. "Killer poisoned it?"

His partner nodded.

Joe crouched down next to the body, felt an urge to place his hand on the sheet. "Any reports of barking?"

"None."

"So the killer might have been known to the family."

"Uh-huh."

Ackerman moved to the large sliding glass door that looked out onto the yard. Beyond was the cornfield. Stalks that shifted silently in the breeze. "This was unlocked when we got here." He slid the door open. A rush of warm air and a sweetness along with it. A childhood scent, a memory trigger. Cowboys and Indians, out in the corn.

Joe stepped into the yard and imagined the killer doing the same. Thirty seconds, walking slow, to reach the fields. He knew; he'd done it countless times himself. He also knew how dark it got out here at night without streetlights, how easy it was to hide in the corn.

It would have been the simplest thing to wait here until the family had gone to bed. Just as simple to disappear back into it once it was over. Forensics would go over every inch of this place, but the yard was scorched brown, the cornfield's earth baked hard as a clay pot. No sense irrigating this late in the season. Good luck lifting a footprint from any of it.

Eleven other houses and not one of them would have spotted a man just strolling through the corn.

Joe ran his gaze over the shadowy crops and thought of the black water at the lake. Pockets of darkness, both of them. Hollow caverns that he'd played in, fallen in, lost himself in completely. Openings to another world from which evil could emerge. It had done so at Cowan Reservoir, and it had done it again here. Just like it had to Joe and his family all those years ago.

Later, when the sun had finally set and the heat had lessened a little, Joe went home. His apartment was on the east side. A small, dirty building on the corner of a rough block. He climbed the stairs slow tonight. The stairwell echoing with the sounds of TV shows and people yelling.

Inside, an old pug came waddling over to greet him. Joe smiled, reaching down and scratching the spot he knew Leo liked, at the base of his neck. The dog groaned happily and pressed his head against Joe's leg, his tail wagging.

A lamp on the foyer table gave off a soft glow. Had he left it on? A question answered by the note next to the phone, neat little handwriting that he recognized straightaway. *Came to pick up some things. I fed Leo.* The plumbing rattled as he read it; a neighbor above him flushing their toilet.

His place was small. A waist-high partition separated the kitchen from the sofa bed in the living room. A punching bag hung by the television set in the corner. Only the bathroom provided any real privacy.

All of which rendered Zoe's note pretty worthless. Now that he really looked, it should've been obvious from the moment he stepped in. Some detective. She'd just taken *some things*, but the place seemed emptied already. A life missing from it. The black strap of a bra peeking out from the hamper the only evidence left behind. Joe stared at it, unsure of what to do or how to feel.

He dumped his holster on the sofa. Poured himself a glass of milk. Leo trotted to his bed in the corner of the room and curled up next to his brown ducky. Joe sat on the floor next to him, resting a hand on his warm back. He stayed there a long while, listening to the sounds of the people living around him. When he finally showered, the water was cool and refreshing, and before long he was asleep, still wrapped in a towel, stretched out across the sofa.

Laura

Laura had already thrown up once this morning. Twice, the night before. A night spent huddled in the undergrowth, waiting for hours in the tall grass that lined the long road out of town. Sitting in the front seat of Francine's car, she could still smell the outdoors on her clothes.

Around them, the world was changing. The dying gasp of the predawn black. Already the fields were taking shape, the morning twilight giving form to the rippling stalks.

They drove in silence. How long ago had Francine picked her up? It seemed that hours had passed since Laura had called her, trembling in the warm phone booth, her fingers dialing the numbers on reflex. Numbers she hadn't dialed in years—was half-amazed she still knew.

The road had started to wind. She gripped the door handle to steady herself. The buildings were far behind them now, the fresh harvest scent replaced by the rusted tang of blood. Her clothes were splattered with it.

"Now listen, when we get there . . ." Francine started, but Laura had bolted upright. Her stomach fluttering, her abdominal muscles going taut.

"Stop," she managed.

And before Francine had pulled over completely, Laura was opening the door and tumbling onto the shoulder. Retching, puking up bile in a thin spray, some of it landing on her hands as she crouched over the dusty road.

She could feel her heart pounding in her ears, could taste the vomit, hot and sour like milk gone bad. Her throat ached. She imagined acid scars trailing down to her belly.

"You done?" Francine said, still sitting behind the wheel. "We should go."

Time passed, back in the passenger seat, curled into a ball as they drove. Francine's hand stroking her forehead. "Everything will be alright," she said. "We're almost there."

Laura nodded, finally finding her regular voice. "I've never done anything like that before."

"I know."

"There was . . ." She trailed off, turning to stare out the window. *There was so much blood.* She'd known there would be, of course. She wasn't stupid. But it hadn't been the blood that had shocked her, not really. It had been the *feeling* of it. The power—the rush that had come over her. The overriding sensation that what she was doing was *right*.

The rows of corn seemed to ebb and throb around them; these living things, pulsing with energy as they traveled deeper into farm country. This far out, it almost seemed like the end of the world. Here and there a long-vacant farmhouse falling in on itself, spared demolition for one reason or another. The scraps the family farmers had left behind after they were finished selling out. Twenty years of slow collapse. A wasteland of vast, commercial cornfields and the occasional massive processing complex.

Laura knew that, in a few hours, ranks of towering harvesters would begin trundling out of those buildings and into the fields, piloted by invisible drivers sealed in their air-conditioned cabs behind smoked glass. She wondered how far she and Francine would need to travel out here before they came across another truly living soul.

There were times she thought she saw lights on the horizon; the hues of red and blue drifting between the golden husks. She watched everything move and shift, and in her sleep-addled mind the fields became their protectors, shielding them from harm. She pictured police cars wandering through them like rats in a maze, the road twisting back on itself to send them in the wrong direction.

When sleep finally took her, the last thing she saw was the endless road ahead of them. It was hard to track how far they'd driven; the last sign they'd passed had been miles back, when they'd left town. Dinged up and hanging at an angle. *Thanks for visiting Cooper,* it had read. *Please hurry back!*

Chapter Five

Joe struggled to get much sleep after the house. Every time he drifted off, Memorial Park brought him back. It burrowed into his brain like a cancer. Cases like this, it was all about how much you could take before you gave in. Some people fed off it. Others burned out. Too soon to tell where he was headed.

He finally snatched a couple of hours. Then the clock hit five and he was more awake than ever. Running through his morning routine: push-ups, crunches, pull-ups on the bar across his bathroom doorway. The punching bag next to the TV; sixteen reps while his coffee brewed. He drank a cup standing by the window in his bare feet.

It was another scorcher. The air in his apartment was heavy and it seemed to press against his lungs, like a dumbbell on his chest. Like it wanted to suffocate him. Opening the windows didn't matter much; there wasn't a breeze. Maybe that's what had kept him up all night. Maybe it wasn't the house after all.

It was a nice thought.

He dressed down a little today; loosened tie, top button on his shirt undone, sleeves rolled up. Not that it helped. He still had a nice glisten on by the time he reached his Pontiac. The AC rattled all the way to the hospital.

Cooper Memorial had been pretty rundown for just about as long as Joe could remember. A big, ugly building, it stood at the edge of what used to be the industrial side of town—before those industries bolted overseas or slunk south to Mexico. Cracked brickwork and rusted pipes, the hospital had never looked like a place you'd go to for help. It looked like a place you'd go to die.

Frank was lying in a bed in a room by himself. Cathy wasn't here but there were traces of her. An old jacket draped over the back of a chair, a half-empty cup of coffee, a toiletry bag on the bedside table.

Joe stood in the doorway for a moment, just watching Frank sleep. Hard to believe it had been so long now. Five months he'd been lying in that bed. Hooked up to machines to help him breathe, help him piss, help him live. If you could call it that.

He moved into the room and sank into one of the chairs by Frank's bed.

"Morning, pal," he said quietly. "Sorry it's been so long. I've been . . . busy."

At first it had been strange, talking to Frank like this. Like he was talking to himself. He'd been self-conscious, worried about being overheard by nurses coming in to collect Frank's piss bags or to give him a sponge bath, each of them wishing the other wasn't there in that moment. But after a while that had faded. After a while it had actually been pretty nice to come here and unload. Frank didn't judge whatever Joe told him. Didn't take offense or tell him he was doing something wrong. Frank just took it all in.

"I been working that new case," Joe said. "Some sicko killed an entire family. Mom, dad, daughter, grandkid even. Bludgeoned most of them in their beds with a tire iron. Who does that? Damn thing's given me the creeps."

He stretched a little, ran his gaze around the room. There were fresh flowers on the windowsill, and a tape deck with a small pile of cassettes next to it. He imagined Cathy listening to them as she sat by his bedside.

The doctors had done a decent job with Frank's face. Ten hours in the operating room picking buckshot out of his fractured skull; another couple of weeks for the swelling to start to go down. The surgeon said Frank had gotten lucky the driver fired before he got any closer. Another ten feet and it would've been a closed casket.

"Oh, you'll be glad to hear Zoe finally moved out," Joe said, settling back in the chair. "I know, I know, you called it months ago. It's my fault anyway. Lately I can't seem to relax, can't seem to just be happy with what I got. Feel like I've been on edge ever since you ended up in here."

There was movement by the door, and Joe turned to see Cathy standing there. She gave him a sad smile as he got to his feet. She was wearing an oversized sweater, the sleeves riding down to her palms. Joe wondered how she wasn't melting in that thing, then realized she probably hardly ever left the air-conditioned hospital. Then he wondered if the sweater had belonged to Frank.

"Morning, Joe," she said. Her eyes weren't red anymore, not like they'd been at the start. At the start she hadn't been able to stop crying. Like there was a faucet inside her that Frank's shooting had broken. But now the water was gone—had been for a while. Joe guessed that was just what happened when something like this went on for so long. Life didn't give you time to cry for five months. Life gave you a couple of weeks, max, then it came calling for your mortgage, your electricity. All the other shit that didn't care about your loss.

"Morning," Joe said. "Just thought I'd drop by and see how he's doing."

She nodded and they embraced. She felt so thin and small, Joe worried she might snap if he squeezed too tight. She went and curled up on the other chair.

"Well, as you can see he's doing fine," she said, gazing at Frank. "Same as ever."

"What about you?"

"Me?" Cathy gave another sad smile. "I'm fine, Joe. Really."

"You eating right?"

"Sure. Why, I don't look it?"

"I'm just asking."

"I don't really have much appetite these days."

"You got to take care of yourself, Cathy."

"So you keep telling me."

"Ah. Sorry."

Cathy let out a heavy sigh as she stared at her sleeping husband. "You know I got a letter the other day?"

"Yeah?"

"From Frank's health insurance. I've missed the last couple payments."

Joe shifted on his chair. "What?"

"You wouldn't believe how much it costs for something like this. Even *with* insurance, I don't have enough to keep him here." Cathy let out a bitter laugh. "He's got until just after Halloween, then his time's up. Not that it matters. Doctors say that after six months, the chances are slim to none of him ever waking up."

"But, what'll—"

"Oh, he'd tell me to just turn off the machines, anyway. And he'd probably be right." She took a deep breath, let it out. "I just can't afford to keep Frank alive after the end of the month."

Joe sank back into his chair. Cathy went quiet after that. The only sounds were the beeps and clicks of the machines, the gentle sighs of the ventilator. There was a sickness to the whole thing that went beyond the physical. An unfairness you couldn't treat. Frank was being kept alive only so he could be left to die. Shot in the face by a scared man with a scattergun and finished off by an insurance broker three states over.

Joe stayed for another ten minutes or so. They didn't talk much after that. Just sat together and watched Frank sleep. They embraced again when Joe left, and he glanced back into the room as he waited for the elevator. Cathy was in her seat, her legs curled up beneath her, her arms hugging her waist. A sudden anger moved through him, and he had to grit his teeth and force himself to swallow it back down.

A stack of newspapers was piled by the exit to the parking lot. The headline of the *Tribune* read MEMORIAL PARK MURDER HOUSE CLAIMS SECOND FAMILY. And underneath it, in italics, *Surviving Son Returns—But Will He Crack Again?* The rest of the page was taken up with a photo of the Richardson house, the front wrapped in police tape, the shot taken just as Joe was stepping under it.

"Gonzalez," Joe muttered. The anger came back hard, and this time he didn't care.

Chapter Six

Captain Harris was a pacer.

He paced around his small office like an animal testing its cage. It was a stress thing. Some folks lose their tempers, shout and slam drawers and pound their fists on tables. Others go real quiet, like they're running calculations in their heads. Joe figured the second type was the worst. He'd once seen another officer calmly listen to the news that his partner had been promoted over him. Guy took it in like it was the local weather forecast. Then he walked out of the station and used a baseball bat to unload on his buddy's windshield.

But Harris was a pacer. He'd grind the stress out through his boots. Joe could see him through the mottled window; a shadow figure gliding back and forth across the glass. And he was a mutterer, too—liked to give off a good, dark diatribe as he paced, especially when things really started pinching him. He was at it now, his stream of consciousness growing louder as Joe approached and entered without knocking.

Harris stopped mid-sentence. Joe caught the words "Bottom-feeding sonuvabitch" before he did. The captain had read the morning paper.

"Get in here and close that door," Harris snapped.

Ackerman was already there, leaning against one wall with his hat dipped, both hands plunged into his pockets. Joe caught his eye and sent him a nod.

"Have you seen this?" Harris said. He pointed to a copy of the *Tribune* on his desk.

"Yeah, I've seen it," Joe said, sinking into a chair.

"Goddamn Gonzalez."

"He's a parasite."

Harris snorted in what might have been agreement. The captain finally stopped moving and scratched at his bald scalp, running a hand over the bare skin. He stared at Joe. "And *you*," he said. Irritation flared and died on the man's face. "Dammit, Joe, did you really have to take this case?"

"It wasn't meant to be mine. Fields phoned in sick, I just picked it up."

"I know Fields is sick. I got half a mind to give it to him anyway."

"I didn't know it was my old place until I got there."

"Which was precisely when you should've turned to Ackerman and begged off. Told him you've got history there."

"It's a coincidence, sir, that's all. Far as I'm concerned, it's just another case."

"Another case that you know the *Tribune* is going to jump all over. Gonzalez is whipping everyone into a frenzy, like we don't have enough to deal with."

There was a silence after Harris finished. The man sat down heavily in his chair. He looked exhausted. He turned to Ackerman. "What do you think?"

"I think I'm playing with half the pieces missing. Be helpful if someone told me what this reporter's hard-on is all about."

Harris blinked. "Christ. You don't know. Course you don't." He sighed and rubbed his face. "Did you read this morning's paper?"

Ackerman glanced over at Joe. "I skimmed it."

"It started with Benjamin West," Harris said. "Teenager shot dead in a playground about three years ago. Couple toddlers found

34

his body on the . . . spinner thing." He twirled his finger in a circle. "The merry-go-round."

"Got it."

"Victim was a local dealer," Joe added. "His family had some connections to organized crime. We figured it was a drug-related homicide."

"Still unsolved?" Ackerman said.

"Don't I wish," Harris muttered. "One of my officers claimed to have gotten carjacked, lost the whole file. Witness statements, forensic reports, everything."

"Ouch."

"It gets better. Few months later, he invites a bunch of us around to his place for a poker game. Someone goes looking for a bottle opener—paperwork turns up in his kitchen drawer."

Ackerman frowned. "Someone paid him to lose the file?"

"Didn't pay him enough, clearly. Shit hit the fan around town after that. People got pissed. Gonzalez appointed himself their spokesperson, made a name for himself."

"For *three years*?"

"Tacked one story onto the next. Kept beating that same drum. Police corruption, ties to organized crime. Far as he's concerned, I'm either dirty or incompetent."

"What's this got to do with Memorial Park?"

Harris grunted and jerked his head toward Joe. "Your partner can fill you in on that later. Suffice to say, I just got off the phone with the mayor this morning. He's asked for someone from Lincoln to come down and—how did he put it—*lend a hand*."

Joe shifted in his chair. "That sounds ominous."

"I've already presided over one fuck-up, Joe. I don't think they'll let me get away with another. Especially not once Gonzalez starts beating that drum again."

"So having me work this case is a fuck-up, now?"

"With that house and your history? Of course that asshole's going to work that angle. You're gasoline on the fire."

"You're giving this prick more credit than he deserves. He's one reporter on a crappy little rag. He's not going to sink your career."

"Not just mine."

"You know, I'm not scared by that slimy shit heel—"

Ackerman cleared his throat. "What if we just neutralized this Gonzalez?"

Harris glared at him. "What?"

"What about giving him an exclusive? First in line to any official updates . . . Opening question at any press conference. Who knows? Might even be able to use him as a tool instead of him being a pain in our asses."

"Coddle the bastard?" Joe grumbled. "What kind of plan is that?"

Harris ignored him. Went quiet, staring at Ackerman's Stetson as he mulled it over. He let out a long sigh. "Fine," he said at last. "Go talk with him. And Joe? I'm not going to take you off this, but I do want to make it doubly clear that Brian is lead detective. He's got more experience than you, it's as simple as that. Think of this as a learning opportunity."

Joe had to fight not to roll his eyes as he stood up. "Fine with me."

"Good. Now check in with Bob when he's finished with the preliminaries. And see if uniforms are done canvassing the area. I want statements from the neighbors—somebody must have seen something. And yeah, do what you can about Gonzalez, but for the love of Christ don't wind the guy up any further."

Outside Harris's office, Ackerman said, "You hungry?"

"Sure," Joe said. "I could eat."

"Great. Let's go finish up with Bob and then get some breakfast. Be good to have a proper talk."

Chapter Seven

The morgue at Cooper PD was in the basement. Down a narrow set of stairs from the main hallway and through a doorway draped in plastic sheets. It was the gateway to another world. Inside, an air-conditioning unit that swirled an icy breeze around white-tiled walls. A light that made you squint. A silence that reverberated in your chest cavity.

And the chill wasn't wholly artificial: Joe spotted what was surely the sheeted Richardsons lying on metal trolleys in the corner of the room. His bare skin prickled. One floor up it would soon be cresting ninety degrees outside, but down here you wouldn't know it. One floor up, the whole damn world might as well have been on fire.

Bob was sitting behind a desk, peering at his computer screen. He glanced up as the two detectives approached. Joe was suddenly aware of the sound of a piano playing softly in the background.

"Morning, Bob," Joe said.

"Morning," Bob said, smiling warmly. He stood up and cracked his back. He looked tired; dark shadows under his eyes, his skin pale. Joe wondered how many hours straight he'd been working down here. Cooper didn't have a big forensics team. Four bodies would keep them busy.

"How you getting on?" Ackerman asked.

"Well, it's slow progress."

"And I'm not trying to rush you. We'd rather it was done right than fast."

"I appreciate that." Bob came out from behind the desk and went over to those metal trolleys. Four sheets pulled tight over four heads. One of them noticeably smaller than the others. Joe tried not to look at it.

Bob selected a trolley, grasped the handles, and pulled it into the center of the room. "I'm about done with David Richardson if you're interested in my findings."

Ackerman stepped forward, notebook in hand. "Very interested, Bob."

Bob snapped on a glove and pulled back the sheet. Richardson's naked body was almost white; a wide chest and a little middle-age spread. Autopsy scars ran down his front like roads on a map. Bob reached up and pulled on a metal chain hanging from the ceiling. A fluorescent bulb pinged to life and everything went purple.

"As I suspected," Bob said, "Mr. Richardson's cause of death was cardiac arrest, brought on by a tension pneumothorax caused by a traumatic penetrating injury. Specifically, a stab wound from a knife that was recovered in situ."

Bob leaned closer. The detectives followed.

"The incision of the blade is on the left side of the chest. It missed the heart by a few inches but it did impact on the left lung, here. Punched straight through to the pleural cavity. The organ would have collapsed almost immediately."

Joe said, "What does that lead to, exactly?"

"Well, once the lung was breached, air would work its way into the space between his lung and chest wall. Without any way to release the building pressure, Mr. Richardson would have very quickly found himself in a lot of trouble. Cardiac arrest, respiratory failure, shock."

"Death?"

"Within minutes."

Ackerman: "What can you tell us about the knife?"

"An all-purpose kitchen blade. The type found in nearly every home in America."

"Has one been found in *this* home?"

"We noted an empty space in a knife block on the kitchen countertop. If the blade fits . . ."

The older detective caught Joe's eye. "Is there any way for you to tell who used the knife?"

Bob gave a wry smile. "I was hoping you'd ask me that. Now, normally in a stabbing death like this, with the stab wound being where it is, the deceased is the victim of a knife attack by a perpetrator. In the case of Mr. Richardson, however . . ."

He trailed off and ran a gloved index finger down the man's bare chest. "Do you see the little nicks here? Around the main wound site?"

Joe squinted.

Ackerman stood up straight. "What are they? Hesitation marks?"

"Full marks for Detective Ackerman," Bob said.

"Jesus."

Joe glanced between them. "Hesitation marks?"

"Yes," Bob said.

"Meaning . . . ?"

"Meaning whoever stabbed Mr. Richardson was nervous about doing so. Rattled the tip of the blade against his chest a couple times before taking the plunge, so to speak. Add in the fact that the only fingerprints we found on the handle belonged to the deceased . . . It's my view that this was a suicide."

"A *suicide*? You're serious?"

"It's not as unusual a method as you might think."

Ackerman said, "Anything on the car?"

Bob leaned back against his desk, snapped off his glove. "Forensic report just came in. Let me get you a copy. The only solid fingerprints found on the steering wheel and dashboard belonged to either David or Marcy Richardson. No one else has driven this car for a long time."

"What about the tire iron?"

"Was taken from the garage by the looks of things. And David Richardson's prints were the only ones pulled from it."

Joe ran through it all in his head. Stared down at the pale face on the metal slab. Imagined him at home, waking up in the night, lying there in the darkness. An urge that had been building inside him finally too strong to ignore.

"Thanks, Bob," Ackerman said, sliding his notebook back into his pocket. "You got anything else?"

"I got some crime-scene photos for you." Bob reached behind him and picked up a folder from his desk. Handed it over, along with the forensics report. "I'm still waiting on the tox screening. Those boys are backed up at the moment. I'll make a start on the rest of the family today. Let you know if anything else turns up."

"Good work."

Together they left the morgue and climbed the stairs to the hallway. When they got to the top, Ackerman checked his watch. It was nearly ten.

"Well then," he said, clamping the folder under his arm, "how about that breakfast?"

Chapter Eight

They headed to a place around the corner, a couple of blocks from the station. The Starlight Diner. Ackerman lit up the moment they were outside, making small talk from the corner of his mouth. A rambling diatribe about closing your windows to keep out the heat. Joe only half-listened.

The houses they passed were decked out in their Halloween finest. Pumpkins and broomsticks, fake cobwebs that stretched above the front doors. Ackerman motioned toward them with his cigarette.

"Seems wrong, doesn't it?" Ackerman said.

"What's that?"

"It's Halloween in less than a week, and I swear I've sweated off five pounds just today. I thought it was meant to be cold in Nebraska?"

"You're so sweaty, why don't you lose that damn cowboy hat? Looks hot as hell."

"Because it's the only thing keeping the sun out my eyes."

Joe grunted. "You'd been here earlier in the year, you wouldn't be complaining."

"All that rain?"

"Wasn't just *rain*, Brian. People building arks, all across the Midwest."

"I got here for the last of it. Soggy mess, I'll give you that. Had me wondering what I'd volunteered for. Just about traded my cowboy boots for hip waders."

"Yeah, well—all this heat now? It's course correction. Just making up for a lost summer."

"So you're saying I should be thankful it's so hot."

"I'm just saying don't complain too much about the weather. People round here might not take your side."

"Duly noted," Ackerman said, grinding the stub of his cigarette into that metal tin of his. "All I meant was, people sure seem jazzed about Halloween. All these decorations. I would have thought a murdered family might put a damper on the festivities."

"No chance of that. It's the Halloween Harvest. Cooper goes all out every year."

Ackerman slid the tin back into his pocket, pushed open the door to the Starlight Diner. "Yeah, well, fun is fun, I guess."

Inside the cool, air-conditioned building, they were greeted by a stocky woman wearing what looked like every condiment they served down her apron. She took them to a booth, fanning her clammy face with a pair of menus. Joe watched her, wondered how she could still be sweating so badly inside. He wondered how old she was. If she was older than his mom had ever been. He blinked the thoughts away as he slid into the booth.

The waitress poured them each a tall glass of water and a cup of coffee. The walk from the station hadn't been short enough; Joe drained half his water in a single gulp, wincing a little as the cold moved down his chest. He sat back and loosened his tie further. Played with his ice as he watched his partner scan the menu, murmuring the options as he went. "The pancake classic," Ackerman said to himself. "The pancake special. The pancake deluxe," and so on.

Joe tuned him out. Let the events of the past twenty-four hours push older memories aside. It was usually a pretty effective way to cope. Hard to feel the impact of the past when the present dulled it almost completely. Course, just now it meant allowing other, more horrible images into his mind. Images that blocked out any thoughts of his mom, of his brother. Of his dad—of being abandoned when he needed a father the most. Maybe that was why he'd become a cop. To see the nastiest stuff he could find. To bathe in it, to let it numb those childhood years just a little. Now the Richardsons flickered behind his eyelids every time he blinked. The bedroom, the baby, the man lying by the black lake.

"Why does everything have to be a combo of some kind?" Ackerman asked.

"What?"

"On the menu, why does it all have to be a *classic* or a *special*? What's wrong with just saying *pancakes*, you know? Let the customer decide what he wants with them."

Joe nodded and ran his eyes over the diner. It was quiet: a man sitting by himself at the counter, a couple over by the window. Joe had been here before, a bunch of times, and he didn't think he'd ever seen it this quiet.

"I mean, what even is this?" Ackerman said, shaking his head. "The French toast sandwich? A *sandwich*?"

Joe sighed. "It's two slices of French toast with a fried egg and sausage in between."

"You've tried it?"

"No, I haven't tried it, it's just that it explains what it is right there on the menu, Brian. Right under the words *French toast sandwich*. You ever use a menu before?"

Ackerman stared at him for a moment. "Well, alright. Didn't mean to get you all riled up."

"I'm sorry. I'm just tired."

"It's the heat, I'm telling you. You get a chance to go home today? Draw those curtains and—"

"Close my windows. Yeah, I'll do that."

"But you've got to remember to open the window up again at night if it gets cooler—that's the key part. Regulate the airflow a little. Hey, you got a ceiling fan, right?"

"It's broken," Joe said, picking up his menu and pretending to study it.

"Got to get that seen to. Forecast says it's only going to get hotter."

"Fantastic," Joe muttered.

The waitress returned, wiping her glistening palms down her apron as she fished for a notepad. "You boys ready?"

Joe ordered an iced tea.

Ackerman cleared his throat before leaning forward. "Now, I'd like the pancake deluxe, but can you hold the sausage and the eggs, and add a side of bacon onto that?"

"You just want pancakes with bacon?"

"Ma'am, that is exactly what I want."

She scribbled it down and collected their menus.

Ackerman looked over. "See? They're overcomplicating matters."

"Right."

Joe took another drink. Ackerman seemed to gaze around the diner for the first time. The TV news played mutely in the corner. Footage of Mandela accepting some peace award.

"It always this quiet in here?" Ackerman asked.

"No, I'd say this is unusual."

"It's after ten. Maybe we're a little late for the breakfast crowd."

Joe shook his head. "It's not just the diner. You didn't notice how empty the streets were this morning?"

"You think the whole town is quiet?"

"Don't you?"

His partner shrugged. "I've only been here six weeks. I'm still trying to get a grip on the place."

"Cooper is . . ." Joe searched for the word. "Unique."

"I get the impression folks around here don't much like outsiders."

"It's a small town, Brian. With a mentality to match."

"Anything in particular I should be looking out for?"

Joe made a noncommittal noise as he lifted his coffee. "People here are suspicious by default. Of people they don't know, of people trying to change things. There's rampant superstition, there's mob rule, there's safety in numbers. Most people in this town own at least three firearms, and nearly every one of them will sleep with it within arm's reach. Year in, year out, our crime rate is ridiculous—robberies, carjackings, hustling. We're *achievers*. You walk certain streets at night, you're almost certainly going to get confronted by a hooker or a mugger. Hardly the norm in a rural town like this. Drug abuse three times the national average. It's a cliché, but this place is a tinderbox. Always has been—in my lifetime, anyway. We've just been lucky enough that it's never truly ignited. And the great majority of the people that live here . . . Hell, they've lived here so long they've forgotten what else it can be, or what it might have been like before."

"And now the Richardson murders."

Joe nodded. Placed his coffee down on the table and leaned forward. "These murders—it's more than just one family. It's the whole town that's affected. We don't solve this case soon? People *will* start taking justice into their own hands. I'm talking newcomers, foreigners, people who don't believe in God. Anyone who doesn't spend their Sundays in church or every other day getting loaded."

"Boy, Cooper sure does sound like a swell place."

The waitress returned with their orders. Placed a large plate of pancakes in front of Ackerman, slid a tall glass of iced tea across the table to Joe. He took a long drink.

"I am absolutely starving," Ackerman said, pouring a thick layer of maple syrup over his breakfast. The smell of it made Joe wince. "I can't believe this is my first time here."

"Where were you before Cooper?"

"Texas. San Antonio. Eleven years."

"Why the hell did you come here?"

"I didn't want to work in a big city anymore. This place?" He waved a wide circle in the air with his knife. "You make it sound bad, and I'm sure it's got its moments, but it's nothing like what I was seeing there. Violence on an unimaginable scale. Cults of crazies burning themselves to death. Gangs—gangs of kids, Joe. Fourteen years old and they're selling crack on street corners. They're murdering each other, and for what? Some bullshit turf war? You know how many drive-by shootings we had last year? Over a *thousand.*" He cut a large slice out of his stack. "There's only so many times you can put the same person in a cell. Watch the same kid get pulled in further and further, until one day you turn up at a crime scene and pull back the sheet and there they are—the end of their story. Nothing ever changes. I wasn't a cop, I was an accountant. A bean counter, except the beans were corpses. Just noting down the violence. I couldn't do anything about it there."

"You think you can do something about it here?"

"Sure. More than I could down south, anyway."

Joe shook his head. "I think you might be in for a surprise, my friend."

"I don't think so," Ackerman said, chewing. "I mean, here I don't get shot at, I don't get threatened by gangbangers. I don't wake up anymore when someone shoots out my front window."

"You sleep through it?"

"Very funny. What about you? What's your story? What's with the whole no-partner thing?"

Joe paused for a moment, a jumble of memories suddenly rushing over him. He wondered how much to tell Ackerman. How much he *wanted* to tell him. After a while, he said, "I had a partner. His name was Frank. Back when I was on patrol, before I made detective."

And Joe went all in—told him the story of what had happened. Five months earlier, the quiet road. The dark night and the taillights; the red eyes dancing in the black. The Buick, swerving side to side across the asphalt.

Ackerman didn't say a word as Joe spoke. Listened as Joe told him about pulling the car over, about Frank tossing the coin to decide who would lead the way. *Your lucky day*, he'd said, smiling, after the coin landed.

"Driver was armed," Joe said quietly. "Some cheap, pump-action piece of shit stashed within easy reach. Guy was either expecting trouble or was looking for it. Had a kid in the back seat, too. Couldn't have been more than ten years old."

He drained the last of his coffee. The morning heat had finally left him.

"Frank didn't even make it halfway to the car. First shot caught him in the side of the head. Second shot shattered our windshield. I was on the ground by then, returning fire, firing blind. I might as well have had my eyes shut. Got off five rounds, severed the guy's carotid artery with my fourth."

"Nice shot."

"Lucky shot."

"Who was the driver?"

Joe shrugged. "James Colfer. Some ex-con, skipped out on his parole. Guess he really didn't want to go back to prison." He played with his empty cup. "Just such a waste. Frank, I mean. Such a pointless waste."

"And the kid?"

"No idea. No record of him that we could find. Wasn't Colfer's, anyway. Social services picked him up. Apparently he's never spoken a word to them."

"Kidnapped?"

"Maybe. We put his description out for months afterward, but no family came forward."

"Where's he at now?"

Joe had been fiddling with his empty cup. He set it down and pulled his hand away. "Foster care, organized by a local church. Lives out with a woman over on Elm Drive. Goes by the name Ethan, wherever they got that from. No ID on him."

"Sounds like quite the mystery."

Ackerman was right, of course. It *was* a mystery. One Joe had been working ever since Frank's shooting. The strange kid who never spoke, who lived with a young woman driving a yellow Ford. How many mornings had he spent following them? Watching her drop him off at the local school? The kid knew something, Joe was sure of it. He owed it to Frank to find out what.

"And your partner?" Ackerman asked.

"Frank's up at Cooper Memorial now. Colfer didn't manage to kill him, but the insurance company's going to finish the job. Poor bastard's got maybe a week before they pull the plug."

Ackerman stared past him. "Christ," he said.

"And now you know why I don't like working with a partner."

"What, you blame yourself?"

"Myself, Colfer, Frank's shitty coin toss, the US Mint, the cashier who broke Frank's twenty . . . It's a long list, but I'm on it somewhere, yeah."

"So what I'm hearing is you want to wrap this up as soon as possible, stop the town from igniting, and get on with saving Cooper single-handedly until someone finally puts you out of your misery?"

"You just hit the nail on the head, pal."

Ackerman nodded, taking a final mouthful of pancake. He fished for his cigarettes. Tapped one out on the table and offered it across.

Joe shook his head. "I'm trying to quit."

"Good for you," Ackerman said, and lit up. He blew out a stream of pale smoke, long and slow, the cigarette never leaving his mouth. He took off his hat and ran a hand through his thick hair. "I'm not sure I could ever quit. I enjoy it too much. Is that weird? Knowing what it does to you?"

"Plenty of people enjoy worse."

Ackerman glanced down at the file sitting at the end of the table. "That they do," he said quietly. He flipped the folder open, started leafing through it. Laying photographs on the table like he was dealing cards. After a moment he stopped and looked up.

"Tell you what," he said, his cigarette rolling as he spoke. "Let's make a deal. You're new to Homicide, I'm new to Cooper. We teach each other what we know."

"Fine with me. Where do you want to start?"

Ackerman placed the last photograph down on the table and pointed to it. "Tell me about Memorial Park," he said.

Chapter Nine

Joe studied each photo as they were dealt.

Polaroids of a badly lit crime scene. A griminess to them, like a voyeur's collection. Blood and flesh, and a presence in the unfocused edges. Something hiding in the poor exposure. The horror, perhaps. Lingering in the latent images, refusing to come out on film.

He felt a little light-headed, sitting there. All of a sudden he wished he'd eaten something. Or maybe that would have made things worse. Ackerman started speaking, swiveling photos around to point at them, but Joe wasn't listening. His full attention ensnared by the filth; his every sense in overdrive. He could feel it even now, here, in the quiet bustle of the diner. It watched him from the corners of the frame. It made him woozy, like he hadn't slept.

He felt a strange urge to return to the house, to stand in the rooms again, to be alone with it. A sudden compulsion to lose himself completely, as he had done before, as a child. Ackerman had said he'd skimmed this morning's *Tribune*. Wasn't a chance in hell Gonzalez wouldn't retell Joe's family's grisly story. Murder-suicides always got readers going, even if the town knew the story by heart.

He'd have to set Ackerman straight. Dispel whatever bullshit Gonzalez had tacked on.

Already he could feel it building in him. The sounds always came back first: the tires of his bike on the dirt road as he cycled home; the sirens as the EMTs sailed past. It had been harvest time then, too, and that sweetness was in the air, same as it was now. And finally there had been the lights—blue from the ambulances, strobing over the tops of the corn. They thudded across his vision, migraine-inducing.

Then he was home, and his mother and brother were gone. His father, too. A neighbor had stayed behind to give him a ride to the hospital.

He blinked the memories away. Moved past them. Tried to let the carnage at the Richardsons' flood back in and sweep everything aside. He thought of the corn behind the house. He thought of the killer walking through it, remembered walking through it himself as a boy. Rattling the leaves and pushing through the stalks as he crossed the rows. Getting spun around until he was encased in it.

As a teenager, he remembered sinking into the black water of the reservoir. Holly Williams, her white skin shining like a beacon. Following her down as she sank below the surface.

There had been something there in the lake that night. Lurking in the depths, watching. A shadow he'd recognized from the cornfields. And now it was back, so close it was a physical presence. Heavy in his chest and tight on his skin. It was there, just down the road, inside the Richardson house.

"Hey," Ackerman repeated, snapping his fingers. "You there?"

Joe blinked, focused. "I'm here. It's just . . ."

"Yeah," his partner said, sighing. "I know."

"You believe what Bob said? That David Richardson was a suicide?"

Ackerman shrugged. "I don't know Bob that well, but he seems to know what he's talking about. The hesitation marks on Richardson's chest support what he says. So, sure, I believe him."

"Doesn't mean someone didn't force him to do it."

"No, it does not." Ackerman studied him, blew smoke out slow. "You don't like the father for the killer."

"And you do?"

"I follow the evidence. That's the only way to be sure."

"I disagree. I mean, look at this guy, alright?" Joe pulled a sheet of paper from the folder. "You see the statement from the neighbor?"

"Stephen Purcell. Yeah, I saw it."

"He told uniforms that David Richardson was a devoted father, loving husband, all that crap. Said he was a good guy. Barbecues for the street, carpools to work—here, read it."

"I said I saw it. What's your point?"

"Look, I know Steve Purcell. I went to school with the guy. He's decent, I don't think he'd make that sort of stuff up."

"I'm not claiming he did."

"If David Richardson really committed these murders? We're talking about someone who—completely out of character—rose from his bed, went out to his garage to collect a tire iron, came back into the house, and systematically bludgeoned every member of his family to death. And then, afterward, he gets a knife from his kitchen, drives across town and stabs himself in the chest. I just don't see it."

"You're applying a level of rationality we don't know exists. We just don't have the data. Maybe he lived with this shit inside him for years. Maybe he rallied against it as best he could, spent every night fighting it."

"Maybe."

"I want to meet with this Purcell, get a feel for him."

"Yeah, fine."

Ackerman finished his second cigarette. Ground it out on the ashtray. "Look, you got chewed out by Harris, big deal. Learn from it and move on."

"Thanks for the advice."

"You're welcome. And there's going to be plenty more, because that's how this deal is going to work, alright? I'm lead detective on this case, and I don't want arguments about how we investigate it. I'm not trying to assert my authority, and it's not a criticism. This is a major homicide and your shield is barely three months old yet."

Joe glared at him. "So everyone seems fond of telling me."

Despite everything, a warm smile managed to work its way onto Ackerman's face. "You know, I reckon we might just make a great team," he said.

Joe rolled his eyes and motioned for the check. "Don't get carried away."

"Tell me, you really grew up in that house?"

"Yeah, and I know you're just bursting to hear the story. Pay for my iced tea and I'll tell it to you on the way."

Laura

A note: long, and stringed, too unwavering to be birdsong, and building in her brain until she woke, gasping, clutching at the sheets and sitting upright. She was sweating. Her dark hair matted to her forehead. For a moment she was completely untethered, and she mentally flailed until the memories of the previous night came crashing over her.

It was strange, the things that stuck in your mind. The feeling of the dusty shoulder under her hands as she threw up was one. The sound of the dial tone as she phoned the farm afterward was another. And there was the blood, of course. She remembered the blood—there had been so much of it, how could she not?

Mason had seemed almost as surprised as her when it happened. Surprised at her scrabbling for the kitchen knife, surprised at her fighting back for once. A look in his eyes that said he thought she wouldn't do it.

The first slice had been the worst. The blade had seemed to barely scratch him, and yet the spray of blood had just about reached the ceiling. He should have backed off after that; left the crazy lady with the knife alone. His day must have been *real* bad to still want to get his shots in after that first slice.

But he'd kept coming, and she'd kept slashing. Her mind gone, her arm moving on reflex. Survival, pure and simple. And when she'd sunk the blade into his side she hadn't even paused; she'd run for the front door before his body had hit the floor.

The blood was still on her. Streaks of it on her hands and arms. Dull, rusted smears that coated her knuckles and wrapped around her fingers. When she touched her hair she could feel it there, too, crusted around the ends in clumps.

She pulled back the covers and slid out of bed, keeping her gaze away from the large mirror on the dresser before she padded down the corridor to the shower room.

The water was lukewarm and wonderful and it ran red. She washed her hair three times until it felt clean, watching the blood swirl around the drain.

Her bedroom was almost exactly as it had been before. The narrow wardrobe, the square bedside cabinet. As she dressed she could hear a sad, slow melody, and from her window she watched a girl stand at the edge of the clearing with her head hung crooked, a violin nestled under her chin. She played her song to the fields. To the dark farmhouse. Laura blinked at the morning light and tried to open her window, but it was locked.

She floated through the room, running her hands over each item. The lamp, the cross, the Bible.

There was a soft knocking at the door and Francine entered, smiling. "Good morning," she said. "Did you sleep alright?"

Laura nodded, and it wasn't until Francine had hurried over, wrapping her arms around her, that she realized she was crying.

"Everything's going to be alright," Francine said quietly, stroking her damp hair. "I promise. You're safe now. You're home."

Francine led her down the long corridor toward the dining room. She led her even though Laura knew the way, had walked it more times than she could count, but then you didn't always lead people because they were lost, did you—and besides, sometimes it was just easier to follow.

They strode past the other bedrooms, furtive glances showing perfectly made beds and neatly folded clothes. Tidiness was one of Rudy's rules, of course. And if you weren't prepared to follow the rules, then your life became very difficult here.

The dining hall was a large, circular room dominated by a lengthy table and a kitchen down one side. Laura remembered that. She remembered baking sponge cakes and roasting chicken on Sundays. She remembered holding hands and bowing her head. Drinking ice-cool water and laughing as Rudy shouted at the girl to play louder on the piano, louder, no louder still, goddammit, until the notes seemed to swirl around the curved walls in an endless loop, until they just about drowned out the clamor from one of the bedrooms, the dull thumping, the shrill screaming.

There were three people standing around the sink now. The girls Laura didn't recognize. Two of them drying cutlery, leaning in toward each other and giggling. The man standing next to them, however, she did.

He was tall and broad-shouldered, and had his hands plunged deep into the soapy water. His sleeves were rolled up, probably more to show off his arms than anything else. Arms made thick by years of chopping wood and tending fields.

Francine cleared her throat and the two girls jerked around quickly, stepping closer together with guilty looks on their faces. The man turned slower, pausing when he saw her. He grinned, lazily, white-toothed.

"Well," he said. "I didn't think we'd ever see you again, Laura."

"Morning, Kyle," Francine said. "Ladies, it's nearly ten o'clock. Shouldn't you be finished with the dishes by now?"

The two girls nodded quickly, peeling themselves away from Kyle and his tousled blond hair, throwing him a look that said everything as they darted from the room. But Kyle barely gave them a second glance. He kept his eyes on Laura as he leaned back against the sink, his hands flat along the edge.

"Does Rudy know you're back?" he asked.

"Rudy knows," Francine said.

"He never mentioned it to me."

"Haven't you got something better to be getting on with?"

"Oh, chores can wait. This is an exciting day! Where on earth have you been hiding, girl? You got any idea what happened here when you left?" Kyle laughed a little, shaking his head. "Course you don't. Bet you never looked back. Bet you even forgot about us a little. How long you been gone anyhow? Four years?"

"Five years. And I never forgot this place."

That seemed to tickle Kyle. His grin widened. "No, I guess the farm isn't a place most people would forget." He sniffed, stretching a little. "You two hungry? You missed breakfast. Morning sermon, too. Rudy was a little put out."

"Kyle . . ." Francine warned.

"Jesus, relax, Francine." Kyle started opening cupboards and rattling pans. "I've got eggs, fresh this morning. Although . . ." He drifted off, turning back to look at them. "It might have to be oatmeal for Laura."

"Don't be ridiculous," Francine said.

"Hey, I don't make the rules. I don't know where she stands now. No one's ever come back before."

"This really doesn't have anything to do with you. She's with me, alright? Why don't you go run after your little fan club and show them how many push-ups you can do. I'll take care of our breakfast, and if Laura wants eggs, then she'll get eggs."

A voice from behind them. "Has anyone asked Laura what *she* wants?"

All of them turned. Rudy was standing in the doorway. Laura wondered how long he'd been lingering there, watching.

"Morning, Rudy," Kyle said. "Look who's back."

"Yes, I know," Rudy said, smiling that dreamy smile of his. He sauntered over, looking tall and lean in his ripped jeans and white tank top. "And isn't it lovely to see her."

"She back for good this time?"

"You'd have to ask her that, Kyle, now, wouldn't you." Rudy stopped in front of her and clasped both her hands in his. "Well?"

Laura felt herself grow hot under their combined stares. Prickles of sweat on the back of her neck. Her hands were starting to ache from Rudy's grip. "I'm not going anywhere," she said.

Rudy beamed and released her. "There—you hear that, Kyle?" He tucked a strand of her hair behind one ear. His nails needed trimming. "We'll have to have a celebration tonight. I think it's time I update everyone about my process. I'm close, Laura, closer than I've ever been."

"I look forward to hearing all about it."

He stepped back, suddenly suspicious. His smile still in place but his eyes giving it away. "Tell me, do you still believe in the end time?"

Laura found the answer quickly. "I do."

He studied her for a moment. She wondered what was going through his head. This woman in front of him, this woman who had vanished for five years and who had now reappeared. The biggest question he must surely be asking himself was *Why now?* And if he wasn't, then that meant he knew—or at least he thought he did. Could be that Francine had told him what had happened. Could be that whoever had answered the phone had said something. What she'd done to Mason would be all over the local news by now, anyway. *Woman murders husband in vicious domestic dispute.*

Or hell, maybe he'd just found a reason for her return in his scripture.

She wasn't sure which made her more uncomfortable.

Rudy finally nodded. Satisfied—either with her answer or with his interpretation of it. "It's been difficult the last few months, Laura, I won't lie. But maybe your return will lift people's spirits a little."

"I'm glad," she said, wanting to ask more but sensing now wasn't the time.

"Good. I can't tell you how happy I am you've returned." He glanced over at Kyle. "Make her some eggs if that's what she wants. It's her first day back. We can work out where she stands later."

Chapter Ten

Memorial Park was still cordoned off. Only a couple of reporters remained, kicking about in a makeshift holding pen. The buzz was already starting to fade.

Joe and Ackerman sat in their car, parked a couple of doors down from the Richardson house. It was funny, how he thought of it as that. *The Richardson house.* Like it had always been and always would be theirs. A defense mechanism, maybe. He really hated reliving this shit.

Ackerman went to open his door, but Joe started to speak.

"My older brother Nicky used to get these nosebleeds," he said quietly. "All of a sudden, right out of the blue. My folks thought we were just playing too rough. What kid doesn't get nosebleeds? But then he started getting tired all the time, would wake up at night sweating. Turned out it was cancer. Leukemia. He'd just turned twelve."

Ackerman let his hand fall to his lap. Stayed quiet as Joe talked.

"He was in and out of hospital for months. Chemo, whatever. And when he was home you'd hear him crying at night. Through the walls, these big fucking sobs. You couldn't sleep they were so loud. And my mom . . . my mom struggled with it, she couldn't take it. My dad could—or at least that's what I thought at the time. I thought my dad could probably take a freight train he was so strong, but we'll get to that. My mom, though . . . She just wanted Nicky to get better. And when the doctors said that wasn't going to happen, then she just wanted him to not hurt as much, because he was hurting real bad by this point, and when she realized that wasn't going to happen either then I guess she just wanted it all to stop, and so one afternoon she baked a fruit pie and she put it in the oven and played all her favorite music and it seemed like the first time in a long time she'd been happy, and I didn't understand it—I was a kid, I was just happy *she* was happy—and I remember dancing with her in the kitchen while this pie baked, this sweet smell everywhere, and afterward she took the pie from the oven and she emptied all of Nicky's morphine bags into the damn thing, and then her and Nicky ate it together and they went to sleep in his bed, and that's how my dad found them, curled up together."

Joe breathed out heavy, his chest rattling. It had been a long time since he'd said any of that out loud to someone.

"I'm sorry, Joe," Ackerman said. "That sounds truly awful."

Joe nodded, keeping his gaze on the house. On the front door, just like he had when he'd left for the last time. "My dad didn't cope so well afterward. Neither did I, really, but I like to blame him a little for that. We moved across town, a little two-bedroom shack. He lasted about a year before he asked the neighbors to look after me and split."

"He left you? How old were you?"

"I was thirteen. Spent the next few years getting moved around until I was old enough to live by myself. Acted out every chance I got. Petty stuff at first, shoplifting or whatever. Worst thing I did happened when I tracked my dad down. I set his truck on fire."

"He press charges?"

"No, which was about the nicest thing he ever did for me. I spent a couple nights in lockup, agreed to go to some bullshit counseling. Six months in a clinic outside of Scottsbluff. People talked about me like I'd gone crazy, but I was just struggling. Funny sometimes—the more support you need, the more everyone seems to disappear."

He'd always figured it was an embarrassment thing. No one really knew how to act around him after Nicky died—didn't know what to say. He'd found himself more and more cut off from the rest of the town. Stares as he walked down the street; conversations hushing as he got close. Most of the time people didn't say anything to him, and when they did, they spoke in clichés. That was the worst. Phrases like *Nicky's in a better place*. Or *his suffering is over*. No one liked to talk about his mom, though. No one ever said *she* was in a better place. It became easier to just retreat from it all, to bury everything deep inside and go through the motions. Something he'd never been very good at doing for too long.

"*Will he crack again*," Ackerman said. The subhead from Gonzalez's article that morning.

"The way that little shit writes about it, you'd think *I* was the one who butchered a family."

"Well, you sure turned things around."

Joe nodded. "Jury's still out on that. Can I get one of those cigarettes?"

Ackerman tapped one out and passed it across. Joe stared down at it, rolling it between his fingers.

"Joe, you know if you ever want to talk—"

"Yeah, thanks. I know." He tossed the cigarette back. "Let's go speak to Purcell."

Together they pushed past the couple of reporters. More flashes of light, a couple of shouted questions. Joe kept his eyes open for Gonzalez but couldn't see him. Probably hunched over his computer, typing up another shot at the Pulitzer.

Stephen Purcell lived opposite the Richardson house. Ackerman banged on the screen door and a disheveled man answered. Dark hair that didn't look like it had been washed in a while; stubble that was more than a couple of days old.

"Mr. Purcell?" Ackerman asked. "Stephen Purcell?"

"Yes," the man said, his eyes darting back and forth between them. Recognition suddenly showed on the guy's face. "Joe Finch?"

"Hey, Steve. Good to see you."

"I didn't know you were . . . I mean, I knew you joined the police. How are you?"

"Been better, I'll be honest."

"Yeah, course, I think we all have. But, uh, what can I do for you?"

Ackerman smiled as he pulled out his notebook. "You mind if we come in, ask you a couple questions?"

Purcell glanced back inside for a moment. "Would it be alright to talk on the porch? My wife is sleeping. She, uh, hasn't been doing so well since, you know, and I'd rather not wake her."

He gestured to a small set of furniture outside. The three men ambled over.

"Sorry to hear about Julie," Joe said as he sat down. "It would have been nice to see her too, say hello."

"I'll tell her you were here. I'm sure she'll be sorry she missed you."

Joe glanced over at Ackerman. "Steve and Julie starting dating in school. Senior year?"

"Junior year," Purcell said, smiling a little. "Seems a long time ago now."

"You know, I still remember you two at . . . Shit, what was his name again? Guy who threw up in the punch bowl at prom."

"Matt Gardner."

"Matt Gardner. I still remember you two at Matt's party." To Ackerman: "Matt made a move on Julie."

"Kid was wasted," Purcell added.

"Oh, completely. Could barely string two words together. And somehow, he manages to corner Julie in the kitchen and starts making this impassioned plea about why they should be together. Everyone's just standing around watching. And Steve comes back from the bathroom and sees this, and goes over to him . . ."

"Not something I wanted to be doing," Purcell said. "Matt had a reputation."

"He earned it, too. Matt had probably been in more fights than everybody else in his class combined."

"Put a football player in the hospital one time."

"So, anyway, Steve goes up to Matt and taps him on the shoulder, all casual-like. Just taps him on the shoulder and says, 'Matt, I reckon that's quite enough'—"

"No, it was just 'That's enough.' You make me sound like a gunslinger."

Joe grinned. "Right. That was it. 'That's enough.' And Matt turns and looks at you, and there's this silence from everyone watching, because we're convinced he's about to put his fist through your head . . ."

"I think some people were *hoping* he was . . ."

"And then he just shrugged and wandered off."

Purcell laughed as though this was hilarious, for a moment transported away from all this. Ackerman looked at Joe like he wanted to ask where the punchline was, but when it was clear that was it, he joined Joe in grinning faintly while Purcell just about bust a gut. When the guy had finally wound down and sighed, the heaviness in his eyes returned, only maybe this time it wasn't quite so heavy. He leaned back in his chair. "So, I can guess why you two are here."

"Yeah," Joe said.

"I already gave a statement to someone." It came out sounding defensive. "But, I mean, of course I'm happy to help."

Joe smiled. "Relax, Steve. This is just routine."

"Alright then. How can I help?"

Ackerman flipped open his notebook. "How well did you know the Richardson family?"

"About as well as anyone knows their neighbor, I guess."

"Did you talk?"

"Now and then, sure. The usual."

"Who with?"

"David."

"How often did you talk?"

"Oh, checking the mailbox, heading off to work, that sort of thing."

"And what is it you do, Mr. Purcell?"

"I work in insurance, over at Nash's place."

Ackerman glanced over at Joe, who nodded. "Yeah, I know it. What do you do there, Steve?"

"Just a broker. Either of you boys want a better deal on your home and contents, I'll take care of you." He cracked a smile that died on his face. The earlier levity seemed to have dried up.

"You ever notice anything out of the ordinary around here?" Ackerman asked. "Anything David Richardson might have mentioned to you?"

Purcell shook his head. "I already went through this with your colleague yesterday."

"Yeah, you told him . . ." Ackerman scanned his notes. "Said David had mentioned something about a set of keys going missing."

"That's right."

"When was this?"

"Oh, months ago. Might be nothing. I just remember him saying he needed to get a new set cut."

"Did he say someone took them?"

"Said they were missing."

"He say anything else?"

"Not that I can recall, no."

"And the night of the murders, where were you?"

"I was at home."

"Your wife will confirm that?"

"Sure."

Ackerman nodded. Let his gaze wander down the street. "It's a nice place, Memorial Park," he said. "I like being so close to the fields. Most towns, they feel claustrophobic to me."

"I guess."

"I stay out on Riverfield," Ackerman said.

"The trailer park?"

"I'm still pretty new in town, trying to work out what I can afford."

"You'll probably get a great deal on that place," Purcell said, nodding across the street. He looked over at Joe. "Must be weird for you, huh?"

It was the question Joe had been waiting for. He could feel his partner's gaze on him, tried to keep his features set. "Sure, a little."

"You know, it was Julie who wanted to move out here. After everything you guys went through . . . Well, at first I didn't want to live opposite it. But then I figured, it's just a house, right?"

Joe stared at him. Saw for the first time a glint of steel behind the man's eyes.

The icy silence was broken by a sudden thumping from inside the house. Everyone's eyes went toward it. Ackerman said, "Is your wife awake?"

"I told you," Purcell said, "she's sleeping."

"Mr. Purcell—"

"Look, she's not well, alright? This hit her pretty hard. She's struggling to cope. And can you blame her? We live right across the street, we see that damn place every morning!"

Another silence. Ackerman closed his notebook. "Mr. Purcell, we're going to need to speak with your wife," he said gently. "Now, it doesn't have to be today, but if you could get her to come by the station sometime in the next few days, that would be great." He reached into his wallet and pulled out a card. Placed it on the little table between them.

Purcell didn't even look at it. "Fine, I'll pass along your message. Now, if there's nothing else?"

Ackerman glanced at Joe, who shook his head. The two detectives rose.

"Thanks for your time," Ackerman said. Then, when they were both back on the street, he added, "Tell me you got the same impression."

"That he's spinning shit? Yeah, I got it."

"Good work with the story about the party. You almost seemed friendly."

"Figured I'd distract him a little, is all."

"What did I say? That local knowledge is going to be useful."

Joe snorted. "You want to know the truth about that party? Julie Purcell was a tease and everyone knew it. You can bet she'd been flirting with Matt all night. Probably just to see two boys fighting over her."

"Sounds like high school."

"Well, let me give you some *local knowledge* to keep in mind," Joe said, slipping his sunglasses on as they approached the reporters again. "In this town, everyone's lying about something."

Climbing into the car, Joe glanced back, narrowing his eyes at the Purcell house. He saw movement in an upstairs window. Saw what might have been a woman, half-hidden behind a curtain, staring back.

Laura

Laura gathered her bloodied clothes and stuffed them into a plastic bag. Then she met with Francine and together they left the farm and went deeper into the fields, past the river's edge, past the small group of trees that marked the start of the fallow earth. There she set the bag down, doused it in gasoline, and set it ablaze.

They sat and watched the clothes burn. There was something freeing about it, the way the plastic squirmed and shrank in the flames, and Laura imagined the bloodstains melting away into nothingness and rising in the black smoke. Without the clothes, maybe it had never really happened. She still had the bruises, sure, but they would heal. In time she might be able to lie to herself and actually believe it.

Francine slid her arm through Laura's as the flames died out. "Good riddance," she said quietly. So quietly that Laura wasn't sure she'd said anything at all.

"Mason bought me that dress," Laura murmured.

Francine squeezed her arm. "Are you going to be alright?"

"I think so."

"You need to tell Rudy what happened. You know he'll ask."

"The way he was acting, it was like he already knew. I thought you might have told him."

"Oh, honey, it's not my place to tell anyone anything about it."

"Not even Patrick?"

Francine looked away, embarrassed. "Patrick's different."

A quiet beat passed as they both stared into the flames. Laura felt herself sag.

"I killed him, Francine," she whispered, her voice barely audible over the sound of the fire. "I killed my husband."

Francine gripped her shoulders and spun her around, holding her tight. "Now you listen to me," she said. "Mason didn't deserve to be called that. Man strangled you half to death. If you hadn't stabbed him, then *you'd* be the dead one."

Laura nodded. The two friends sat and watched the fire burn itself out. When it was done, the bloodied clothes were gone.

"What did Rudy mean that the last few months had been difficult?" Laura asked.

Francine grunted. "Some people are . . . losing faith, I guess. Gossiping behind his back, saying he's struggling to understand the text anymore."

"I'm not sure he ever could."

Her companion glanced around them uneasily. "Don't let some of them hear you say that. As far as they're concerned, Rudy is making *great* strides in decoding God's message, and anyone that says otherwise is an apostate."

"Do you still believe him?"

"That he's a presence foretold in the Bible? That the Book of Revelation has this hidden text only he can read?" Francine shook her head. "I swear, I'm starting to wonder how I *ever* believed something like that."

"Don't be too hard on yourself—we all did. Have you ever thought about just leaving?"

"And go where? Do what? I can't just up and leave without some sort of plan, Laura, I'm not like you. Besides, I've got Arthur to think about."

Arthur. Her boy.

Laura nodded, poking at the smoldering remains with a stick. "I nearly had a baby, you know. Out there."

Francine stared at her. "You *what*?"

"I had an abortion in the end."

"Oh, Laura, I'm so sorry. Was it Mason's?"

"That's why I *had* the abortion. I couldn't bring another person like him into this world. Mason made my life hell, Francine. What if his child did the same to someone else? That would be my fault."

"You can't blame yourself for the actions of others."

"Not if I can do something about it."

Francine sighed and got to her feet. "Come on, we've been gone a while," she said. "People will start to notice we're missing. Why don't I give you the tour, show you what's changed."

Returning through the fields, Laura saw a man approach. He looked like he was panting, even though the walk here was short and the ground level. The man stopped when he spotted them and leaned on his knees to catch his breath. Laura smiled as she recognized him.

"Patrick!" she said as they approached.

"It's good to see you," Patrick said, giving her a welcome embrace. "I couldn't believe it when Kyle said you were back."

Patrick was an older man, in maybe his early fifties, with thinning hair and a slight paunch. He had a large, rounded face that tended to go red whenever he exerted himself too much.

"Are you staying?" he asked.

"I don't know. I haven't really thought that far ahead."

Patrick nodded, his head at a sympathetic angle. "Francine told me what happened with Mason," he said quietly. "Sounds to me like you did what you had to do. I'm glad you're alright. I'm glad you're here."

"I am too," Laura said.

"Thanks again for looking after Arthur," Francine said to him. "I know it was short notice."

"Oh, don't worry about it." Patrick smiled goofily. "We always have fun."

"Well, I guess. He was talking about you all morning. I barely managed to get him to finish his breakfast."

Patrick beamed, and Laura suddenly realized exertion wasn't the *only* thing that made his face redden. She wondered how much she had missed in her time away.

"Where are you guys headed to, anyway?" he asked.

"I was just going to show Laura around," said Francine.

"Mind if I tag along?"

Laura smiled and shook her head. "Not at all. It'll be nice to catch up."

They spent the next hour wandering around the farm. Francine pointed out the makeshift greenhouse and poly-tunnels that they'd set up.

"You guys grow so much more than I remember," Laura said, gazing at the neat rows of fruit and vegetables.

"We've also got a whole bunch of livestock for meat and dairy," Patrick said. "It's all about being self-sufficient. The only way to truly elevate ourselves is by leaving our old lives behind."

"Alright, easy there," Francine said. "She's aware of the whole elevation thing already."

"Do you guys still go into town?" Laura asked.

"Now and then, sure," Francine said. "There's supplies we can't make ourselves. We've stopped working there, though."

"You quit the Starlight Diner?"

Francine nodded. "Nearly six months now. And let me tell you, I don't miss it one bit."

"What do you do for money?"

"Oh, we get by," Patrick said. "Every so often some of us go into Cooper and sell stuff at the market. Extra food, fresh milk. If you're smart about it, you'll be amazed how little money you actually need, though."

Listening to him, she heard Rudy. The man had a gift for packaging up soundbites and making others spit them out like it was something they'd come up with themselves. Course, you had to really buy what Rudy was offering for it to work. Patrick had always been a firm believer as far as she could remember, and from the sounds of things, not much had changed.

"See, look at this," Patrick said, motioning to a small group of women sitting in a circle on the grass. The women were all stitching little bundles of fabric, talking and laughing amongst themselves. "You have no idea how popular these are in town."

Laura watched as he went over excitedly and held up one of them.

"People don't want mass-produced, child-labor goods shipped over from China anymore," he said. "They want local products, handmade and unique."

He tossed it over to Laura and she caught it, turning it over in her hands. It was a small bear, with little glass beads for eyes and an open mouth. Something about it seemed off; the angle of its features, perhaps. Like the animal was laughing at her. Or worse, maybe it wasn't a laugh at all but a scream.

She handed it back. Patrick offered to show her the new cooling shed, where they hung the animals they trapped or shot, but she told him she was tired, which was true, and she went back to her room and slept until dinnertime.

Chapter Eleven

That night, Joe headed out. A little bar a few blocks from his apartment. Stacey's. A bland name that was both the beginning and the end of any attempt to appeal to female drinkers.

He sat on a worn leather stool and ordered a beer. Drank it watching the local news report on the Richardson killings. He usually got a shot, too, but not tonight. A message from Zoe on his answering machine. *I've got some of your stuff to drop off.* An awkward phone call afterward. She wanted to meet somewhere public—least that was the impression Joe got. He wasn't sure how to feel about that.

"Terrible thing," the barman said, pausing as he hung wine glasses to nod at the TV set. "You working this one?"

"Yeah, I'm working it."

"What kind of sicko does something like that?"

Joe shook his head.

"You ask me," the barman said, "it's the parents' fault. Bet he was one of those kids who liked to burn ants with a magnifying glass."

"I think I used to do that."

The barman waved a dismissive hand. "Ah, you're different, Joe. You can always spot the kids who are going to be trouble. They stand out. People like to pretend that's not true, but you ask me? This guy was dangerous from day one."

Joe made an agreeable noise and took a sip of his beer. The barman, presumably satisfied, went back to his glasses. Joe swiveled to check the clock on the wall, noticing as he did so how quiet the place was. Stacey's wasn't exactly the pounding heart of Cooper's upper-west side, but it usually had a better atmosphere than this.

A shout of triumph from across the room. A man whooping at a second television screen. Some football game. The man's wife sat next to him, looking about as interested in the game as Joe was, her gaze blank and expressionless. Across from them sat a small group of men, all three of them smoking and drinking whiskey and hunching forward as they spoke. And in the corner sat an old man, a bottle of beer and a book on the table in front of him. A flash of white on the man's collar. Joe tried to remember if it was the same priest he'd seen yesterday, standing outside the Richardson house.

Joe turned back to the news. The mayor was giving a statement. He was outside his home, dressed in sweatpants and a T-shirt. Accosted by a reporter as he took out the trash. He looked sweaty and nervous, his large glasses magnifying his beady eyes to comic proportions.

"Doesn't exactly make you feel like we're in good hands, does he?" the barman said.

"No, he does not."

"You ever met him?"

"Nope."

"I wonder how this is all going to end."

"Just keep your doors and windows locked tight, let us do our jobs."

"Oh, I'm not worried. I've got my protection."

The barman lifted up his shirt. Joe tensed, expecting a gun. Got a tattoo instead. A black symbol of some kind; a hand with an eye set into the palm.

"What's that?" Joe asked.

"It's the evil eye, man. Wards off demons, keeps me safe."

"How long you had that for?"

"About as long as I been here."

"Does it work?"

"Sure, but you got to believe in it, you know? Hey, if you're interested, I got a buddy—"

"I'm good," Joe said. "But I appreciate the offer."

The barman grinned and nodded. "We each got to find our own path."

Joe raised his bottle in mock agreement as the door swung open and Zoe walked in. She paused at the entrance, her eyes finding Joe's and crinkling slightly as she smiled. Tentative, nervous. Joe raised a hand, suddenly glad he hadn't had that shot.

Zoe slid onto the seat next to him and ordered a beer.

"Put it on my tab," Joe told the barman.

"No, that's alright," Zoe said. "Thanks, though." She was carrying a small grocery bag. She passed it over. "I think this is everything."

"Straight to business."

"Sorry, I—"

"No, it's fine. No point dragging it out."

The barman slid a bottle in front of Zoe and she dropped a couple of bills down. Joe glanced inside the bag. A sweater, a few shirts, and an assortment of toiletries.

"Doesn't seem like much," he said, letting it fall to the floor. "Your stuff filled a suitcase."

"You never spent that much time at my place."

Joe wasn't sure how she meant that. Didn't want to find out. "How've you been?"

"Fine." She shrugged. "I mean, pretty shitty, but, you know." She took a long drink. "How's Leo?"

"He's good. Still loves that duck you bought him." Joe smiled, thinking about him. "I feel bad. I haven't seen him much these past few days."

"Busy with work?"

"I'm on the Richardson murders."

Zoe paused for a moment, her bottle suspended. "What's that like?"

He weighed up how much to tell her. "About as miserable as you'd expect."

"God, it's so awful, isn't it?"

"I don't think God had anything to do with it."

"You know what I mean."

He knew. Knew under that black top she'd be wearing her silver cross.

"You see that priest over there?" Joe said, nudging his head toward the old man in the corner.

"Yeah."

"I think I saw him before. At the crime scene."

"What, is he a suspect now?"

"Course not. I just don't like it, is all."

Zoe rolled her eyes. "You don't like anything to do with religion, Joe."

"Did you know the barman's got a protective tattoo?"

"No."

"Well, he does. Ask him to show you."

"I'm alright."

"Says it keeps him safe."

"And that's better than going to church?"

"At least he keeps his beliefs to himself." Joe jerked his thumb at the priest. "Him? He'll feed off shit like this."

"Don't be ridiculous."

"I'm serious. Nothing like a murdered family to kick-start some Catholic guilt. Collection plate will be spilling over this Sunday."

"Joe!"

Zoe's tone was sharp; he'd taken things too far again. The bored wife across the room blinked slowly and looked over at them.

"Sorry," he said. "I'm stressed."

"You still working alone?"

"No, I got a new partner. Brian Ackerman. I ever mention him to you?"

"I don't think so."

"Guy lives out of a trailer. Wears a cowboy hat, Zoe, I swear to—"

She shot him a look. He waved his hand through the air. Picked up his bottle.

"I really never mentioned him?"

"I don't know, maybe."

"Yeah, maybe." Joe drained his beer, motioned for two more. "Anyway, he's only been in town six weeks or so. I'm showing him around, he's showing me the ropes. Sort of a quid quo pro thing."

"Pro quo."

"Huh?"

"Never mind. What's he like?"

"Fine. Bit full of himself, maybe. I'm going solo again once this case is done."

"He know about Frank?"

"Yeah, I told him. I said I can't work with a partner."

"You always were happier alone."

Joe scowled as the barman put two beers down. "I didn't mean it like that."

"I know. Sorry. Listen, I should get going . . ."

"Oh, come on, Zoe. You just got here. I just got you another drink."

"I said I was only coming for one."

"You didn't even let me tell you what's happening with Frank."

It was a cheap trick. The sympathy ploy. His pride would be hurting in the morning.

Zoe sighed, picked up her original bottle. She'd barely drunk a third of it. "What's happening with Frank?"

"His life support's getting turned off."

"Oh, Joe." For the first time, she really looked at him. "Joe, I'm so sorry."

"Thanks."

"When?"

"A few days. Happy Halloween, hmm?"

"Poor Cathy. I can't imagine what she's going through. What a horrible decision to have to make."

"It's not a decision, that's the worst part. Even with insurance, she can't afford the care."

"There's no way she can borrow it from somewhere?"

"You kidding? Cathy can barely afford to pay her mortgage. Every moment she's not working she's down there, sitting with him. Her life's over, Zoe, just as much as his is, maybe. And they say he can't understand things, can't hear what people are saying around him, but what if they're wrong? What if he's trapped in there, screaming at them not to flick the switch? What if . . ."

He trailed off, suddenly unsure where all this was coming from or where it was going. He let out a long, shaky breath. Took a drink to calm himself.

Zoe reached out and squeezed his arm. "You can't think like that."

He relaxed a little, glanced down at her hand. She took it back. Started pulling on her coat.

"I'm being selfish," Joe said. "I haven't even asked about you."

"Sure you have," she said, sliding to her feet. "You asked."

"How are your folks?"

"They're fine. Look, I need to go, alright?"

"Zoe—"

"Please don't make this any harder."

But Joe wasn't sure he knew any other way. He studied the label on his bottle. When she told him to take care of himself, he responded without looking up. Finished his beer, finished hers. Sitting there a while, he felt it in his guts, like acid reflux. He finally ordered that shot. Ordered a couple of them. Getting up to leave, the old priest in the corner caught his eye and raised a glass.

It was quiet as he walked home. No sign of the heat letting up. He was sweating, the day coming off him in waves. Cigarette smoke and beer, stale coffee and something sweet. The maple syrup on Ackerman's pancakes, maybe. Stress, too, if it had a smell. His hands shook with it.

The trip to his apartment should only have taken a few minutes, but twenty passed and he was still walking. Down narrow streets and dirty alleyways. The sidewalk glistening with moisture and the stench of piss. The day's warmth radiating from the ground up.

A few blocks over, someone shouted. A man. Laughter and car horns. Joe looked that way, saw a figure in a rocking chair gazing back from a front porch, a shotgun laid across his lap.

When he finally arrived at Elm Drive, the yellow Ford was parked outside. He glanced up at the house, at the church it stood next to. It was late. All the windows were dark. He pictured the kid again, the kid that hadn't spoken a word since Frank's shooting.

The barman had said you could spot the kids who were going to be trouble. Said they stood out.

Joe thought back to the day it happened. Saw the child's face as he approached the car, the blank gaze from the back seat. Splattered with blood from the dead guy up front. Just taking it all in like it was a Saturday morning cartoon. Oh, he stood out alright.

He told himself he hadn't meant to come here. But then he was at the yellow Ford, and his hands still shook, only now they held his service weapon. He turned it over so he was gripping the barrel. A quick, criminal's glance to make sure he was alone. A hard, sharp blow to break the car's taillight.

The pieces scattered into the dark. In the house, someone turned on a light, a figure appearing at the window.

Laura

There were no clocks allowed at the farm. This was one of Rudy's rules.

Time was what he referred to as the "Ultimate Master." It was the sort of phrase only a man like Rudy could get away with saying, for reasons Laura hadn't quite understood at first.

The logic (according to Rudy) went something like this. Time dictated that people set their lives to it: when to sleep, when to eat, *what* to eat. Without time, he argued, everyone was free. A concept that had seemed almost revelatory to Laura when she'd first joined. The idea of unshackling yourself so completely from your previous life that even *time itself* didn't have a say.

Later, of course—much later, years maybe—you would be lying in bed, and you would see the posturing in his words. The high-school philosophy, the faux-intellectual smugness. The only Ultimate Master here was Rudy himself. But back then, he could have told her to sprout wings and fly and she would have thrown herself off a cliff for him. Rudy had seemed something more than a man to her at that time. Had seemed something very close to a higher being.

But capturing people was the easy part. Keeping them was harder. Laura saw the logic in Rudy wanting to abolish

Time, because Time was all it took to realize how much bullshit he talked.

And now she was back. A part of her life that she'd tried her very best to bury these last five years. Only not very deep, it would seem—the farm had been the first place she'd thought to run to after Mason. Was it a weakness? A part of her that was broken? Or was it just Rudy's programming, kicking in again after all this time?

But sitting here, around the great fire, Laura gazed into the flames and wondered if it wasn't something more. The knife had seemed to shiver in her hand as it slipped inside him. She could feel it, even now, every time she closed her fist. A tremble that ran up her arm, that made her heart race. There was a strength inside her, a strength she hadn't known existed until that moment.

"You alright?"

It was Francine, turning away from Patrick mid-sentence to lean in.

"I'm fine," Laura said. "It's just strange, being back."

"It won't take long to settle in. Less than the first time." Francine laughed lightly. "*That* was a culture shock, huh? I remember Patrick took nearly six months before he was able to hold a conversation while maintaining eye contact."

"That was a withdrawal period, brought on by stress," Patrick hissed, his face reddening. "And it wasn't six months, it was a week."

"Oh relax, I'm kidding."

Patrick rolled his eyes and hunched forward over the fire. Laura and Francine shared a smile. It had been easy to forget these little moments. Easy to forget there was more to the farm than just Rudy. Like the sound the wind made as it rippled through the corn in the fall, just before harvest time.

A gentle rustling that Laura had always found soothing. And there was beauty here, too; you could see it in the dying light as it trickled through the branches of the scattered trees at dusk. It was in the vast spread of stars that came out at night, that seemed to only exist out here, free from streetlamps and car headlights. It was in the mist that sometimes settled across the dipped plains for an hour or two in the early morning.

Laura knew she'd tried so hard to forget certain parts, that now she worried she'd accidentally forgotten it all.

Movement from across the fire. One of the girls by the sink she'd met on her first morning, getting up and stretching. Beside the girl, Kyle sat cross-legged. He watched her leave, and when he turned back he stared at Laura.

"You ever going to tell us why you ran away, missing girl?" He smiled. "You ever going to tell us why you came back?"

"It's none of your goddamn business," Francine said. "Last time I checked, you weren't—"

"She left because she became disillusioned," Rudy said.

With a start, Laura realized he'd been sitting off to one side this entire time. His back against a tree trunk, long legs stretched out in front of him. He ran his dreamy gaze around the group, his eyes unblinking.

Kyle started to speak but Rudy interrupted again. "She started questioning what we were doing out here. She let doubt enter her, let it grow until it became denial. And once you become infected with denial, then you are lost beyond my reach."

Murmurs around the fire, people nodding their heads. Laura saw Patrick watching Rudy, his eyes wide, drinking in every last word.

"But she came *back* to us," Rudy continued, rising to his feet. He started to walk around the fire. "She came back to us. She spent five long years away, and she realized that denial was the *Devil's work.*"

A couple of people cheered. "Drive out the Devil!" someone shouted from the darkness.

Rudy laughed and pointed in their direction. "Yessir, you've got to drive it out! You've got to *purge* it from yourself. Purge the denial, the doubt, the dissent. You've got to find your way back again, find *faith* again! The people out there, they look at you and they say you're brainwashed . . ."

A smattering of laughter.

". . . they say you're *conditioned* . . ."

More cheering.

". . . but *I* say *they're* the ones who are brainwashed! *I* say that you all have common sense, you've all got free will. Free will to make your own decisions, to look at the information that's right in front of you. And I know it's scary—leaving your old lives behind, giving yourself over to something bigger. Believing in something that can't be quantified or measured. But that's why no one here is doing it alone. I'm with you; I'll lead you. All I ask is that you follow me, all the way to the very edge. And I promise you—I *promise* you—that, once you have faith? You are *unstoppable.*"

It sounded as though everyone was cheering now. Raised voices that filled the night, that seemed to swirl around Laura from all directions. A sudden claustrophobia, even though she was sitting outside. She closed her eyes to drown it out.

Someone took hold of her hands. Laura looked up to see Rudy settling himself down in front of her. The crowd hushed as they watched.

"I am so glad to have you back with us," Rudy said. "I always knew this was where you belonged."

Up close, she could see that he'd changed a little over the years. The lines around his mouth were etched deeper; there were creases along his forehead that she hadn't noticed before.

But Rudy was the same. That faraway look in his eyes, that slow, easy smile, like he was just getting the punchline to a ten-minute-old joke. His skinny frame, his long arms and legs. The way they seemed to fold around him when he sat down, like he was a dying spider. But Rudy had strength in those limbs, and he moved with a kind of grace. A special sort of confidence that seemed to just ooze from his bones.

On some people, his body might have been disturbing. On Rudy, it was otherworldly.

"I know what happened while you were gone," he said softly. "I know what you did out there." Rudy raised one hand and ran his fingers through her hair. His long nails raked the skin on her neck. She shivered involuntarily and he smiled as he felt it. "You know your place again now, don't you."

It wasn't a question.

Laura nodded. "I do."

"I want you to come to my room tonight. Understand?"

"Yes."

"Good."

He released her and rose to his feet. As he strode away, Laura forced herself not to rub at the spot on her neck where he'd touched her. She could feel the group staring. Some of them with what—with envy? Francine took her hand and squeezed it tight, and Laura watched as Rudy vanished completely into the darkness. She thought again about Mason and about the knife, how it had shivered in her hand as it entered him, and how her arm had trembled and her heart had raced.

Chapter Twelve

It was seven a.m., and the mercury was already pushing eighty. Hard to believe that just a few months ago the place had felt like it was about to be washed away. Back then, people had joked about it being the End Times. Judgment Day, all that crap. The very same lines they were repeating now. Said with smiles and raised eyebrows, like they didn't actually believe it. Like they weren't getting down on their knees and praying every Sunday. People only made these jokes because it was in their heads to begin with.

Joe felt sluggish today. Last night's shots still working their way through him. The air felt heavy. It got inside your brain, it fogged up your thinking. Joe drove in a daze, his windows down, the pressure a thudding roar that threatened to blow out his eardrums.

Unease stalked the town like a predator. The near-empty school bus rolling down the quiet streets; the subdued chatter of the local talk radio. The Richardson murders had taken more than just a family. It had stripped away some of the glue that held Cooper together.

At the station, Ackerman was already there. Had been for a while, by the looks of things. The meeting room was transformed: crime-scene photos pinned to one wall, a couple of whiteboards set up in the corners.

Joe stepped in with two cups of coffee and an aspirin between his teeth.

Ackerman looked up from a stack of folders. "Morning," he said, his eyes dropping to the coffee. "One of them for me?"

Joe handed a cup over and swallowed his aspirin.

"Rough night?" Ackerman asked.

"It's this heat. I don't sleep right."

"You tried—"

"I swear, if you tell me to close my windows one more time, I'm going to empty this over your damn head."

His partner smiled.

"What's all this?" Joe asked.

"I got Harris to give us some private space. Didn't feel right keeping all this out in the open."

Joe nodded. Staring at the photographs, it was hard to disagree. He motioned to the folders. "Bob finish his reports?"

"Forensics on the rest of the family members, the house, and the car."

"You read them?"

"Just about. You want the rundown?"

Joe took a seat and stretched out. "Sure."

Ackerman opened the top folder and moved over to the photo wall. "Marcy Richardson, her daughter Emily, and grandson Jacob," he said, motioning to their pictures. "All three killed by blunt force trauma to the skull. Bob's confirmed that the tire iron found at the scene was the weapon. Marcy got it the worst. Multiple contusions, multiple fractures. She was likely struck close to twenty times, although she would have been dead for most of them."

The new photographs, taken on the autopsy table, were somehow even more upsetting than those from the crime scene. They were cold, clinical; all emotion stripped away. In the house there had been a lingering anger, a residual sort of mania that almost felt alive. Bob's photos showed otherwise. A collection of parts, held together by muscle and bone and bound up in skin. It was hard to believe there had ever been life there.

"Emily Richardson died in a similar fashion. Her son was . . ."

Joe didn't want to look at that third picture, but he forced himself to. Little Jacob was so small he'd fit into a high-sided metal tray. His body curled on its side, his head reduced to nothing more than a bloodied smear. Joe felt his stomach slither and he pushed his coffee away.

"What about the house?" he said.

"Forensics didn't find much," Ackerman said softly, closing the folder. He dropped it onto the desk and stepped away. "Still cross-referencing fingerprints, we'll have more in a couple days."

"Any sign of forced entry?"

"None. Both front and back doors were unlocked."

"David Richardson said to Steve Purcell that a set of keys had gone missing a few months back."

"You believe Purcell?" Ackerman asked.

"Hell, I don't know." Joe pushed a fingertip against one temple. "Guy's lying about something."

"Well, listen to this. Tox report came back on the victims. David Richardson tested positive for trace elements of something called zolpidem."

"What's that?"

"It's marketed as Ambien. Started out in Europe, been in the States since last year. His doctor prescribed it to help him sleep."

Joe frowned. "A sedative, then."

Ackerman nodded. "It'll make you loopy, report says. Or it can, anyway. Pretty common. Hallucinations, memory problems."

"So he was drugged up? On his own, or someone spiked him?"

Ackerman shook his head. "Who knows? Apparently this stuff stays in the body for up to thirty-six hours. Guy had them in his bedside cabinet. He might have just taken some the day before he died."

"Or he was sedated, driven out to the reservoir, and stabbed to death."

Ackerman shrugged.

"What about the blood smear on the upstairs wall?"

"Tested as belonging to both Marcy and Emily Richardson. From the force of the blows, Bob reckons the killer would have been drenched in blood."

"And he only leaves one mark on his way out? This guy's covered in it, what'd he do with his clothes?"

Ackerman paused. "They found traces of blood matching all three victims in the bathroom drainage system."

"He . . . showered when he was done?"

"Most likely explanation."

"Maybe he did a load of laundry while he was at it."

Ackerman shrugged. "Maybe he brought a trash bag and a change of clothes."

"What the hell kind of guy are we dealing with here?" Joe said as he watched his partner turn to scribble something on one of the whiteboards. "Someone who knows just how much mess they're planning on making, who brings a change of clothes. Someone who factors in time for a *shower*."

The scribbling stopped. "Joe, I know you don't want to hear this, but maybe Bob's right."

"David Richardson did not do it."

"Don't know how you can feel so sure. He knows the house, he's got the time, he's got the spare clothes in an upstairs drawer."

"*I* know the house, Brian, does that make *me* a suspect?"

Ackerman rolled his eyes. "Or, you know. Aliens."

Joe stood up and walked over to the window, slid it open. The air was hot but it was better than what they were trapped with in here. He thought about the house, remembered climbing the stairs. How the fourth step had creaked. Was that something the killer knew? Maybe Marcy Richardson was a heavy sleeper. Or maybe Ackerman was right and she heard it just fine. No reason to worry when you know who's coming up the stairs.

"You alright?" Ackerman asked.

"I'm fine."

"It's a rough one. Maybe the roughest I've worked."

Joe gazed out across the quiet parking lot. They weren't high, but even from here he could see over much of the town. In the distance he could make out the faint dust cloud that hovered above the sawmill. It sparkled a little in the morning sun.

"Anything else?" he asked.

"One thing. They found a shoe print in the soil underneath Emily Richardson's bedroom window."

Joe turned. "What kind?"

"Sneaker. Probably male, looking at the size."

"It belong to any of the family?"

"No."

"You got a photo?"

Ackerman passed it over. The print was nestled in a flowerbed, facing away from the house.

"Could have been left by someone dropping out of the window," Joe said. "Bob find anything on the frame?"

"Not sure yet. Might be nothing."

"Might be our first lead. What about the car?"

"Forensics are still working on it. No trace of blood yet."

"But those bloodied clothes had to go somewhere," Joe said. "They didn't just vanish. Do we know the route David took to the lake? We should check CCTV for the night of the murder."

Ackerman looked impressed. "Worth a try."

Joe glanced at his watch. "Great. We can talk to Dispatch on the way."

"Where are we going?"

"I arranged for us to speak with Daniel Gonzalez this morning. Thought we could scare him into being less of a pain in the ass."

"You really think that will work?"

"I doubt it," Joe said, managing a grim smile. "But it sure as hell will make me feel better."

Chapter Thirteen

They met Gonzalez on his home turf. Downtown, by the warehouses. Rusted buildings and the relentless grind of industrial machinery. A place most people avoided during the day. At night, the area became something altogether more sleazy. A carrion call to Cooper's hustlers and streetwalkers; a safe space for the curb crawlers and drug pushers. The *Tribune* sat on a small patch of land by the river.

Most of the space inside housed the printing presses, which were loud, dirty, and just starting to spool up. Reels of newsprint ran through rollers, inked rubber spinning out whatever crock of shit the journalists upstairs had cooked up the day before.

It got hotter and more cramped as Joe and Ackerman climbed the narrow stairs. Metal walls kept the heat close. A door at the top led through to the editorial offices and a handful of reporters. All of them hunched over their desks, their wastebaskets full of discarded fast-food wrappers and empty pop cans. Above them, the ceiling peeled away in yellowed patches.

Joe stepped inside with Ackerman on his heels. The door didn't do much to cut the racket of the machines below them. They found Gonzalez squatting by the only open window. Back of the room, farthest from the noise downstairs. He gave them an oily grin as they approached.

"Morning, gentlemen," he said. His handshake was limp and wet. "I have to say, your phone call came as quite the surprise."

"We figured it would be helpful to make sure we're all on the same page," Joe said.

"Oh, of course." Gonzalez kept grinning, his five o'clock shadow stretched wide. "Just so long as this isn't some attempt to silence the press."

Joe exhaled. Ackerman stepped in. "Cooper PD isn't about to impose on your constitutional rights, Mr. Gonzalez. We're here to ask for your help with an active investigation. If you're not interested, that's no trouble."

Gonzalez flicked his gaze from cop to cop. The guy was antsy. Bouncing with nervous energy. "Why don't we talk in private?" he said. "And please, call me Daniel."

They hunkered down in a tiny meeting room. It was even hotter than the rest of the building. A sourness to the air—the stench of days-old sweat. Gonzalez struggled with the window, his weak arms trembling as he tried to lift the sash.

"Please," Ackerman said, taking over and smoothly sliding it up.

Gonzalez nodded a thanks and threw himself into a plastic seat, wiping at his forehead with the crook of an elbow. "Jesus, this heat," he sighed. "It's October, for crying out loud."

The room was decorated with various framed pages from the *Tribune*. GIRL FROZEN IN LAKE BREATHES AGAIN, one proclaimed. Joe remembered that story.

Gonzalez must have seen him staring.

"Little Paula Kaplan," he said, nodding at the frame. "Doctors said she was clinically dead for nearly four hours."

"I seem to recall it being a little less than that," Joe said.

"Obviously I stand by the *Tribune*'s reporting."

"Obviously."

Gonzalez stared at Joe for a moment. "My paper prints the truth, Detective Finch. I'm sorry that it makes you uncomfortable."

"The truth doesn't make me uncomfortable. Your paper's version of it does."

"Well, I think this is shaping up to be a very short meeting."

Ackerman leaned forward between them both. "Alright, gentlemen." He sent each man a withering look. "I only know the vague particulars of the gripe between you two, but quite frankly I don't care. Once this is over, by all means feel free to go right back at it—but once it's *over*, understand?"

Gonzalez shrugged. "If you boys have got something to say, I'd appreciate it if you'd spit it out. I've got a story to be getting on with."

"We want to work with you," Ackerman said. "Directly. Use the *Tribune* to help us with an ongoing investigation."

"The Richardson murders?"

"That's right."

"The *Tribune* isn't a police resource. You can't just call us up when you can't solve a case."

"We're asking for your help, Daniel."

Joe watched the two of them, disgust building in his throat. Any help Gonzalez gave them would only be in service to himself. The man knew why they were here—why they were really here—and he was going to wring every last drop from it.

There was something physically revolting about the fat little reporter. It might have been the near-constant sneer he wore. Or the permanent line of sweat that sat above his upper lip, and the way his tongue snaked out to lap at it. His sliminess was ever-present.

Thick in the hot air. The clock said 10:45, and already Joe wanted another shower.

When Ackerman had finished, Gonzalez rolled his beady eyes over to Joe. He nodded at another framed headline. "It still rankles, doesn't it?"

Joe had to swivel in his seat, but he already knew what he'd see. COOPER POLICE IN CARTEL POCKET. In slightly smaller print underneath: *Detective Paid by Organized Crime to Sink Case.*

"After that story broke," Gonzalez said, "I found that the people of Cooper PD were suddenly very hostile toward this newspaper. And after all this time, now you come to me for my help."

"You painted a one-sided narrative," Joe said, his voice even. "He was one bad apple. You made it sound like we were all on the take. You know how much uproar you caused?"

"I report the world as it is, not how you'd like it to be."

"Oh, please. You report whatever sells."

Ackerman shot Joe a look. "What my partner is trying to say is that, instead of a repeat of all that, we want to use the *Tribune*—with your permission, of course—to assist us in drawing the killer out. To catch whoever murdered this family. At the very least, we can try and keep the town under control. People start calling for our heads, it just makes our jobs harder."

"Well, sure, I get that," Gonzalez said, digging out a packet of cigarettes. He tapped one out and lit up, not bothering to offer them around. "But like I said, the *Tribune* isn't some state-sponsored paper. I'm not just going to print whatever articles you boys hand over."

"We're not looking to write your stories for you," Ackerman said.

"Alright," said Joe, leaning across the table. "Here's the deal. You stop printing your usual inflammatory *shit*—"

"Joe . . ."

"—and urge people to come forward with any information they might have. In return, we'll give you access to the Richardson house. Walk around, take your pictures, whatever. We'll also let you have first question at tomorrow's press conference."

Gonzalez's eyes bulged slightly at that, the corners of his damp lips twitching. Joe had been expecting a grin. He could only imagine the restraint. The reporter sat back in his chair, making out like he was considering it.

"There's going to be press here from Lincoln, Omaha, Kansas City—hell, probably Denver. It's going to be a shit show." He started pumping his fists, over and over like he couldn't contain himself, then fixed Ackerman with a stare. "You look right at me, call me by name. Say 'Daniel Gonzalez, *Cooper Tribune*.'"

"Done."

"And I want first question and a follow-up."

Joe groaned. Ackerman said, "Fine."

"I want my access to the house to be exclusive," he went on. "And I want the police to formally adopt the 'Bedtime Bludgeoner' in all their future press releases."

Joe pressed his fingers into the table so hard he thought they might snap. "*What?*"

"Every one of these sickos has to have a nickname, don't they? You know: Night Stalker, BTK, Son of Sam, whatever. People couldn't tell you their real names. But their *alter egos*? That stuff lasts."

"Jesus. *Alter egos?* This is a violent killer, not some superhero."

"Oh, sure, I know that. But someone's got to coin one for this guy. All I want is for the *Tribune* to be the paper that does it."

Joe got to his feet. Ackerman rose beside him and said, "No nickname. You call him whatever you want, but you're on your own with that. You'll get your exclusive access and your follow-up question. We have a deal?"

Gonzalez was just about squealing with delight. "Oh, Joe. If only you could see the look on your face right now."

"Daniel," Ackerman said firmly, placing both hands flat on the table and bending down to his level. "Enough of the bullshit. You don't want this? We'll go find another paper that does."

"Oh, relax, detective. Do we have a deal? When do we *start*?"

Chapter Fourteen

A few days had passed since the Richardson murders, and Memorial Park was quiet. The crowd of reporters was gone, a trampled patch of lawn left behind. There was only so long you could film an empty house. Besides, the real story wasn't in the bricks.

Joe could feel the eyes of the street on them as they rolled slowly through. Neighbors watching from their windows, staring at the police cruiser and the old, dented piece of shit that trailed them.

He'd insisted Gonzalez bring his own ride. Said it was standard procedure. Joe wasn't having the slimy reporter sitting in the back seat, sweating into the upholstery.

They parked outside. Watched as Gonzalez heaved himself out, his car rocking with the effort. A plastic food wrapper drifted with him, caught midway to freedom by the slamming door.

"It's hard to believe this guy has so much sway over this town," Ackerman murmured.

"People just want to be told what to think," Joe said. "It's frightening, having to do it on their own."

Gonzalez went to his trunk and returned a few moments later with a large camera slung around his neck and a bulge in his pockets that Joe could only pray was extra film.

The yellow police tape outside had come loose. It lay in bunches on the front lawn. As they got close, Joe noticed the security seal across the doorjamb had been sliced through. Ackerman caught his eye for a moment before going inside.

The house was a mess. Furniture was upended, drawer contents scattered. The aftermath of Cooper PD's forensics team.

Despite the mess, it wasn't like before. Last time there had been a darkness, a physical presence. Now, with the blinds open and the light streaming in, it was somehow just a house, and the only thing Joe felt was sadness. For the Richardsons, for himself.

Did another family dying in this place erase the ones that had died before? Did it wipe away his connection here? It wasn't like Nicky's murder had a monopoly on any of this—and that's what it was, murder, despite how some people tried to dress it up. How his father had tried to dress it up. Like it had been a kindness, like his mom had been doing his brother a fucking *favor*. It was an attitude that had bled into every part of their relationship afterward. William Finch's increasing inability to accept what had really happened in this house. His increasing need to stand up to the neighbors, to Cooper in general. To defend his wife's honor, like she'd been publicly insulted or accused of a petty crime.

At first they had let him get away with it. *The wound's still raw, he doesn't know what he's saying.* Platitudes that made people feel better. Safe in the knowledge that it was just grief working its way through him.

But then weeks turned into months, and his father kept it up. Maybe some of them agreed with him—though if they did, they kept quiet about it. And so what had started with sad smiles and nodded heads, with sympathetic squeezes and trite words, became anger, became hostility. People didn't want to hear about how a mother had committed the worst sin imaginable. When his father tried to argue that what she'd done took strength, it was thrown back in his face. Real strength would have been to trust in God's plan. What she'd done was weak and sick, and he was weak and sick to agree with her.

The final stage in his father's downfall was to be shunned. Ignored by everyone in Cooper. William was now the local weirdo, the man who rambled to anyone that would listen about how his wife had saved his boy. He refused to let it go, to let the town move on. People avoided him—avoided Joe, too. Because of course he was just as much of a weirdo as his father in their eyes. Just as damaged, just as deranged. Maybe that was why Joe had lashed out. Theft, vandalism. Anything to draw a different sort of attention. His mom had abandoned him and he'd grown to hate her for it. When his father finally left town, the only thing Joe had felt was relief.

A sudden flash and a high-pitched whine. Gonzalez prowled past them with a sickening eagerness. Stooped forward, his camera raised. Tragedy surveyed through the detached gaze of a viewfinder.

"Was all this done by the killer or am I witnessing you boys' fine handiwork?" he asked.

"Forensics are thorough," Ackerman said defensively, his mind surely on the sliced-through security tape on the front door.

Joe wandered behind them, detached. It was strange, returning like this. Memories resurfaced that he'd left long-buried. A woman's laughter; his mother in the kitchen. Baking, the rolling pin in her right hand, a giggle that went on too long and became strained, a mania in her wide eyes.

He placed his hand flat against the living-room wall. It was a cheap job, and the paper bubbled slightly under his palm. He wondered how many layers were still underneath. What he would find if he peeled it back.

His fingers found a raised edge. He picked at it, started to tear a small strip. Leaned in closer.

"Joe."

He turned quickly. Ackerman was watching him from the doorway. "Yeah?"

"He wants to go upstairs."

"Go for it. I'm going to stay down here a while longer."

"Alright," Ackerman said, in a tone that made Joe wonder whether his new partner thought he was soft. Like he couldn't take seeing the bedrooms again. Shit, maybe he couldn't.

Once he was alone, Joe glanced at the wallpaper. A floral pattern lay underneath the top sheet. He didn't recognize it. Wasn't really sure what he'd been expecting to find. Some trace he'd lived there, maybe. A part of him buried and left behind.

He floated slowly through the house. The whine of Gonzalez's camera punctured the stillness. The reporter must have taken close to fifty photos already.

The door to what had once been his father's office lay open. Peering inside, he remembered the big desk that had once sat by the window. His father didn't tend to bring his work home with him—he'd been the manager of a small pharmacy out by the hospital—but Joe had often found him sitting here in the evenings, reading the sports pages or listening to music. A brief refuge from the frantic lives of two young boys; and then, later, from the unrelenting pressure of Nicky's cancer.

Another high-pitched whine from upstairs. Gonzalez probably hunched over a blood spatter. Joe wandered into the kitchen and remembered his mother standing there on the day it happened. The smell of the pie in the air. A certain kind of syrupy scent that still caught him off guard, even now.

Into the dining room, and the mess continued. Chairs upended, lamps tossed to the floor. Ackerman hadn't been kidding about Forensics being thorough. The uniformed officer manning the line would have sealed the house up when he left, but that would have been days ago. Someone had forced the front door open since. But for what?

The thought was there before he had time to process it. He moved through the kitchen and into the small laundry room. Crouched down next to the washing machine. Upstairs, Gonzalez was really going for it. The whine was like an air-raid siren. Guy was in the master bedroom, getting hard over the king-size.

Joe ran his hand along the baseboard. His fingers scrabbled for that little notch, and then one swift thump with his closed fist and the board popped out. The little nook where he and Nicky used to hide their secret shit. Their action figures they weren't meant to have, their bad report cards. Innocent stuff that seemed so important when you were a kid.

Only now, when Joe reached his hand inside the space, he didn't find a half-broken GI Joe. His fingers closed around something long and smooth; an envelope. Pulling it out, he was surprised to find it wasn't even that dusty. Thing hadn't been there long.

Chain of custody! a voice screamed in his head. Still crouched, he pulled on a latex glove and used it to slide a black-and-white photograph from the envelope. The shot had been taken through a zoom lens, the focus a little off. But it was clear enough to make out what mattered. David Richardson stood in a parking lot, next to a man Joe didn't recognize in sweatpants and a hoodie. Both of them leaning against the trunk of a car—Richardson's SUV from the reservoir. Both of them holding what could only have been chunky bricks of cocaine.

Joe stared down at it, trying to make sense of it all.

The sound of a camera made him jump. He turned, the high-pitched whine still ringing in his ears, to see Gonzalez standing over him with a grin.

Chapter Fifteen

Joe sprang forward, snatching at the camera. Gonzalez darted back with a yelp.

"You give me that film," Joe snarled, "or I'll smash that thing."

"We had a deal," protested Gonzalez.

"You fucking *rat*—"

Suddenly Ackerman was there, his hand on Joe's shoulder. "Calm down, both of you. What's going on?"

"What's going on," Gonzalez said, "is that Detective Finch is reneging on our arrangement."

Ackerman looked first at the reporter—standing nervously guarding his camera like it was a newborn baby—and then at Joe. Finally, his eyes fell on the photograph.

"What's that?"

"It's evidence," Joe said. Then, to Gonzalez: "And off limits, asshole. Give me the film."

"I can't take it out, I'll ruin the rest of the roll."

"Tough shit. You've got enough to spare."

"This is censorship!"

Ackerman sighed. "Alright, that's enough. Now listen—"

Joe stepped forward, and in one fluid movement grabbed the camera clean out of Gonzalez's hands. The reporter yelped.

"Give that back!"

Joe ignored him. Popped the back of the camera off and tore out the roll of film. Tossed the empty camera back. "You got your pictures, now get lost," he said. Stepped forward as he did it. Gonzalez moved away.

"No wonder people in this town don't trust the police," Gonzalez spat, hurrying toward the front door. "Don't think I won't be writing about this."

"You write one word about this photo, I'll personally raid your office every other day until I find something that sticks. Understand?"

Gonzalez glared at him from the safety of the doorway. His face was red, his shirt collar damp with sweat. Then he turned and scurried off.

They waited until the sound of his rattling car had faded, then Ackerman pointed at the photo.

"What's this?" he asked.

"I found it hidden in the baseboard. It was a spot me and my brother used to use when we were kids."

"Let me see it."

Joe handed it over. Ackerman studied it. David Richardson and a young man handling bricks of cocaine.

Neither of them spoke for a moment. Then Ackerman said, "Alright, what are you thinking?"

Joe ran the argument through his head one last time, then came out with it. "I think Richardson was moving drugs for someone. That man he's standing next to, most likely. My gut feeling? He had this photo taken to use as leverage."

"For what?"

"Protection against whoever he was in business with. You know, 'I wind up dead, this photo makes its way to the cops' sort of thing."

"Do you know who the guy in the hoodie is?"

"No, but looking at those bricks, organized crime would be my first guess."

Ackerman nodded.

Joe peeled his latex glove off with a snap. "Which probably connects to the broken seal on the front door."

"How's that?"

"Hoodie-guy busted in, looking for the photo. Cartel must have known Richardson had it. Leverage only works if everyone's on the same page."

"You're losing me. The cartel murders the Richardsons . . . Then what? Comes back to find the photo?" Ackerman shook his head. "That seal on the front door only goes on *after* Forensics is finished. How did they know we didn't already pick it up?"

"Because it was never logged into evidence."

Ackerman watched him for a long moment. "So now it's a *cop* who's after the photo."

"Brian, whoever came back here knew the photo was still in the house. Thanks to Gonzalez, it's an open secret Cooper PD had officers on cartel payroll. Maybe it still does."

The two men stood in the quiet house. Ackerman gazed down at the photo, frowning, a look on his face like he knew where this was going. Finally, he nodded.

"Good. It's a solid theory," he said. "But that's all it is right now, alright? We keep this between us for the moment. The press conference is tomorrow and the last thing this town needs right now is Gonzalez with another corruption story. Captain's on thin ice as it is. You mind if I keep this?"

"Fine with me. I'm not going back to the station anyway."

"Where are you going?"

Fitting the baseboard back in place, Joe said, "To blow off some steam. If I don't, I'm worried I'll end up killing that fat shit when I see him tomorrow."

Chapter Sixteen

Leaving the Richardson house, Joe's mood was dark. Working this case was harder than he'd imagined. Photographs in the baseboards stirring up shit his brain would rather stay buried.

Probably it showed on his face. Dropping him off at the station, Ackerman told him not to do anything stupid. Like his mind wasn't already halfway made up. Couple of beers at Stacey's closed the gap.

Joe parked across the street from the church. The yellow Ford was sitting outside, the taillight still broken. *Elm Drive. Memorial Park.* Nice names that papered over the cracks that ran through this town. His thoughts drifted, as they often seemed to do lately, to the cornfields and the reservoir. And, now, to the wallpaper at the Richardson house. He remembered the feeling of it beneath his fingers. Layers of the past, covered up and forgotten.

He blinked. Forced himself not to peel it back. To leave it be. He brought his mind forward: Frank lying in the middle of the road. Marcy Richardson lying on her bedroom floor.

Across the street lived the boy from the back seat of the Buick. The mysterious boy who had never spoken a word since the shooting. And not for lack of trying; by investigators, by social services.

Joe had clung to the idea that the boy from the back seat might have an answer—something he'd kept away from all the other cops and social workers, something he'd kept just for Joe. The truth about where he came from, or why he'd been in that car to begin with.

It took another forty-five minutes for them to appear. Early evening now, Sarah Miller leading Ethan by the hand toward the Ford. Joe stayed still and watched as they pulled off from the curb. Waited until they were a block away before following.

Once they reached the road out of town, he kept a car or two between them. Sarah Miller was a nervous driver; slow to accelerate and never coming close to the speed limit. That was alright. He wasn't in a rush.

Finally, the Ford turned off onto a side road. Straight and empty, flanked by rotting farmhouses and flat, dry fields. Joe followed them, the only car behind her now. He put his foot down. Closed the distance fast. When he got close enough to read her license plate, he reached for his portable police flasher unit and tossed it on the dashboard. The bulb spun blue, her eyes jumped to it in her rearview. She slowed and pulled over.

This was a bad idea. He knew that. It wasn't yet night, but the sun was well on its way. Its light starting to fade but its heat hanging around. He let his car rattle into silence. Sitting on the shoulder, the dust settling in the air. For a couple of seconds he thought he might just drive off. Knew that's what he *should* do. Then he saw the back of the kid's head through the rear windshield, just like the last time they'd met. He popped open his door and climbed out.

Her window was rolled down by the time he got there. Up close, he could tell she was nervous. Might have been the first time she'd been pulled over by a cop. The kid was clutching a set of crayons, drawing. He didn't even bother looking up.

"How can I help you, officer?" Sarah Miller asked. Her voice sounded dry, her first few words coming out in a near-croak. She kept both hands on the wheel, like she'd heard stories about what might happen if she didn't. Her gaze snapped back and forth between Joe's and the horizon. Unsure what made her look more guilty.

"Do you know why I pulled you over?" Joe said, adjusting his sunglasses as he leaned against the side of her car.

"Is it the taillight? Because honestly, I just noticed that this morning. I mean, it must have just happened. Somebody must have smashed it. I haven't had the chance to get it seen to yet."

"Where is it you two are heading?"

"We're off to get some dinner. Ethan wasn't feeling well this morning so I kept him home from school. Thought a picnic might cheer him up a little. He's doing better now, though. Isn't that right, Ethan?"

The kid in the back seat said nothing.

"He missed out on a playdate with some friends," Sarah said quietly. "I was hoping this would take his mind off it."

Joe glanced over at Ethan. He found it hard to believe the boy had any friends, the way he was. He tapped on the window. After too long, Ethan turned his head to look at him. His light-brown hair fell about his face, his dark eyes wide in the dim light. The last time Joe had been this close to him, the boy had been soaked in another man's blood. Amazing what a good shower and five months could do.

"Evening, son," Joe said. "How you doing back there?"

Ethan kept on staring at him. A crayon was clutched in his right hand, held still. No tremble. No nervousness. Joe wondered if the kid recognized him. If he did, he didn't let on.

"You miss school today, huh?" Joe said. "Your mom tells me you're feeling better now though." He leaned closer to the glass. "I used to pull that trick when I was a kid, too."

The boy went on saying nothing.

"He's shy," Sarah said, twisting around to look at him from the front seat. "He doesn't talk much."

Joe smiled. "Maybe he will for me." He nodded at the drawing. "Nice dragon you've got there."

Ethan glanced down at the picture in his lap, then back at Joe. A beat passed.

Nothing.

Joe leaned even closer to the glass. Took off his sunglasses. "You remember me?"

Ethan's mouth opened a crack, his lips moving like he wanted to say something. Joe saw the kid's fingers tighten on the crayon.

"Officer . . . ?" Sarah's voice sounded concerned.

"There something you want to tell me?" Joe said to the kid. "Now's your chance, Ethan. That's your name, right? *Ethan?*"

"Look, if there's a problem here, I'd rather you spoke with me," Sarah said sharply.

Joe stood up straight. Slid his sunglasses back on as he glanced up and down the road. Still no one. "License and registration please, ma'am."

She reached into the glovebox and handed over her documents. Joe made a show of reading them, like he didn't already know her details. He kept flicking his gaze toward Ethan. The boy had returned to his crayons, his head bopping back and forth slightly as he drew. For the first time, Joe wondered if maybe he'd been wrong about the kid. If maybe there wasn't anything more to him after all.

But he clearly wasn't going to get those answers today. Ethan was lost in his own head, probably always would be. Maybe it had started back in May. Maybe Frank wasn't the only one who had been shut out from the rest of the world that day.

Joe stood up straight and handed her documents back. "You get that light seen to as soon as possible," he said.

"Of course. Thank you, officer."

Joe walked slowly back to his car, then sat in the front seat and watched as they drove away. The sun glinted off the metalwork, and the dust and the dry dirt glittered in the air for a long time after they'd gone.

Laura

Laura kneeled on the rough earth and dug at the soil. The trowel was old and rusted, and the dirt came away in thin layers. It was hard work. Her back ached with the effort.

She sat up and gazed out across the fields. The sun was low, its amber light just skirting the tips of the tallest trees. A couple of tractors rolled lazily along the horizon. Around her, others stooped here and there, and she wondered if they were having any more success than she was.

Tending the fields hadn't been her first choice. Rudy had asked her what she'd wanted to do—how she wanted to contribute. Said it in a way that made her skin crawl. A low drawl, his body close. *Con-trib-ute.*

That had been last night, in his room. She wasn't naive; she knew what he wanted. Only this time, she wasn't some wide-eyed young girl, taken in by his shitty wordplay or claims of power. Now she saw him for who he was.

"I'm the vessel, the messenger," he'd said, standing by the door, watching her as she walked inside. One long arm draped across his chest. "I'm doing as well as any man who dares to have religious views outside the mainstream. How are *you* doing?"

Laura had regretted asking the question almost immediately. Small talk was not something Rudy excelled at. Not enough opportunity for grandstanding.

"I'm tired," she'd told him.

"Of what?"

Of men like you controlling people like me. "Just tired."

Rudy smiled as he closed the door. "Don't worry, I won't keep you up late."

His room was far more extravagant than hers—than anyone's, in fact. A big bed sat in one corner, a wide desk taking up an entire wall. On it were open books and piles of papers—folded, rolled up, paperclipped together. All of them covered in scribbles. The rantings of a madman.

"How is your work coming?" she asked him. She didn't really want to know; she just wanted to get him talking. Once you got Rudy talking, he sometimes forgot about why he'd asked to see you.

"Slowly," Rudy said. "Slower than some people would like."

"Not enough for them that you're chosen by God?"

"It wasn't enough for you."

Laura picked up some of the papers, tried to read the scrawled handwriting. She managed to make out words like *passage* and *ascension*. It was the same stuff he'd been peddling since she'd known him.

"If I didn't believe all this," she said, "I wouldn't have come back."

"I told you, I know why you came back," he said. "And it wasn't to rejoin this community." He moved from the door now, unfolding himself as he drifted closer to her. Slowly, like molasses. Laura had to fight the urge to step away from him—that's what he wanted her to do. That would take her closer to the bed.

"So why *did* I come back then?" she said, pretending to study the scroll of paper she was holding.

"You came back because you murdered a man. Because you thought my farm would be the best place to hide."

"Word travels fast."

"And thoughts faster. I could always read you, Laura."

"Yes, you could," she said. "I was young when I first came here. I was searching for . . ."

She knew to let her voice trail off. An irresistible opening for Rudy.

"For truth," he said. "You were searching for truth. Which is what everyone wants, and yet when it is presented, most turn away from it. People cry out, 'Is this all there is to life?' and I answer them, I tell them of what we are doing here." His voice was vibrating now, his long legs taking him over to the window. "I am *close*, Laura, closer than I've ever been, to unlocking the text of Revelations. Once I have a full understanding, once I have fulfilled God's wish, I will open the doorway for us all."

This was it. His big push. His theory about the End Times—that God had asked him to round up the true followers for the next step on humanity's journey. Laura was embarrassed to look at this room—at the collection of well-worn books and scribbled thoughts—and know that at one time she had believed it all.

She wasn't sure who was worse: someone like Mason, who had enjoyed controlling people simply for the pleasure of it, or someone like Rudy, who did it while truly thinking that he served a higher purpose.

"You know, there are those on the farm," Rudy said slowly, "that say you being here—now, when we're so close—is no accident."

Laura finally looked at him then. Standing by the window, gazing out at the dying fire across the field. "So why do *they* think I'm here?"

Rudy shrugged. "The Devil is very clever, Laura. It's universally accepted that he'll send people to sway others. To test them. To try and convince them to turn away from God's light."

"They think I'm the Devil?"

"More like working for him. Personally, I don't put much stock in it, but I suppose I can see where they're coming from." He sighed. "I just hope they don't get too carried away. An angry mob is so very hard to control."

He said it in such an off-hand manner that Laura felt the skin at the back of her neck prickle. Was he warning her? Were people really thinking that about her, or was this just another of Rudy's mind games? Either way, maybe the farm wasn't as safe a hiding place as she'd imagined.

"I'll keep that in mind," she said, moving toward the door. His eyes on her reflection the entire way. "But like I said, I'm tired, Rudy. I'd like to go to bed now."

She was almost at the door when he slid past her in a flash and placed his palm flat against it. Those long legs. He was so close she could smell the fire from him, smoky and acrid.

"I asked you here tonight so I could warn you, Laura." He glanced at the door. "You go out there alone, you might be alright. Or one morning you might wake up to find a crowd standing over your bed." He took his hand away

114

and stepped back. "You stay with me, I'll put you under my protection."

She forced herself to meet his gaze. To hold it. "I guess I'll just have to put my faith in their hands," she said.

Rudy's mouth had twitched a little at that. A smile, maybe. Before he could say anything further, however, Laura opened the door and slipped out, rushing through the darkened corridor toward her room.

The dinner bell brought her back: to the grim field, to the cool sun. She stood, wincing at her back. She made her way across the narrow rows of dirt and into a bathroom. Locking the door, she washed her hands in the small sink. The water was ice-cold. Her fingers red from the exertion. In the mirror, she saw streaks of soil across her forehead and did what she could to wash it off.

When she opened the door, she found two girls waiting to go in. The same girls who hung around Kyle every chance they got. One of them stared her down as they stepped past her and entered the bathroom.

Her friend met Laura's gaze and smiled, embarrassed. "Hi."

Laura considered her for a moment. "I don't think we've been introduced," she said. "I'm Laura."

"Oh, I know."

Course she did. Everyone did.

"I'm Katherine," the girl said. "My friend in the bathroom is . . . Louise."

She said it weird, like she wasn't used to saying it.

"Did you choose it?" Laura asked.

"What?"

"*Katherine*. Did you choose it, or did Rudy give it to you?"

"Erm, he . . . he gave it to me." She paused, shifted her weight. "It's strange, right? Having to take a new name?"

Laura shrugged. "It's all part of the rebirth. You've got to leave all your old life behind, or whatever. Up to you how much you want to believe it. To me, a name's a name."

"Yeah, I guess."

Katherine looked younger than her—early twenties, maybe. Maybe even younger. The girl fidgeted as she stood, one hand slid deep into the pocket of her jeans, the other clutching a tattered Bible to her chest.

"How long have you been at the farm?" Laura asked.

"Oh, not long. Just a couple months or so."

"You like it?"

"Sure, it's neat."

Laura smiled thinly. *Neat*. This girl was from another world. "What brought you here?"

Katherine shrugged. "Kyle, I guess. Me and Louise, we met him in town. He told us about this place. We were just traveling through, looking for work. Figured we might as well give it a try."

"You should watch yourself around Kyle, alright? He's an asshole."

Katherine looked away, embarrassed. "I mean, it's not like I'm looking for a serious relationship. I know he's got other girls in town. I heard he got one of them pregnant."

"I'm not just talking about him screwing around. He's got a real nasty streak in him. I've seen him with trapped animals, he damn near—"

The girl had shaken her head.

"Look," Katherine said. "No offence, but I shouldn't even be speaking with you."

"What?"

"I don't know your history here, and honestly I don't really care. I'm new here. I don't want to give people the wrong impression."

Rudy's warning last night floated to the front of her mind. *He'll send people to sway others.*

"You worried people see you talking to me, they'll think—what, I've corrupted you?"

Behind her, the bathroom door opened. Laura turned around to see Louise standing there. The young girl smiled coldly. "Leave my friend alone," she said. "And don't talk to us again."

Laura rolled her eyes. "Fine, whatever. I was just trying to help."

"We're not the ones who need help. If I were you, I'd start locking my door at night."

Laura turned on her heel and marched off. Quickly, before the girls saw her face flush. She squeezed her hands into her pockets to hide their trembling. Behind her, she could hear the two of them whispering to each other. It took all of her strength not to look back.

Chapter Seventeen

They held the press conference in the church downtown. The Blessed Virgin Mary. It sat overlooking the river. Anywhere else, it might have been for the views. But not in Cooper, where the water ran dirty brown, where the long summer had dried the stream to little more than a trickle.

It was late afternoon, but it was still light. Joe and Ackerman stood by the entrance, at the edge of a surprisingly neat lawn. It was the best spot to watch the townspeople arrive. Events like this, you never quite knew what you were looking for. Something you'd recognize when you saw it. A nervous habit, a shifting gait. A stare that was just *off*, somehow. Joe eyeballed every person who passed by, and after five minutes he was ready to arrest every single one of them.

Top of his list was the man at the front door; handshakes for a select few, warm smiles for everyone else. It was the priest from Stacey's a couple of nights earlier. And from the crowd outside the Richardson house.

Joe stared at him, knowing it was nothing more than coincidence. But his brain was lit up already, and he was too wired to shut it off. A beat later and the priest's eyes slid through the crowd and onto his. Joe turned away.

Ackerman nudged his arm, motioning with his head. "Look who decided to leave the house."

They watched as Steve Purcell ambled through the entrance, his elusive wife by his side. Julie looked awful: dark shadows under her eyes, her hair unkempt. She gripped Steve's elbow with what looked like all the energy she had.

"Come on," Ackerman said, glancing at his watch, "let's get inside."

As they entered the church, the priest reached out and placed his hand on Joe's arm.

"I remember you," the man said.

Joe grunted. "Likewise. Not often you see a priest in a bar."

"We all have our weaknesses, detective."

"You'll get no argument from me on that, Father . . . ?"

"Brading."

"I see you outside the Richardsons' too, Father Brading?"

The priest's smile faltered. "Yes. I was there to ask God to watch over the family."

Joe felt his face harden. "Shame God wasn't there a few hours earlier. He might have been able to do something."

Then Ackerman's hand was on his shoulder. "Thanks again for letting us use the church, Father. We'd best be getting inside."

"Oh, of course." Father Brading's smile was back in place. "I do hope you're able to find the people responsible for this tragedy. The town needs to heal."

"Well, that's what tonight's all about," Ackerman said, pushing them both inside.

"I've been praying for them," the priest said. "The Richardson family."

"Make sure to send some of those our way, Father," Ackerman replied over his shoulder. "We could use all the help we can get."

Once they were inside and had left the priest behind, Joe turned and said, "You sure like going out of your way not to piss anyone off."

"I seem to be doing a pretty bad job with you."

"You believe any of that crap?"

Ackerman shrugged. "Sunday school as a kid. It never really leaves you."

"Well, I don't like the guy."

"I'm not sure you like anyone."

Joe snorted at that. "Come on," he said. "Let's stand where we can get a good view. I want to keep my eye on people."

Captain Harris was sitting at a long table at the front of the room, next to the mayor and some stranger in a smart suit. Some city councilman, maybe. But no, too polished for that. Someone rolled in from Lincoln—governor's office, state legislature—intent on making sure folks saw how serious it was all being taken.

Joe remembered what Harris had told them earlier. That the mayor had asked for someone to lend a hand. Politics-talk for *keep an eye on things.* On Harris, on all of them. Last thing they wanted was another dirty cop in charge of something like this.

The first few rows of chairs were taken up by the press. Reporters from all over, most of whom Joe had never seen before. They clutched recorders and notepads, leaned in and whispered to one another. Their news vans parked outside, satellite-linked back to Lincoln or Des Moines or Kansas City.

And sitting right in the middle of it all was Daniel Gonzalez. No one was talking to him; Joe liked to think the guy's reputation preceded him. Or maybe his smell had. The church was hot, and the reporter was already sweating. Swiveling about in his seat to watch the townspeople streaming in, scribbling notes. His eyes roamed the room and found Joe's, and the two men stared at each other for a couple of moments before Gonzalez hunched forward, pen moving fast.

As Joe and Brian took their positions at the back of the room, the mayor leaned forward and tapped his mike. A dull thud echoed around the church.

"Good evening," he said solemnly. "I'd like to start off by saying thank you to everyone who's been able to join us. It's our aim to share what information we have and to answer as many questions as we can."

The last time Joe had seen the mayor it was on the TV at Stacey's. Awkward footage caught by a reporter as he took out the trash. Stammered responses, eyes magnified behind giant glasses. He'd decided to wear his contacts tonight.

"Now, I'm going to let Captain Harris of the Cooper Police Department speak, but first I'm going to hand you over to Sam Lemire."

He slid the microphone over to the man in the sharp suit.

"Thank you, Mr. Mayor. And as you've just heard, my name's Sam Lemire. For those that don't know me, I'm your district's state senator."

Lemire paused there, eyeballing the room. A hundred people and not one person made a sound.

"Now, I want you all to know that I am listening, I am seeing what's happening in your community, and I am going to make sure that the police and your good mayor here have everything they need in order to resolve this situation. So, without further delay, I'm going to hand you over to Captain Dale Harris, who's going to give us all an update on where we're at with the investigation and what the next few days will hold. Captain?"

Joe shook his head. Lemire was good. Trying to push as much of the weight onto the captain's shoulders as he could, all the while making himself sound like he was just one of the townsfolk. Joe would bet a thousand dollars this glossy specimen spent the absolute minimum number of nights sleeping in the crap-ass little district he'd convinced to vote him in. An insufficient density of cocktail bars and bespoke tailors.

Harris smiled grimly before reaching over and sliding the microphone across the table.

"Thank you, Sam. Good evening everyone, I'm Captain Harris. I'm here today to talk about the deaths of the Richardson family, which took place on October twenty-fifth, in their home out on Memorial Park. I want to make sure we're all up to date on what's happening in our investigation. There will be some time for questions at the end. Now . . ."

The captain spoke slowly and carefully. He walked the crowd through what had happened, starting with the discovery of David Richardson out by the reservoir. He told them that while David had died from a stab wound to his chest, the rest of the Richardsons had been killed by bludgeoning. At this point, he paused and glanced over at his detectives.

"Our forensic examinations lead us to believe," he said, clearly choosing his words carefully, "that due to the evidence found on the body of David Richardson, he inflicted his own injuries on himself. And . . ."

Harris paused as the voices in the room swelled.

". . . *and* that it is to be the report of the coroner's office that the cause of his death be officially ruled as suicide."

Joe heard words and snatches of phrases as people muttered to each other. Words like *unbelievable* and *ridiculous* and *murdered*. A man turned to the woman next to him: "Who the hell stabs themselves to death? The man was killed, just like his family." Through all of this, Joe watched as the color drained steadily from the face of Steve Purcell. His wife had practically collapsed onto him. Shock, or something more? Joe gave himself a mental nudge—*question Julie Purcell.*

"Please," Harris said, holding his hand up. "I know this is hard to understand. Hard to hear. Upsetting. I'm just sharing with you what the evidence tells us up to this point. Our understanding of the events that took place on October twenty-fifth inside the Richardson house is still unfolding. What we are certain of at this point is the following: Marcy Richardson and her daughter, Emily—as well as Emily's baby son Jacob—were murdered in their beds. They were killed with what we believe to be a tire iron taken from inside the home. Thankfully, it appears that their deaths happened quickly."

The crowd continued to murmur and shift around in their seats. Truth often made folks uncomfortable. Joe knew this, knew that the truth about what had happened in that house was maybe the most uncomfortable thing most of these people would ever hear.

Which was probably the reason the captain had just avoided telling it. Because the truth was that they hadn't all died quick, and Emily Richardson had torn the hair from her scalp to prove it.

"We do have a number of pieces of physical evidence collected at the scene," Harris went on. "Obviously, I'm not about to divulge the exact details of an ongoing investigation. What I can say, however, is that there were a number of distinctive items left behind by the killer or killers—the staged nature of which would indicate this was a planned attack. We also found a shoe print of an unknown male on the property. Whoever left that print is a person of interest and we would ask them to come forward to eliminate themselves as a suspect.

"There was no sign of forced entry into the house. Whether this was because the attacker or attackers had keys to the property or they were let in, we don't know. They might well have just been lucky and found an open window or door."

Joe walked slowly along the wall of the church. Past the rows of people sitting in their plastic chairs. He scanned their faces, watched their movements, their postures. Noted if they'd come alone, and whether they looked scared, or angry, or excited. Across the hall, Ackerman did the same. And all the while, Joe saw the crime-scene photos behind his eyes, every time he blinked. Their grimy images were burned into his brain. It was his fuel.

Then Harris cleared his throat and said, "I'd like to now open up the floor to any questions."

The rows of reporters erupted. People shouting out their names, their news organizations. They raised their hands. A couple of them even jumped to their feet. An eagerness that made Joe sick. He found Gonzalez in the throng. The guy was sitting quietly, his pen in the air.

Joe thought about the photograph from the baseboard, wondered whether Gonzalez would keep his mouth shut about it. He shot Ackerman a worried glance.

The captain motioned toward the reporter. "Mr. Gonzalez," Harris said, barely hiding his disdain.

The rabble quieted down. Gonzalez—never one to miss an opportunity to make an impression—rose slowly to his feet. He even managed to pause for a moment for effect.

"Daniel Gonzalez, the *Tribune*," he said. "You said that you believed David Richardson killed himself out by that lake, although I have to say, in all my years of reporting here in Cooper"—pointed glance at the man from Kansas City three seats over—"I've never heard of someone committing suicide by stabbing themselves in the chest."

The murmurs grew behind him. A man near the back in a base-ball cap stood up and shouted that it was all a load of horseshit, that David Richardson had been murdered plain and simple. Joe's eyes swung toward him, trying to memorize his face. Gonzalez certainly knew how to get his readers going.

"Is there a question, Mr. Gonzalez?" Harris said.

"Is it your theory that David Richardson murdered his family before committing suicide?"

"At this point, we're not ruling anything out."

It was the third time someone had made reference to David Richardson killing himself, and third time was the charm. More people vaulted to their feet, shouting. A woman dressed in camo pants accused the captain of ignoring the truth. "This is the work of *outsiders*," she crowed, her friends stamping their feet in agreement. "We welcome them into our town and look what they do. No God-fearing white man would do this to his own family—"

"No *Christian* God-fearing white man—"

"—and everyone here knows it 'cept you."

Another round of cheering. More voices piping up.

"Your police department couldn't find a missing *shoe*, never mind solve something like this—"

"*Corrupt*, you boys are all *corrupt*—"

Joe was starting to lose track of who was shouting now. People getting themselves riled up, mob mentality overriding basic dignity. So much for using Gonzalez to keep people under control.

Harris put his hands up and tried to calm things down.

"Please," he said, leaning into the microphone rather than rais-ing his voice. "It's just a theory, one of many. This is *preliminary* evidence."

"You oughta be questioning those homeless tramps down by the river," a woman yelled. "They were looking at me the other day like I was a cut of meat!"

"Now, I'm not *racist*," a large, red-faced man began, "but—"

Harris cut them all off. "Everybody, I promise you, we are not focusing on any one suspect at present."

"But David Richardson *is* a suspect?" Gonzalez asked loudly. "In the deaths of his family, *and* in his own?"

"He is a person of interest," Harris said. "One of many."

The captain was getting angry now. It was a thankless task, Joe knew. People wanted to feel safe, wanted an investigation like this to be wrapped up quick. To see the person responsible arrested or dead. But at the same time, if something seemed too neat, if something didn't fit their narrow view, they didn't trust it. And once trust was lost, it almost didn't matter whether they arrested the right guy or not.

Gonzalez's voice cut through the chatter once more. "You refuse to confirm whether you have any suspects, captain," he said, and Joe froze, knowing what was coming next. "But what about the photo—"

"You've had your two questions," Harris said sharply. "I want to give everyone a chance to ask something. Ms. MacNeill?"

A woman a few seats over stood up and started asking about an increased police presence on the streets. Gonzalez sat down hard, his face set. Joe breathed out a sigh of relief.

The conference didn't last much longer. Harris got his main points out. More visible police, especially at night. A recommendation not to be out after dark. A reminder to check your doors and windows before going to bed. Fairly tame advice, all things considered. It wasn't like he had much else to go on.

Joe waited for Ackerman outside. The sun had set, and he watched as people hurried through the parking lot, their righteous fury evaporating in the warm night as they scattered to their cars and the safety of home.

Chapter Eighteen

Harris had wanted the press conference to make a splash, and it did. He assigned a junior officer to man the phone lines. In total, just over sixty people called the hotline over the next twelve hours. Cranks, every one of them. People with nothing better to do than waste police time from a phone booth halfway across town.

A few of them genuinely wanted to help. The mystics and the telepaths, mainly. The ones who reported visions of baby Jacob naming his killer in their dreams. The junior officer dutifully noted down each one on a small square of paper and passed them along to Ackerman and Joe. Their meeting-room command center was starting to look messy.

"Someone better go speak to Bob," Ackerman said, leaning back in his chair and raising one of the little squares. "Apparently David Richardson himself's been on the phone. Turns out he's not dead at all, and wants to confess."

Joe grunted as his partner scrunched up the paper and tossed it into the trash. "I think he's phoned a couple times already. Dispatch pulled his address. Want to go knock on his door?"

"Captain doesn't want us antagonizing the population any more than they already are."

"No thanks to Gonzalez."

"Please don't say that man's name in this hallowed space."

Joe smiled grimly. There was a certain satisfaction in knowing that the reporter had gotten under Ackerman's skin.

Since the press conference, the *Tribune* had already put out an article on the supposed mistakes that Cooper PD had made in their investigation. Witnesses unquestioned, theories ignored. It didn't matter what the forensics reports said, the paper had reached its own conclusions. Mainly that David Richardson was innocent, that he'd been murdered along with his family, and that the police were currently covering up for the killer. Joe even got a mention; taking that roll of film from Gonzalez was tantamount to suppression of free speech, apparently.

In all of this, the sad part wasn't really the bullshit that the *Tribune* pumped out. It was the number of townsfolk only too willing to listen.

The blessing, if there was one, was that Gonzalez hadn't printed anything about the photo from the baseboard. Not yet, anyway. It made Joe uneasy, like the reporter was building up to something.

He held the picture out in front of him now. "We need to talk about this," Joe said.

Ackerman glanced up at the door. "Not here."

"It's just us."

"In the room, yeah."

Joe blinked. "You think this place is bugged?"

"I don't think we should be taking any chances, that's all."

"The tech we use? Trust me, you'd know if people were listening in. There'd be a tape deck the size of my television in the corner of the room."

"Humor me, will you?"

"Alright, you win." Joe held his hands up. "Let's go to the diner. Unless, of course, they're in on it too."

"Already eaten," Ackerman said, rolling to his feet. "Besides, I want to talk to Emily Richardson's friends today. Kill two birds."

"Unis already took a bunch of statements."

"I know, but I want to get a feel for them. Look them in the eyes when I talk to them."

Joe nodded, snapped his notebook shut as he followed Ackerman back into the main office, then out to the parking lot. "What are you thinking?"

"I'm thinking Emily Richardson was a seventeen-year-old with a kid, and I have no idea who the father is. Those statements you're talking about? Not one of them knew who he was."

"They lied?"

Ackerman shrugged as he climbed into his car. "They're kids. This stuff is scary, makes them clam up sometimes." The car started with a throaty growl. "Understanding why kids do what they do is one mystery I will never crack."

The radio played country as they drove. It had never really been Joe's thing but he was grateful for it now. Gave him something to focus on other than the quiet streets around them. Lone cars waiting for traffic lights; diners with empty tables by the windows.

At last night's press conference, people had been angry. An anger that had made them bold, made them stand up in a roomful of strangers and say nearly anything. Things they might not have known they had in them. Things they might not have known they even believed—or worse, things they knew they didn't.

But once they were out of that room? Once the anger faded? Then all they'd be left with was fear. And fear could be crippling. Fear could build, until it was too much to bear. Until the anger came back to take the strain, sometimes in ways they wouldn't expect. Beating on a stranger because he looked at them funny, or because he was walking down the wrong street. Right now, Cooper was quiet. But Joe sensed the fear was building, and it was only a matter of time before it broke free.

Ackerman reached for his cigarettes. "You know, back in San Antonio I had a case," he began. "A missing girl. Aged seven. Mother and father went on the news channels, begged whoever had her to give her up. Offered money and everything."

"What happened to her?"

"Couple weeks went by—nothing. Then one day, a neighbor of the kid's *grandparents* hears a child yelling inside. They knock on the door, ask if everything's alright. Find the missing girl inside, playing Atari. Turned out the mother had made the whole thing up. Gave the daughter to her folks to keep hidden for a while."

"Why the hell would she do something like that?"

"Just wanted to get on TV, I guess."

Joe blinked as his partner lit up. Saw the Richardsons again. Marcy's head buried in the crook of her arm.

"What happened to this family, it was personal, Brian. I can't prove it, but I know it. The killer had a reason to be at their house that night. We find that reason, we find our man."

Ackerman squeezed the wheel and drove faster.

O'Bannan High School sat off the main street. A low, squat property with a bunch of boarded-up windows along the front. The building looked more like a factory than a school. Joe remembered coming here as a kid; place had been halfway to condemned even back then, and time hadn't helped matters any.

They were met at reception by a stocky woman. Late fifties, with bags under her eyes. She ushered them into a side room. Fast, embarrassed. Joe got it: police at a high school were bad enough. Homicide detectives were worse still.

She set them up in a science classroom. Bunsen burners and posters of the periodic table. A funny smell in the air—chemicals and teenage sweat. Joe stared out the window at the empty school-yard. Everything seemed so much smaller now.

Ackerman sat down at a desk in the middle of the room. "This will do fine," he said.

The woman nodded. "Who do you want to speak with first?" she asked.

◆ ◆ ◆

Some people, they just had a look about them. Some you could tell were going to be assholes before they opened their mouths. Something in the way they walked into the room. Like they were looking forward to it. Those were the ones Joe liked to crack the most.

Then there were the others. The people scared shitless before you'd even started. The kind of person that would sign whatever piece of paper you slid in front of them, just to get it to stop.

Joe and Ackerman spoke to a handful of students, and they pretty much hit both types. There were a couple of tough ones—ones who'd go back to their pals and brag about how they'd told some cops where to go. A badge of honor they'd polish for years to come.

Most of them, though, were decent kids. They understood what had happened in their town. Wanted to help if they could. The biggest trouble, it turned out, was Emily Richardson herself.

"She really dropped off the map when she left school," one girl said. "Like, I hadn't seen her for weeks before . . . before she . . ."

"Did Emily ever talk about her son? About Jacob?" Ackerman asked.

"She didn't want people knowing her business," another girl said. "She only told people she was pregnant when she couldn't hide it anymore."

"How did she seem after she got pregnant? You notice any change in her?"

"Besides the obvious?"

"Sure," Ackerman said, smiling. "Besides the obvious."

The first girl again: "Emily had always been private. More than a lot of people. But I got the impression that being pregnant . . . It made her happy." A furtive glance toward the floor. "Well, maybe not toward the end."

"What happened at the end?"

The boy grinned at them as he leaned back in his chair, spinning a lighter between his fingers. "Rumor started around school that Emily's *dad* was the father. I mean, it was bullshit, but we all just wanted to know who it was. Had to be a reason she kept it so quiet." He laughed, still playing with that lighter. "That rumor made her so mad, I think she just decided not to show her face to anyone for a while."

Joe stared at him. "Can you see why a rumor like that might make someone mad?"

"Yeah, I guess I can see." The boy shook his head. "Man, she thought she was all that."

And then there was Mel.

Mel had a look about her, but it wasn't like the rest. To Joe, she looked loyal. The type of girl that maybe didn't have many friends, and worked hard to keep the ones she did. The type of girl who would keep another's secret.

She was a small, timid-looking thing in thick-rimmed glasses. She stood by the doorway, too nervous to sit down.

"Please, have a seat, Mel," Ackerman said. "You can pick anywhere you'd like."

The girl nodded and moved immediately to the nearest desk. Sat with her back straight, like she'd been summoned to the principal's office. Something that probably didn't happen to her all that often.

Ackerman leaned forward, smiling warmly. "Hi Mel. My name is Detective Ackerman. This is Detective Finch. I'd like to thank you for taking the time to speak with us today."

"That's fine."

Her voice was timid, too. She picked at a fingernail.

"I know all of this is pretty difficult," Ackerman said.

"Yeah."

"You guys were friends, right? You and Emily?"

"Yeah."

"How well did you know her?"

"Pretty . . . pretty well. We're good friends. Were good friends."

"You saw her a lot."

"I guess. I mean, I didn't see her as much, not since she . . ."

"Since she left school?"

"Yeah."

Ackerman nodded like he understood, and sat back in his chair. Joe watched as Mel visibly relaxed. He had to admit, the guy was good at this sort of thing. Had a softly-softly approach. Something Joe had always struggled with.

"Your teachers tell me that Emily left because of her baby. Because of Jacob?"

Mel nodded.

"Did you meet him after he was born?"

The young girl smiled sadly and nodded again. "Yeah, I met him a few times. He was really cute."

Her words caught in her throat and her hands moved to her face.

"I'm sorry," she said.

"Don't be," Ackerman said. "It's a sad thing, what happened to Emily and her family. A terrible thing. And that's why we're here. Right, Joe?"

"We just want to find whoever it was that did this, same as you."

The detectives waited a couple of moments as Mel collected herself. Then Ackerman leaned over his little desk again.

"Mel, do you know who Jacob's father was?"

She glanced away, her cheeks reddening.

Joe studied her face. It was always hard with kids. They got embarrassed easily, got hung up on the inconsequentials. They lied about silly stuff so they didn't get in trouble with their parents. And everything was served with a layer of drama that you just had to push past.

"It's alright," Joe said, flashing what he hoped was a reassuring smile. "It's alright if you don't know. But if you do, it might be helpful."

"We don't want to cause anyone any trouble," Ackerman said, picking up the thread. "We just need to make sure we look at everything."

Mel nodded. "I . . . I only saw him once," she said quietly.

Ackerman flipped open his notepad. "Was it someone from school?"

"No."

"Do you know his name?"

"No."

"When did you meet him?"

"I didn't really meet him, I just . . . saw him. With Emily."

"Where were they?"

"You know MacFarlane's farm?"

Joe grunted. "Sure."

Alistair MacFarlane was a bit of a legend around Cooper. An old hermit farmer, his place was out in the middle of nowhere. And while the farms around him had slowly been bought out by bigger and bigger outfits—then finally by faceless agribusiness corporations—MacFarlane had held out. The man had insisted on harvesting his crops all but single-handedly, signing up drifters and local misfits for a week at a time when he needed help with his aging machinery. Most of these guys had never worked anything more complex than a beer can in their life. Every so often one of them went off the rails, and local law enforcement was sent to round them up. Joe had nearly gelded himself one time, chasing a big man from Arkansas over a barbed-wire fence.

So yeah, he knew MacFarlane's farm.

Mel shifted in her seat. "Well, that's where she said he lived. He and the rest of them were helping the old man. There's so much land there. Why didn't he just sell some of it? Rich guys offered him a good price a couple times."

Joe smiled. "Because it's not always about the money. Some people just like doing the work."

"Well, if *I* had that much land, I'd sell it and use the money to get out of here."

Mel faltered as she said it. Guilt flashed on her face, like wanting to leave Cooper was such a terrible thing.

Ackerman was scribbling in his notebook. He looked up. "*He and the rest of them?*"

"What?"

"You said *he and the rest of them* were helping work MacFarlane's land. Who are you talking about?"

Mel shrugged. "There was a group of them out there. I don't know how many."

"And you went there, too? What were you doing out there?"

"Giving her a ride, this one time. I didn't stay long. She didn't want me to meet him, kept asking me to go home."

"You get a good look at him?"

"Not really. Tall, blond hair. That's all I saw."

Joe said, "Why didn't she want you to meet him, Mel?"

"I guess she knew her dad wouldn't approve."

"He older?"

"Yeah."

"How old? As old as my partner here?"

Mel shook her head. "Not *that* old. Uh, I mean . . ."

"I know what you mean," Ackerman said, shooting Joe a faint smile. "When was this?"

"A long time ago. Maybe a year? Emily had just found out she was pregnant, I think. She stopped seeing him before the baby came, though."

Ackerman scribbled in his notepad. "You know why?"

"No. Emily and I, we didn't really hang out after she left school."

"How did you guys become friends?" Joe asked.

"Oh, study group," Mel said. She smiled a little, visibly relieved to be back on safe ground. "I was helping her with some classes."

"Would she have told any of her other friends about him?"

"I don't think so."

"Emily would tell you stuff she wouldn't tell other people?"

"Yeah."

"Why?"

Mel looked away. She seemed to sag a little, sitting there. "I don't know."

Joe bobbed his head. "Seems like you do, though. It's okay to tell us."

The girl swallowed, looked around. Searching for someone to bail her out, maybe. "I'm not that popular, I guess. I don't have a lot of friends. I think she thought she could trust me." She gave a weak smile. "I didn't really have anyone I could tell this stuff to anyway. And now look at me."

She sank even further into her seat, distressed.

Ackerman closed his notepad gently. "You're not betraying her, you know. If Emily knew whoever it was that did this, I think she'd want you to help us catch him, don't you?"

"Yeah, I guess," Mel said, wiping at her nose. "I just don't know what else I can tell you."

Ackerman reached into his pocket. Pulled out the black-and-white photo from the baseboard. He slid it partway inside his notebook to hide David Richardson, and then held it up.

"Was this the man you saw?" he asked Mel.

She stared at it for a long while, then shook her head. "No, I don't think that was him," she said. "Sorry."

Ackerman nodded and put the photo away. "That's alright." He glanced over at Joe. "I think that's probably everything. You can head back to class now, Mel. And thank you for today—you've been incredibly helpful."

Mel smiled. That feel-good approval from authority flooding through her.

Laura

Several days had passed at the farm, and Laura had spent almost all of them alone. At meals she sat at the end of the long table, sandwiched between Francine and Patrick, eating little and talking less.

She could feel the gaze of more and more people on her each day. It had gotten so bad that one night she'd returned to her room to find a note from Francine lying on her pillow. *Everything will be alright*, it read, in neat little writing. She'd fallen asleep reading and rereading that damn note, had woken up with it still clutched in her fingers. Part of her screamed to get out, to grab her few possessions and just hike back to the highway. The rest of her pictured patrol cars parked outside her home, prowling the roads in search of her. She'd murdered someone. They would never stop looking.

"You need to get a routine going," Francine had told her. "Something to occupy your mind. You keep replaying that night, you'll go crazy."

She was right, of course. But beyond chores, there wasn't much to do. So Laura had thrown herself into the farm work. She worked longer than the others, and with fewer breaks. She planted carrots and broad beans. She harvested cabbages. At the end of each day, she showered in cold water and collapsed into her bed, falling asleep near instantly. Too tired for the nightly bonfire, too busy to sit with the others for lunch. It was an isolated situation, and a situation that suited her just fine.

Francine hadn't said what night she should stop replaying. Hadn't had to. Mason and all that blood sat there, in the front of her mind, every second of the day.

He worked at the sawmill. *Had* worked. Her thoughts about him, they tended to flit back and forth between the past and the present. His handsome smile at the bar the night they met; his hands around her throat the night she left.

"You really don't know anyone else here in town?"

"I really don't."

Their opening exchange. He was the guy at the bar who had seen her sitting alone. It was the same day she'd left the farm. She'd volunteered to go into town with Kyle, had spent the entire car ride with her leg shaking she was so nervous. He'd put his hand on her knee, given it a squeeze. Laughed, like she was just so goddamn excited to be with him.

It had been easy once they got to the store. They'd split the shopping list, she'd tossed her half straight into the trash and slipped out the door. Hid inside a TV repair place, spent an hour watching him from across the street, watching him walk up and down the little row of stores, his steps growing more and more irate, until he'd pounded both fists on the hood of his SUV and left.

"Where you staying?" the guy in the bar had asked.

"At the moment? Nowhere."

"You got a job?"

139

"I've got nothing."

He'd laughed at that. Told her his name was Mason. Said he'd never met anyone like her. This strange girl, who seemed to have been dropped into Cooper from orbit. It wasn't that far from the truth.

He'd bought her a drink. A cocktail, like a girl couldn't just drink a beer. Gin, green chartreuse, maraschino liqueur, and fresh lime. He'd said it was called a Last Word. Grinned as he'd said it—a line she hadn't really got at the time. "Women," he'd said, sliding the drink across to her. "They always get the Last Word." Later it would become his joke, his party piece for making others laugh at her expense.

"I got a buddy," he'd said. "Runs the motel out on Corolla Drive. He's been looking for someone to do housekeeping. Change sheets, clean bathrooms, that sort of thing." He shrugged. "It's nothing great, but it comes with a room."

She'd known then that she would end up with him. Looking back now, she wondered if there wasn't some part of her that was broken. This need to be taken care of. This inability to function by herself. When the bar closed, he took her home like it wasn't even a question. Where else was she going to go?

But now, kneeling in the hard fields, scraping soil under the sun, she wondered if that was true. She sat back and stared out across the plains. Course, it was easier to think like that. To play the victim. To shrug off any responsibility for what had happened. She'd spent years at the farm before meeting Mason. Years watching Rudy work his manipulative charm on everyone around him.

Had she really been a helpless woman that night in the bar, on the run from Kyle? So inexperienced that she had to latch onto the first guy who wanted to take her home? Or had she simply turned a night on the streets into a warm bed? Replaying it all in her head, it was easy to lose track.

She popped open the flask of water sitting next to her and drained it. The water was ice-cold and wonderful. Some of it ran down her neck, and she half-considered just pouring the whole thing over her head.

"Laura?"

She turned. A younger man whose name she hadn't learned yet was standing there.

"Yes?"

"Rudy wants to see you."

She set the flask down and sealed it back up. "In his office?"

"By the trees."

Bundling up her equipment, she stood, brushing the dirt from her pants and stretching her back. She trekked across the fields toward the treeline. After a couple of minutes, she could make out Rudy standing there. Leaning against a trunk, his body draped over it. He raised his hand as she got close.

Laura did the same. "You wanted to see me?"

Rudy smiled, pushing himself slowly upright. "Good morning to you too. How's the field today?"

"It's fine."

A brief pause, then he said, "Come and see what Kyle caught."

She followed Rudy deeper through the scattered trees, where they found Kyle in a small clearing, grinning, his hands in his pockets like he didn't know what else to do with them. A nervous energy that put Laura on edge.

He was standing over a simple spring trap, the type that littered much of the area around here. A small rabbit was caught, its foot snared in the device. It wasn't dead yet. It lay on its side and whimpered, panting quickly.

"Well done," Laura said, staring at the animal. "It'll make a nice dinner. But you shouldn't leave it like that. It's hurting."

"Then why don't you put it out of its misery?" Kyle said.

"What?"

"Use this." And he held out a metal tire iron.

Laura glanced over at Rudy, but Rudy didn't say anything. Just kept on watching her, kept on leaning against tree trunks like he couldn't stay on his own two feet without them.

She reached out and took the tire iron. The dull metal was cool in her warm hands. The ends of it crusted in what she might once have thought was rust. After Mason and the kitchen knife, she knew better.

Kyle snickered. "Don't worry about the mess on it. I shot a deer a few nights back, took a few turns with the thing to put it down for good. Rabbits don't take as much effort. One good swing ought to do it."

Laura felt her stomach tighten. "You keep that deer for yourself, Kyle?"

"Huh?"

"I don't remember eating any venison the last couple days."

Kyle spat into the brush. "You barely been down for dinner the last couple days," he said. "And besides, you

142

got to hang it a while before you butcher it, otherwise the meat stays tough."

Rudy cleared his throat and finally spoke up. "Come on now, Laura. Don't let that thing suffer."

The rabbit gazed up at her, its eyes wide, its belly rising and falling in quick movements. She tightened her grip on the tire iron. It was a kindness, she knew that—or at least she told herself so. Sometimes it was better to murder something than to let it live. They called it a mercy killing.

She crouched down next to the animal. Raised the iron. She could feel Kyle and Rudy watching her, could swear they were panting almost as much as the rabbit. Waiting on her to fail, to chicken out. To show them she'd gone soft.

She hadn't gone soft.

The iron made a little whistle as it flew. A soft crack, and the whimpering stopped. The rabbit's belly went slack. She tossed the bloodied metal on the ground and stood up.

"We done here?"

Neither of them said anything at first. Then Rudy started to laugh. A great, slow laugh that kept building until he was just about bent over.

"Well, I did not expect that," he said at last. "Did you, Kyle?"

"She's always been full of surprises," Kyle said slowly.

Laura kept her eyes on Rudy. "Can I go back to work now?"

"Course you can. I'll walk you back. Kyle, take care of this." He flicked the back of his hand toward the rabbit.

Silently, Laura fell into step beside him as they left the clearing. When they were nearly at the fields, Rudy spoke up.

"You've always had something that a lot of others here don't. A spark inside you. Something that scares me a little. Scares you too, I think."

Laura kept quiet, unsure how best to answer. Not that it mattered. Rudy sure did like the sound of his own voice.

"Don't tell the others," he said, "but I finally finished decoding the message."

She gave him a sideways glance as they walked. "You did? What did it say?"

"That the day of ascension is close, Laura. Real close." He grinned. "I'm going to announce it soon. Tonight, maybe."

"Well, congratulations, Rudy."

"How have the others been treating you?"

"They've been ignoring me mostly."

"That might change when I tell people about the message. Closer we get to the big day, the more people are going to worry about the wolves in our midst trying to stop it."

Whatever that meant. "I'll be careful," she said.

Rudy nodded as they neared her patch of field. "My offer still stands. You want my protection, you just come knock on my door. Doesn't matter if it's the dead of night."

Laura kept her gaze forward. If Rudy wanted to, he could have her dragged from her bed and into his with a snap of his fingers. Hell, he could just walk into her room, simple as that.

But that wasn't how he liked to play things. It was one thing to force someone through violence. It was another to engineer a situation where they came to *you*.

She thought again about that night she'd met Mason. Maybe in the end she wasn't all that different from Rudy.

144

Maybe she *had* done to Mason what Rudy had done to her. Manipulated him, exploited him.

Course, you took that line of thinking and ran it down the track a few years, and where did it get you? A cramped little kitchen at two in the morning, with your husband's hands crushing your throat. The years in between filled with Mason drinking—drinking in bars or until he passed out in front of the TV, coming to bed stinking of sawdust or beer, or sex. The first time he'd punched her he'd cried and said he was sorry. Said he would change, and he did. He didn't cry after that.

But if she was so smart, why had she put up with it for so long? If she'd exploited him that first night, then he'd sure as shit turned the tables on her. She'd tried to control Mason and failed. She couldn't do it, not like Rudy, not long-term. She wasn't strong enough. The only permanent solution she'd ever found was at the sharp end of a kitchen knife.

They stopped at her field and Rudy smiled. "I'll see you at dinner tonight," he said, and then he was gone. Striding back toward his room.

Laura watched him until he had disappeared inside, then turned to see Kyle standing a ways off. He was staring at her, the rabbit trussed up over one shoulder, the bloodied tire iron hanging down at his side.

Chapter Nineteen

Driving back to the station from the high school, the streets were quiet. Inside the car it was quieter still. It was early afternoon, but Joe was already feeling tired. He was glad his partner was behind the wheel.

Ackerman, mulling it all over, said, "So. Next stop, we go talk to this guy MacFarlane. See if he can't shed some light on all this."

Joe laughed. "Good luck with that."

"Oh yeah? Why, he some kind of hard-ass?"

"He's dead. MacFarlane had a heart attack back in April. One of his hired workers found him pitched over a fence."

"Shit." His partner slid a fresh cigarette into his mouth and lit up. The man was a chain-smoker. "Who's looking after the land now?"

"Who knows. Farm's locked up in probate. Last I heard, they tore his house down. Place was condemned. Any workers living there are long gone now."

Ackerman sighed and cracked his window. The dry afternoon air whipped at his hat. He took it off, tossed it on the back seat. Ran a hand through his hair. "So, according to a schoolkid, we've got Jacob's dad living out in the fields somewhere, him and a whole bunch of others, and they're going into town to butcher families." He paused. "Does that setup ring any bells?"

"Don't say it."

"You know what it sounds like, Joe."

"Brian, I swear, if you try to compare this to some kind of Manson family bullshit—"

"You don't see it?"

"Not like you do. People want to go sing 'Kumbaya' in the middle of nowhere, that's fine with me."

"What if it's some kind of religious cult, hmm? What if we've got some Branch Davidian nutjobs hoarding modified AR-15s? Christ, from the sounds of it, who knows *what* goes on out in those fields?"

"Corn, mostly. Some soybeans."

Ackerman smacked his palm off the steering wheel. "This isn't funny, Joe! Six months ago, I watched that David Koresh freak bring hellfire down on himself and his idiot followers. You asked me why I left San Antonio? Because of shit like that! It happened not three hours from my front door!"

Joe went quiet. Ackerman had a point. That Waco shitshow was something he'd want no part of.

After a couple of moments, his partner flicked his half-smoked cigarette out the window. "I'm sorry. Didn't mean to go off on you."

"No, I get it. I didn't mean to poke fun."

They slowed at a set of lights. Ackerman leaned across and started rummaging through the glovebox.

"What you looking for?" Joe asked.

"Cigarettes."

"How many of them do you get through a day?"

"Too many." Then, pulling a pack out from under a badly folded map: "You want one?"

"I told you, I'm trying to quit."

"That's right. Good for you."

They drove in silence the rest of the way. Wasn't long—a couple of minutes, maybe.

"We could try and speak to neighboring farmers," Ackerman said as they pulled into the station parking lot. "Maybe they saw something."

Joe shook his head. "MacFarlane's land is out in the middle of corporate hell. I promise you, no one out there knows shit about any field other than the one they're being paid to churn through." He unclipped his seatbelt. "You ask me, the photo's our priority."

They left the car, barreled through the main doors, and headed for the meeting room.

"We could try recanvassing the people on their street," Ackerman went on. "If the guy in the photo with Richardson is a pusher, he might be involved in prostitution. Might even be an idea to . . ."

His voice trailed off as they entered the room. Captain Harris was standing by the back wall, peering at the various photographs and scribbles they'd pinned up. He turned to them and smiled coldly.

"You two. Close the door and take a seat. We have a lot to discuss."

Chapter Twenty

Harris paced. Up and back along the wall, peering at scribbles and highlighted sections of forensic reports.

Joe slid uncomfortably into a seat and watched in silence.

"Hell of a mess you've made in here," Harris said.

Ackerman perched on the end of the table, took off his hat. "We're covering every lead, sir."

"And?"

"It's . . . still scattershot just now. None of it points anywhere conclusive yet."

Harris finally halted and turned toward them. His gaze moved back and forth from detective to detective. Then stopped on Joe.

"Tell me about the footprint," Harris said.

Joe cleared his throat. "It's a male shoe print, size nine."

"I know that. Whose is it?"

"We, uh, haven't managed to identify it yet."

Harris smiled and picked up a folder that Joe didn't recognize. "You boys clearly aren't abreast of current developments."

Ackerman frowned. "What's that?"

"Forensic report. Bob handed it in this morning when you two were out. Where were you, by the way?"

"O'Bannon High. Speaking with Emily Richardson's friends."

"Were they of any assistance?"

"A little, yeah. But again—"

"Nothing conclusive," Harris finished for him. His smile was still in place, only now it looked plastic and fixed. Like the guy had seen someone smile once and figured he'd give it a go.

"What did Bob find?" Ackerman asked.

Harris flicked open the folder and started leafing through the report. "Forensics confirmed that the print found on the property belonged to the neighbor, Stephen Purcell."

Joe sat up. "How did they find that?"

"Well, I'm no expert, but I believe it's fairly simple once you have a shoe to check against."

"But we don't—"

"I sent a couple uniformed officers around yesterday to go through his trash. Weren't they surprised to find a perfectly good pair just lying there." The captain tossed the folder onto the table. "Almost as surprised as I was to discover you hadn't even thought to do the same."

Ackerman said, "Sir, this is our investigation. You should have checked with us before—"

"Before what, detective? Before trying to get this godforsaken mess under control? What is all this?" He motioned to the wall behind him. "All these photos and statements, theories scribbled on whiteboards. It's been almost a week, and still you're no closer to making an arrest."

"You want us to bring Stephen Purcell in for questioning? Fine, we'll—"

"No, I do not want you to bring Stephen Purcell in for questioning. I want you to *arrest* Stephen Purcell."

Ackerman paused. Joe watched his fingers tighten on the brim of his hat.

"With all due respect," Ackerman said, "on what grounds?"

"Are you serious? Purcell was at the town meeting. He hears about the shoe print, decides to toss his sneakers. There's your grounds."

"It's circumstantial, sir. We don't know when he threw them out."

"Well, we know it was after he left the goddamn print."

"He was their neighbor. There might well be a perfectly normal reason for his footprint to be there."

Harris stared at him incredulously. "Trampled in the flower-beds, next to a downspout not three feet from Emily Richardson's bedroom window?"

"It's not enough for a warrant, sir. The DA will never agree—"

"Then skip the DA!" Harris barked. "You can hold him for forty-eight hours before his first arraignment. This is *basic* stuff, detective. Stop jerking me around."

Joe watched his partner struggle to keep his cool. This from the guy who less than ten minutes ago had pointed the finger at Steve Purcell himself. A sudden realization that Ackerman really hated to miss even the most basic procedure.

The captain dropped the report on the table in front of him. He reached into his inside pocket and pulled out a photograph. Held it up. Joe felt his stomach twitch.

It was the photo from the baseboard.

"Would one of you mind explaining this?" Harris said.

"Where did you get that?" said Joe.

The captain glared at him. "Why, I found it right here. Amongst all this mess."

Joe glanced over at his partner. "You made a copy?" he asked.

"I make a copy of a lot of stuff," Ackerman said. To Harris: "We found that behind a baseboard in the Richardson house. It shows David Richardson meeting someone. We don't know who yet."

"And why the hell am I only hearing about this now?"

"We wanted to wait until we had something more concrete."

"More concrete," Harris echoed softly. He slid the photo back into his pocket. "You want to hear something concrete? I *will not* allow this investigation to be the end of me. Do both of you understand that? I know this is all circumstantial, Ackerman, I *know* that. But while you two are out chasing rumors and speculation, I've got the governor's office *and* the state legislature breathing down my neck. I've got Gonzalez printing incendiary trash as fast as he can type it. I've got men spending their nights with shotguns on their laps, wives sleeping with scissors under their pillows." The captain let out a sigh, rubbed at his face with a hand that Joe thought he saw tremble, just a little. "I've been on borrowed time for a while now, gentlemen, but I'll be damned if I get shown the door by some oily state senator twisting this thing to make a splash at my expense. Now, you've got your orders, and I don't want to hear anything further."

After he was gone, Joe slumped back in his seat and looked over at his partner.

"Now what?" he said.

Ackerman grimaced and reached for his hat. "You heard the captain," he said. "We go arrest Stephen Purcell."

Chapter Twenty-One

Joe stared through the one-way glass at the man sitting in the inter-rogation room. Steve Purcell was slumped forward, hands splayed out on the table in front of him. Did he look guilty, sitting there? Did he look like a man who had slept with his neighbor's daughter, who had fathered her child, who had murdered them all to keep it quiet?

On paper there was a certain logic to it. A route from start to finish. But looking at him now, Joe wasn't sure. Hell, it wasn't just what was going on through the glass, either. It was all those years they'd spent together at school. Insider knowledge filtering his per-ception. Memories coloring his thoughts. And so it came back to the same question, the one Joe had been asking himself ever since Steve had answered his front door. *Did he look guilty?*

"You ready?"

That was Ackerman. His back to the glass, standing by the door. Joe followed him out of the room.

In the corridor, he spotted Julie Purcell. She was on a plastic seat. Her head bowed, her hands in her lap. He could see them shaking from here. She'd followed them all the way to the station; the way she'd drifted, Joe was amazed she hadn't crashed.

He turned to his partner. "Give me a minute."

Ackerman nodded and leaned against the wall.

Julie looked up as he approached, her face crumpling a little. "Joe, I . . ."

Joe smiled as best he could. Took the seat next to her. "How you doing? Can I get you a coffee or anything?"

"I just want to know what's happening."

"Well, we're about to go have a talk with Steve now." He watched her face closely. "Is there anything you think we should know before we do?"

Julie looked away, shifting her weight on the seat. Joe stared at her, felt that same question bubbling up. *Did she look guilty?*

"Julie?" he said gently, glancing back at his partner. Ackerman was still standing there, watching. "Julie, the night of the murders, was Steve with you?"

She kept her gaze on the floor. He got the impression of something hardening within her. "No. Not all night."

"Where was he?"

"You'd have to ask him that."

Joe let her answer fade out. Finally, he nodded and stood up. "If you want, I can grab you a pop from the machine?"

"I'm fine."

Joe studied her for a moment longer, then nodded and headed back toward Ackerman. Got halfway there before Harris turned the corner ahead of them. Talking to a man in a well-cut suit: Sam Lemire, the state senator. The two of them were smiling. Sure looked like the captain was getting squeezed, alright.

Harris offered some friendly advice before Joe and Ackerman entered the room—"Make sure you nail this guy"—and the last thing Joe saw as the door closed was Lemire's toothy grin.

Ackerman opened with an offer.

"Can I get you something else to drink, Mr. Purcell? I'd say coffee, but the stuff our machine puts out is absolutely repulsive. Or maybe it's just the water supply here. I'm sure we can find you a soda if you'd like."

Purcell shook his head, barely raising his gaze. Joe caught Ackerman's eye. Glanced at the mirrored glass. Pictured Harris and Lemire, staring back.

They both sat at the table. Ackerman set out a thin folder in front of him. His fingers moved over the surface of the folder, trying to decide whether to dive in.

Joe cleared his throat. "Julie's here," he said. "She's worried about you."

Purcell looked over at him. Gave a resigned smile. "Who would have thought, back when we were at school, that one day we'd be sitting here like this."

"One of life's little quirks," Joe said.

Purcell leaned back. He was dressed in loose jeans and a dark T-shirt. He was pissed, too—wasn't trying to hide it. Joe had known him almost all his life, but still struggled to get a read on the guy.

Purcell said, "I've been thinking a lot about the past recently. Ever since your visit, I suppose. A lot of people try to leave this town after high school. Not sure I can blame them."

"Cooper's not for everyone."

"But it's home, isn't it. For people like you and me."

Joe shrugged. "I get the allure of a big city. Small-town living, people knowing your business . . . I guess maybe most just want to disappear a little."

"You like it, though, don't you? Being the big fish."

Joe had to smile at that. "Can't see how I quite qualify, there. More like a little sunfish. A perch, maybe. Bass, at most."

Unamused, Purcell nodded, his eyes still on Joe. "You ever think about the old days?"

At first Joe reached for the easy answer, *no*, but then caught himself. Recently it felt like that was *all* he'd been able to think about. His mother singing as she baked, that sweetness in the air. Dancing in the kitchen with her as she cooked her poison. Her last act with him, and he hadn't known. Hadn't had the chance to say goodbye. But *she'd* known; she'd known and she'd looked him in the eyes and laughed and spun him around—

He blinked. Brought himself back. Suddenly he was standing at the edge of the reservoir, flashes of white skin on a dark night. A girl's smile as she slipped under the water.

"Actually, yeah, I have been thinking of the old days lately," he said. "Holly Williams, she was a year ahead of us. You might not—"

"I knew Holly," Purcell said, and he flashed a smile. "Reckon a bunch of the guys did, you get my meaning."

Joe gritted his teeth. "Clear enough."

"They used to say she had a thing for taking guys' virginities. I heard she had a scorecard at home, used to tally it up, like it was some competition." Purcell tilted his head, his grin widening as realization dawned. "Oh, don't tell me . . ."

"Then don't ask."

Purcell put his hands up in mock surrender. For a moment Joe saw it; the inkling of something harder in the man, something nastier beneath the surface. For a moment he wondered if he'd been wrong about Steve Purcell.

"Whatever happened to Holly, anyway?" Joe asked.

Purcell's smile faltered a little. He sniffed, said, "You didn't hear? She moved out to Kansas City. Killed herself a couple years back. Loaded a bunch of rocks into her pockets and just walked into a lake."

Joe blinked. "Jesus."

"Life's little quirks, right, Joe?"

An uncomfortable silence settled over the room.

Ackerman shoved the conversation back on point. "Did you kill the Richardson family, Mr. Purcell?" he asked.

The question landed hard. Purcell's head snapped at it. "No," he said.

"You know who did?"

"No."

"Okay." Ackerman opened the file and pulled out a photo, slid it across the table. It was a picture of a footprint embedded in soil. "Do you know what this is, Mr. Purcell?"

Purcell glanced at the photo, his face impassive. "Looks like a shoe print."

"That's right. It was left behind at the crime scene. I think it was mentioned at the press conference. Was Mr. Purcell at the conference?"

This last part was directed at Joe, who nodded. "Yeah, he was there."

"Great, so you already know that part," Ackerman said. "So now we have this shoe print, alright, and we're wondering how on earth we're ever going to find the person who wears the shoe. I mean, there's a lot of people out there."

"Even more shoes," Joe added.

"At least twice as many," Ackerman conceded. "Hell, lots more than that, you think about it. Most people tending to have more than one pair."

Joe nodded soberly. "That checks out."

"Can we please get to the point?" Purcell said.

"Sure." Ackerman leaned forward. "Now, after we came to see you the other day, some officers swung by and had a look in your trash—"

Purcell perked up. "You searched my trash?"

"I didn't search it myself, but yeah, we did."

"Don't you need a warrant for something like that?"

"To go through your garbage? No, Mr. Purcell, we don't. What do they call it? Your reasonable expectation of privacy? You put your trash out, you're basically accepting that any number of animals or scavengers might go poking around in there. Hell, you're leaving it for a stranger to collect, after all, right? So no, we don't need a warrant to go through your trash—and when we did, this is what we found."

Ackerman slid a second photograph across the table. It was a picture of a pair of brown sneakers. He tapped the edge of the picture.

"Recognize these?"

Purcell stared at the photo, his face pale.

Joe leaned forward, flashed a sympathetic smile. "You know what's coming next, Steve. Don't draw this out."

"Let me guess," Purcell said. "It matched the shoe print you guys found."

Ackerman said, "I asked you already if you killed the Richardsons, but now I'm going to ask you again."

Purcell sank into his chair a little. "I didn't kill them," he said.

"Then why was your shoe print at the scene?"

"I don't know. I go over there sometimes. I'm their neighbor."

"You go walking over the flowerbeds? This print wasn't left on the garden path, you understand me? It was left under a window. Emily Richardson's window. You hear her dad getting back early, have to make a quick escape?"

"What?"

"Were you having an affair with Emily Richardson, Mr. Purcell?"

"Of course not."

"That why your wife didn't want to speak with us? You knock up your seventeen-year-old neighbor?"

"This is bullshit. You couldn't be more wrong—"

"What did she want? Money? Was she threatening to tell her father about you? Threatening to tell the *police?*"

"You think . . . you think I'm Jacob's *dad?* You think I killed my own son?"

Ackerman shrugged. "Maybe you're not his dad. Maybe Emily got around." He gave a slight smile. "You seem to know the girls that do."

Anger flushed Purcell's face. "Who the hell are you to ask me these sorts of questions? You're not even from around here, are you?"

"Texas. Was it the hat?"

Purcell turned on Joe. "Who the hell is this cowboy, Joe? Are you hearing him, what he's saying?"

Joe nodded yes, he was hearing him, then asked, "Where were you, Steve, on the night of October twenty-fifth?"

Purcell blinked at him. Once, twice. Sat back in his chair. "At home."

"I told you Julie was outside, remember? I told you I talked to her already. You want to answer that one again?"

Purcell started to speak, then fell silent. His gaze drifted.

Ackerman started pulling out more photos. "Maybe this will jog your memory a little," he said quietly. He spread them out on the table. Crime-scene photos, the Richardsons, butchered and bloodied.

"Stop," Purcell said, turning away from them. "I don't want to see those."

"This is the one that I struggle with the most," Ackerman said, and tapped the photo of David Richardson, lying flat at the reservoir's edge. "Did he really do it himself? I mean, I've heard that people do stab themselves to death, but I've never actually seen one before."

"I didn't—"

159

"Were you nervous, was that it? That why the body had those hesitation marks? Couldn't quite bring yourself to slide that knife home?"

"Detective—"

"Course, you must have been wearing gloves. No other prints on the knife but David's. How did you get him out to the lake?"

"I didn't kill him!"

"Then start talking!" Joe banged the table hard enough to make the photos jump. "You say you're innocent? Then where were you the night of the murders? You give us something to go on, or there's nothing I can do to help you. Do you understand what I'm saying?"

But if Purcell was holding anything else, he wasn't sharing. Joe watched as acceptance seemed to settle on the man's shoulders. He glanced back at the mirrored glass as Ackerman scooped up the photographs. Displeasure sat uneasily in his chest, its origins unknown. Harris, maybe, for being right. Or Purcell, for not putting up more of a fight. Or maybe it came from himself, for not seeing what had been right in front of him this whole time.

Chapter Twenty-Two

That night, the heat that had strangled Cooper for so many weeks finally broke. Rain clouds rolled in as the sun set, thick and dark, and what started as an evening drizzle soon turned into a full-blown thunderstorm.

Joe stood under an awning behind his apartment block. Watched the water soak the overgrown yard. Flashes to earlier in the year, to rivers bursting their banks, to flooded fields. He hoped to hell they weren't going to get a repeat.

It was too wet even for Leo, who hung back by Joe's feet, staring mournfully at his favorite patch by the wooden fence.

Inside, the storm still made itself known. In the rattle of the windows, in the slowly spreading damp patch above his kitchen. And there was a smell of something rotting; an animal, maybe, decomposing beneath the floorboards. A lesser man might have seen it as a sign. Omens of things to come.

Purcell's arrest was the headline story on the local news. But Joe couldn't shake that dissatisfaction, that feeling that Purcell wasn't everything the captain wanted him to be. Unanswered questions swirled around in his brain. How had Purcell gotten Richardson to the lake? How had he killed him?

Joe ate dinner and watched video footage of Harris behind a podium lined with microphones. Statements of reassurance, promises that a killer had been caught and that people could sleep easy in their beds. The evening storm would wash away the heat, he said, and tomorrow's Halloween Harvest festivities would go ahead in full. Behind him, State Senator Sam Lemire stood in his well-cut suit and smiled.

◆ ◆ ◆

Later, Joe lay awake in the early hours, notions of portents and warnings from above leading him to Zoe and her silver cross necklace. He'd never liked religion, never liked the way it changed people. Had seen firsthand how it got under people's skin and made them feel like shit just for trying to live. Like living in Cooper wasn't hard enough already.

His mom had been the only one in the family who believed in it. Enough to get down on her knees and pray to God every night to save her son. His dad had ignored it, along with most else that was going on around him. Shutting yourself off from the world was one way to deal with it.

His brother's illness had been big news. Kid dies slowly from cancer? Small-town folks ate that shit *up*. There'd been a time when they could barely get to the damned grocery store without getting stopped every five minutes by some well-wishing churchgoer. He'd even gone to church himself a couple of times—they all had, dragged there by his mom, ecstatic that the priest was going to mention Nicky in his sermon.

And he had. Had got everyone to bow their heads and say silent prayers, had waxed on about the reason God chose to make a young boy sick. Joe had perked up a little at that bit, but in the end it all came down to the same shit. *Belief.* Everything was a test, and the answer never seemed to change. To Joe, the whole thing had seemed like a scam. Afterward, the collection bowl did the rounds, and he watched teary-eyed women emptying their purses to help keep the cancer from their doors.

He thought now of Father Brading. The beaming priest with a soft spot for taking in strays, for visiting crime scenes and drinking hard liquor in rundown bars. The type of conundrum that usually kept a couple of skeletons in the back room.

Frank had always said that things were easiest when they were kept at arm's length. Harris had wanted the case closed, and it was. Maybe that was all that mattered.

The next morning brought a cool breeze and the tentative first steps toward fall. Joe got to the station mid-morning to handshakes and back slaps. He plastered a smile on his face so fake it hurt, and pushed through to the meeting room. Ackerman was already inside.

"Morning, partner," Ackerman said.

"Morning."

"How does it feel to be the hero for the day?"

"Back slaps aren't really my thing. What are you doing here so early?"

Ackerman motioned to the walls. "Taking all this down. Captain needs the room back."

Joe nodded and started to help. Crime-scene pictures, memos, hand-scribbled notes. It didn't take long to come across the photograph of David Richardson with the unknown man. Joe stared at it, then looked over at Ackerman.

The older cop was hunched over a table, shuffling documents into folders. All of a sudden Joe thought of Harris, that first day. The concern that Joe had picked up the case instead of Fields. The assigning of a new detective to run point.

Joe glanced back at the photograph in his hands, his sleep-addled brain sparking connections he knew he should ignore. The broken seal across the Richardsons' front door; the theory that a cop on a cartel's payroll had come back to search the place.

Packing the picture away, he said, "You must be pretty pleased with how all this turned out."

Ackerman answered without turning around. "How do you mean?"

"Steve Purcell charged, everything else just put in a box."

His partner stopped and looked over at him. "We skipped some steps to get here," he said, "and that doesn't sit right with me. But, end of the day, it's Harris's call. Buck stops with him and it's his ass on the line if he's wrong, not ours."

"Pretty simplistic view of the world."

"Things are always simpler if you just follow the rules. That's why they exist."

Joe grunted. "You think we'll ever find out who sliced that security seal over the Richardsons' door?"

"Whoever it was, it's not our concern anymore. I'm going back to routine traffic stops, and after all this, I'm looking forward to it."

"Traffic stops don't tend to make the front page."

"And all the better for it, I promise you." Ackerman smiled as he sealed up the last box. "Well, I guess that's it."

"I guess so."

They stacked the boxes in the middle of the room. Ackerman held out his hand. "Been a genuine pleasure working with you on this one."

Joe shook it. "Likewise," he said. As if he could say anything else.

Of course, the truth was he could say a lot more. Could ask him how well he knew the captain. Could ask him why Harris had really brought him onto the case. Was it to clean up a cartel trail? To keep any trace of organized crime away from reporters like Gonzalez?

Ackerman went for the door, made it halfway before turning. "Say, you got any plans for tonight?"

"Not particularly."

"Why don't you come around for some dinner? Celebrate our success with a couple beers. I know I live in a trailer park, but the stove works fine and I make a pretty mean bowl of chili."

Joe paused. Went to say no, then figured this would be as good an opportunity as any to find answers to those questions. He smiled. "Sure," he said. "Why not."

Chapter Twenty-Three

That night, Joe drove slowly through town. A six-pack of Budweiser clinked in the passenger footwell. It was dark, a little after seven, and the streets were filled with costumes. Packs of ghosts in white sheets roamed alongside dark-cloaked vampires, undead zombies, animals, and an assortment of other shit that Joe didn't recognize.

Joe rolled past them, windows down even though the heat had faded. The cool air helped him think, let him keep tabs on what was going on around him. He could hear laughter and music playing, the constant chatter of excited kids, car doors slamming and parents yelling.

A few blocks over, at Eaves Park, he knew there would be another party kicking off shortly. Older kids only this time; their music a little louder, their costumes more revealing. Police tended to let them have their fun till around midnight. Not that it was usually anything that serious. A bonfire, some drinking, the usual things that kids got up to. This sort of stuff was like a safety valve. You let folks blow off a little steam now and again, they didn't build it up. And after the last few days, people had earned their right to relax.

Leaving downtown behind, Joe swung his Pontiac out onto the backroads and bounced along for another couple of miles until he hit the trailer park. The place was packed out; rows of mobile homes stacked end to end, with what seemed like only a few feet between them. Down the center was a long passageway. Kids raced along it, shouting and running under strings of Halloween lights and carved pumpkins.

Joe spotted Ackerman's car and pulled in alongside it. Grabbed the six-pack and thumped on the flimsy front door. Ackerman swung it open and grinned.

"Welcome," he said. He spotted the beers. "Stick them in the fridge and help yourself to a cold one."

Joe climbed inside and glanced around. The trailer was small. One end was for living—miniature couch and easy chair, galley kitchen, tight little dining nook. The other end was the bedroom and some kind of bathroom, he presumed. No door, just a cloth partition to separate it.

A pot of chili stood on the tiny stovetop, bubbling, the smell of it thick and meaty in the cramped space.

"It's not much," Ackerman said as he closed the door after him, "but it works."

"How long did you say you've been living here?"

"About seven weeks now." Then, with a laugh, he added, "When I first arrived, I thought it would only be for a week or so. Just until I found a real place. Then I got my first paycheck."

"Suddenly this trailer seemed real enough."

"Exactly." Ackerman raised his bottle and they clinked. "Cheers."

Joe took a long, slow drink. The cold beer rolled through him. "So, I'm guessing Cooper PD doesn't pay as much as Texas," he said.

"It pays about half."

"Ouch. Still, they can't be paying me more than you, not with my experience. There must be somewhere better than this you can find."

Ackerman shook his head. Took another drink as he stirred the chili. "The pay is alright, really. Gives me enough to pay rent, food, and still have a little left over to blow at the gentlemen's club out on Wodega. What's that place called again?"

"I wouldn't know. But if you're the one doing the blowing, you should definitely be able to afford an apartment."

"Oh, you're a stitch," Ackerman said drily. "Here, pass me that masa harina. I just need to stir it through right at the end."

"Masa what?"

"It's like cornmeal. Cupboard on the right."

Joe pulled out a hefty packet and handed it over. "You mind if I use your bathroom?"

"Course. Just past the curtain there. Can't miss it."

When Joe was out of sight, he took a moment to think. Any intention he'd had to search the place tonight was gone. Place was so small he wasn't even sure where a guy would hide anything to begin with. And hide what? Was he really expecting Ackerman to have some signed letter from Harris, instructing him to report back on his young partner's movements?

Joe sighed and pressed his palms against his eyes. Even if Ackerman *had* been told that, Joe didn't have the first clue as to why. And was there anything wrong with Harris wanting to make sure a fresh detective didn't get in over his head? Again, his mind landed back on the baseboard photo. He didn't even know, he realized, what it was he didn't know.

When he returned, the steaming pot seemed just about ready. Dark, rich-looking chunks of meat sizzled amongst charred onions and garlic. Joe felt his stomach flutter.

"You know," he said, taking a seat at the little dining booth, "I'm sure I read somewhere that the authentic Mexican recipe for chili does not use any cornmeal."

"And I'll bet the authentic Mexicans don't drink Budweiser, either. No cornmeal?"

"No cornmeal, no tomatoes."

"Well, I'll give you the no tomatoes," Ackerman said, taking a drink. "That's a lazy way to make a sauce and stop it burning, and you lose out on the taste. But no masa harina? That's just ridiculous. Your chili would be watery as all hell. Who said that? Mexicans?"

"So I read."

"Huh. Well, we're not in Mexico, we're in America. And this is *Texan* chili, you understand? We like it hot and dry. You need some liquid to moisten it up? Friend, that's what the beer is for."

Joe raised his bottle. "No argument here."

He ran his eye over the trailer again. The longer he sat there, the more Ackerman just didn't add up.

"You ever see yourself going back to Texas?" he asked.

Ackerman shook his head. "I don't think so. I left a lot of baggage behind there. It's not just the crime . . ." He trailed off, took another drink. "Truth is, my paycheck is just fine. Problem is, most of it I don't get to keep. I've got an ex-wife and kid back in San Antonio."

Joe lowered his beer. "Ah."

"*Ah* is right."

"Shit, man, I shouldn't have pried."

Ackerman waved his hand through the air. "Don't sweat it, it's not a big deal. Just is what it is."

"How old's your kid?"

"She's twelve. Name's Becky."

"You miss her?"

"Oh, like crazy. Me and her mother, though . . . We've got issues that can't be fixed. God knows we tried. But she's a good woman, and she'll do right by Becky. If I'm honest, my money does a better job of taking care of them than I ever did."

Joe drained his beer. "Sounds like you're doing right by them now," he said.

"Maybe. Becky knows where I am, knows that I'll always want to see her if she ever wants to see me. You want another beer?"

"Sure."

Ackerman passed over another cool bottle from the fridge. Leaned against the stove as he opened one for himself. "Still feels a little like I've failed her, you know? All the parental politics, and Becky just gets caught in the middle."

"Kids are resilient," Joe said. "She knows you're providing, best way you can. Trust me, even though you're not with her right now, it's not the same as abandoning her."

"Spoken from experience?"

Joe grunted. "My dad set the bar for how *not* to parent. I mean, he basically took it and just tossed it onto the floor. That's how low it is. So long as you're doing better than him, you're fine in my book."

"Sounds like you guys had to deal with a lot, though."

"Yeah, we did, but that's not an excuse." Joe took a drink, those memories starting to simmer inside him. "Guy left me to be raised by strangers, practically. *That's* abandonment."

"Your dad still alive?"

"Far as I know. Up in Minneapolis."

"Big change from Cooper."

"Large enough to get lost in, I think is the point."

Ackerman nodded and turned back to the stove. "You should go visit him, while you can."

Joe blinked away the past, took a long drink before answering. "How's dinner coming along? I'm starved."

"Good, because this hot, dry, cornmeal-filled, tomato-banned chili is just about ready to eat."

Ackerman had turned to start serving when his pager began buzzing and skittering around on the kitchen counter. He frowned, went to pick it up just as Joe's joined in.

Ackerman said, "It's Dispatch." He snatched his phone off the wall and called it in. "This is Ackerman," he said. Then, "Shit."

Joe turned off the stove. Dinner was over.

"I'm with Detective Finch," Ackerman continued. "Can confirm we're both en route. Will meet first responders at the scene." He caught Joe's eye, jerked his head toward the door. "Set up a roadblock around the property. I want every vehicle stopped and searched that tries to leave."

Ackerman hung up and followed Joe outside, pulling out his keys.

"Let's take mine," he said.

"You want to tell me what's going on?" Joe said, climbing in the passenger side. "The suspense is killing me."

"Uniformed officers responded to a report of a home break-in," Ackerman said, starting the engine. The car jumped as the tires spun. "Another family's been attacked."

Chapter Twenty-Four

It wasn't hard to find the right address. They could hear the screaming from a block away.

Ackerman had to dump the car at the end of the street; costumed partygoers were spilling out of houses onto the road, pushing and jostling as Joe and Ackerman hustled toward the scene. In the distance, Joe could see the red and blue lights of parked cruisers.

People were mainly trying to get the hell away from whatever was up ahead. The detectives pushed through the bodies. For a second Joe thought he was clear, then some kid in a Freddy Krueger mask knocked into him, nearly sending both of them flying. Joe grabbed him and spun him away. All around, Joe could hear the sound of people shouting and crying.

"Move!" Ackerman shouted beside him. He was waving at parents standing in the middle of the street, one hand on his hat. "Move! Out of the way!"

It was like swimming against the current. The air was alive with yells, with car horns and police sirens. That bad dream where you just can't get across the road fast enough. None of these people would know what was happening. But they'd see cruisers and uniformed officers, and with the Richardsons haunting their sleep, they'd know enough.

Eventually they reached the police tape. They flashed their badges and ducked underneath. Ahead of them sat a couple of squad cars and an ambulance. EMTs were loading a woman on a stretcher into the back.

An officer ran over. "Detectives?"

"Finch and Ackerman," Joe said. "What's going on?"

"This is the Taylor residence. Some trick-or-treaters heard a gunshot go off inside the house. A few minutes later someone jumped out the upstairs window."

"The woman on the stretcher?"

"No, the perp. Landed in some garbage bags and took off into the crowd."

"Who fired the shot?"

"*That* was the woman on the stretcher. Patricia Taylor."

Ackerman readjusted his hat. "She scared him off?"

"Looks like it."

"She get a description?"

"Tall, slim, wearing a Halloween mask."

"She badly hurt?"

The officer shook her head. "More shaken than anything else. Perp landed a couple blows with one of her kids' baseball bats."

"Who else was in the house?" Joe asked.

"Just Mrs. Taylor. Her husband and two kids were out trick-or-treating."

They moved toward the ambulance. The EMTs were about to close the back doors.

"Mrs. Taylor?" Ackerman asked as they approached.

The woman on the stretcher was trembling. Her blonde hair was matted to her scalp with sweat, her makeup smeared with tears. The EMTs eyed them warily but didn't try to stop them.

"Mrs. Taylor?" Ackerman repeated, softer this time. He took his hat off like he was paying his respects. "I'm Detective Ackerman, this is my partner, Detective Finch. You mind if we ask you a couple questions before you go?"

Patricia Taylor shuddered and Joe noticed her fingers digging into her thighs. Her gaze took a few seconds to lock onto them.

"Have you seen my children?" she said quietly. "My husband, he was with them . . ."

Ackerman turned to the officer behind them. "Have we been able to locate the family?"

"Yessir, they just picked them up. They'll meet Mrs. Taylor at the hospital."

"You hear that, Mrs. Taylor?" Ackerman said, turning back. "They're fine. Everyone's fine. Now, I'm going to have a look inside your home, alright? I need you to tell my partner here what happened tonight."

"It was Rudy," she said. "Oh God, it was Rudy . . ."

Joe pulled out his notebook and started scribbling.

Joe found Ackerman bent over in the upstairs hallway, plastic wrapped around his shoes, peering down at something on the floor. A backpack, Joe realized, as he got closer.

"What have you got?" he asked.

His partner stood up straight. "I think this was left behind by whoever broke in."

"Patricia Taylor said he dropped it on his way out the window. How'd you know?"

Ackerman used the tip of a pen to open the bag. Joe crouched down to look. Inside were four little teddy bears. The exact same kind they'd found on the bodies of the Richardson family.

"It was him," Joe said quietly.

"What else did Mrs. Taylor tell you?" Ackerman asked.

"Not much, she's pretty out of it. Her ex-husband is Rudy Hoffman, he's the kids' father. Said he was abusive when they were together, back in Wichita. She remarried a few months back."

"Rudy Hoffman . . . That name ever come up before?"

"Not that I can recall, but listen to this. She said he started up some sort of religious group when they were together. Bible study, followers he'd pick up off the street. Hobos, mostly. Runaways. He even visited a bunch of prisons, convinced cons to join when they came out."

"A religious cult? This is starting to sound familiar."

"Brian, they'd stitch together animals for his kids as presents. She said it used to creep her out. When she tried to leave, he got violent with her. Beat her in front of the others."

"What happened?"

"She left. Took the kids one night when he was out. Drove them across the state and ended up here."

"When was this?"

"Nearly ten years ago."

Commotion at the top of the stairs. Bob appeared there, dressed in his white forensics suit. "I'm afraid I need both of you boys to leave," he said. "You're contaminating my crime scene."

Ackerman pointed at the backpack. "I want that done first, you understand me? You let me know as soon as it's ready."

"Fine. Now *out*."

As they headed back out onto the street, Ackerman asked, "What are the odds this Hoffman character set up shop with his groupies out at MacFarlane's place?"

"That was my thought, too."

"Did Patricia Taylor think she managed to hit anything?"

"Shot went wild, she said, but it was enough to scare him off."

"She said he was wearing a mask?"

"Plain white hockey mask. Michael Myers, I think."

175

"Jason Voorhees. If she didn't see his face, we don't know for sure it was her ex. And why all of a sudden does Hoffman go after her, after ten years?"

"No idea. But damn, he's ticking a lot of boxes. A history of violence, handmade teddy bears? Jesus, Brian, from the sounds of it, the guy started up his own cult."

"And I left Texas to get *away* from all this Waco bullshit."

When they reached Ackerman's car, Joe asked the question that had been on his mind since they'd left the trailer park.

"What does this mean for Steve Purcell?"

Chapter Twenty-Five

Ackerman drove. Fast—or at least as fast as he could with the crowds. His high beams on, dashboard light spinning blue.

"I don't think Purcell ever had anything to do with these killings," Joe said.

"We don't know that for sure," Ackerman said. "If it *is* some cult, maybe Purcell's a member. Maybe one of his buddies took over from him tonight."

They were out of the suburbs now, heading across town. The crowds of trick-or-treaters had thinned down here, and Ackerman put his foot down.

"I don't think he's involved," Joe said again. "And I don't think Purcell's a member of any cult. Whoever killed the Richardsons went to ground, waited until we'd signaled the all-clear. Christ, a goddamn press conference to let him know we were no longer looking. Harris telling him it was safe to kill again."

"What do you think our next step should be?"

Joe grimaced. "I want to go have a conversation with Steve Purcell. But first . . ."

Ackerman sighed. "Yeah."

◆ ◆ ◆

Captain Harris was a man whose entire life was unraveling in front of him. The guy looked shell-shocked, leaning against his desk, shirt crumpled like he hadn't had time to iron it. Like he'd slept in it, maybe.

Outside, Joe could hear the slamming doors of news vans. The excited chatter of journalists with a story. Two families attacked and a possible wrongful arrest; Cooper had blood in the water, and Harris was carrion for the scavengers.

Joe pressed his argument once more. "Sir, we should release Stephen Purcell now," he said. "Get him out the back, away from the press."

"Phones haven't stopped ringing," Harris said. "Whole town is going to explode over this."

"The longer we hold him, the bigger this is going to get. If we can—"

Harris shook his head, pushed himself to his feet. Started pacing. Pausing every so often to glance out his window at the growing crowd. Joe watched him, thinking about all the people who had to be breathing down his neck. Thought about the mayor. Thought about Sam Lemire and his fancy suit.

"Let's just think this through a moment," Harris said breathily. "Now, you said Patricia Taylor named this Rudy Hoffman as her likely attacker?"

"Yessir. Said he started collecting followers when they were together, back in Wichita."

"And Emily Richardson's friend told you about a . . . a what—a community of people living out in the middle of nowhere?"

"That's right. Possibly the same group started up by Rudy Hoffman."

"Well, for all we know, Purcell is one of them."

The man was desperate to hang onto Purcell for the Richardson murders. Joe glanced over at his partner. Ackerman was leaning quietly against the back wall, playing with the brim of his hat. He caught the captain's eye and said, "We don't have any evidence for that, sir."

"Then find it!" Harris said, glaring at them both. "That's your jobs, isn't it? To find evidence? Look into this Hoffman. I'm not releasing Purcell until I know for sure he's not involved. I *will not* be the captain who let some Waco asshole back onto the street."

The captain was panting now. Sweat marks on his shirt. He picked up a half-done tie and slipped it over his head, turning away. "In fact, I'm having him moved to the state pen."

"Jesus, already?"

"Dammit, Joe, I can't have press vans camped outside like this! Sam Lemire has gotten Lincoln to agree to hold him on a temporary basis, just until all this calms down."

"But we're not done talking to him yet!"

"Even if you *did* have any say in the matter, detective, I don't have a choice here."

"Says who? That asshole Lemire?"

Harris batted his lamp across the desk. It crashed to the floor, flickered and died. The room fell quiet. In the half-darkness, Joe watched the captain's shoulders rise and fall.

Joe said quietly, "Just give me five minutes with him, sir. Please. Before you ship him off."

Harris didn't answer for a few moments. When he did, he didn't bother turning around. "Transport's already on their way," he said at last. "Clock's ticking, detective."

Joe bolted from the room. He could hear Ackerman close behind him.

"Tell me you've got a plan," his partner said.

"Go get Purcell," Joe said. "Get him into an interrogation room. Once he's gone, we'll lose him. Maybe for good."

"Where are you going?"

"To get something from storage."

They parted at the base of the stairs. Joe raced across the main office and down another floor into the basement. The storage room was packed full of cardboard boxes, stacked just about to the ceiling. He moved from shelf to shelf, searching for the Richardson papers. Of course nothing was filed away in the correct location; it was easier to spot the newer boxes from their lack of dust.

He found the files he was after near the back of the room. Pulled them out and flipped open the lids. Tossed papers until he had it. The photograph from the Richardsons' baseboard. The black-and-white picture of David Richardson and the unknown man.

Not bothering to stuff the boxes back, Joe ran back up the stairs. The interrogation rooms were on the other side of the station. At the main entrance he saw reporters blocking the steps. A sudden flash of cameras; Sam Lemire moving through them into the building, his face stern.

Ackerman had put Purcell in the same room he'd been in when they'd interrogated him. He was guarding the door. He gave Joe a questioning look, but Joe just pushed past him into the room.

"What the hell's going on?" Purcell asked. The guy must have heard about the Taylor attack. He was all nervous energy, full of that awful kind of hopefulness that comes from someone else's tragedy. Joe knew he had to crush it.

"Steve, listen to me. We only have a few minutes. I need you to look at something."

Ackerman closed the door behind them. Stayed standing with his back to them as Joe slid into a chair across from Purcell and placed the photograph on the desk.

"Did you take this?"

Purcell's face froze. His eyes dancing.

Joe leaned in. "I don't have time to piece this together, alright? You need to help me here. I'll lay it out, you tell me how I'm doing. We know that David Richardson was involved in something bad.

Cartel, we're guessing. He had this picture taken as leverage to make sure he was safe. Hid it where nobody would find it. Now, you lived across the street, you were friends. He let you in on what he was up to, or maybe you found out on your own. He asked you for help, asked you to take this photo. How's that so far?"

Commotion now outside the door. Voices in the corridor. Ackerman picked up a chair, jammed it under the handle.

Joe took Purcell by the arm and shook him. "Dammit, Steve! They're coming to take you to Lincoln, okay? And once they do, you're out of our jurisdiction. If you want us to help you, now's the time to start talking."

The door handle rattled. The chair held. Someone began banging on the door. Ackerman looked over at them, worried.

Joe said, "We talked to Julie, remember? She said you weren't at home the night of the murders. Where were you?"

"A motel."

At last.

"You're having an affair? That why you kept your mouth shut all this time?" When Purcell stayed quiet, Joe pounded the table. "Christ, Steve, no one here cares about who you're screwing. If you don't start talking they're going to *hang* you for this—"

"It was David, alright?"

Joe stared at him.

"I was having an affair with David," Purcell said, louder than he needed to, and slow, like he was amazed at the sound of the words. "No one knew."

OK. Didn't see that one coming. But suddenly things made a little more sense. The guy had been in a relationship with a dead man, too scared to admit it. To his wife, to the town. Maybe to himself. Then a thought struck Joe and he frowned.

"Wait, you were with David Richardson the night of the murders? What time did you get home?"

"Late. Two in the morning, maybe." It was coming out of him fast now. "Julie asked me where I'd been, I made up something stupid. I should have had an excuse ready. The look she gave me . . ." He shook his head. "We were getting sloppy."

"Sloppy enough to leave a footprint in his garden?"

"Huh?" He blanched. "Yeah, maybe."

"What was that, a previous visit? You climb out the window when Marcy came back?"

"She was supposed to be out with her girlfriends. That was when we decided it was safer to go to a motel."

"After the motel, did you see anything when you got home?"

"No, we took separate cars. I waved to him from across the street before going inside. God, do you think his family were already—"

"Where was the motel?"

"Some place over on Maple, I don't remember the name."

"And the photo?"

"I took it. David worked for that man, that piece of—"

"A *name*, Steve."

"Anatoly Marchenko. He's a cartel guy, down in Omaha. They use empty farmhouses, barns outside Cooper to store their product. David was a mule—ran drugs and money between here and Omaha. Last couple trips, he started getting scared something might happen to him."

"David thought he might end up dead?"

"He was . . . Jesus, he was skimming money from the cartel. Every other transport, a little here and there. We . . . we were going to run away together."

"How much, Steve?"

"Two hundred grand, all told."

Joe closed his eyes, tried to think it through. A crash against the interrogation-room door that made the desk shiver. The chair started to slide. Ackerman jammed a boot against it, caught Joe's eye, shook his head. Time was up.

Purcell said, "Joe, listen. David gave me notes. A ledger. It's all in my desk drawer. Please, if there's anything—"

Another crash and Ackerman stepped back, letting the chair finally lose purchase. It slid away as men in black combat fatigues burst in. Ackerman's eyes widened at the show of force, and Joe saw hands grab his partner before they grabbed at him, too. He twisted, reached up to fend them off, but was lifted out of his chair like a child, and pinned against the wall.

"Get your damn hands off me!" he shouted.

"Easy, detective," came an acid-washed voice at his back. "We've got orders to transport this man to Lincoln. I let you go, I don't want any more trouble."

The pressure faded and Joe shoved the man clear. The guy was dressed like he was boarding the next flight to Fallujah, three of his buddies kitted out likewise by the door.

"*Damn*," Ackerman said. He was off to one side, his hat askew. "And I thought *Texas* was crazy."

Joe watched Purcell as they hauled him away. There was panic in his eyes.

Out in the corridor, Sam Lemire watched everything unfold. He stared at the detectives, his face impassive, before leading Purcell out the station's main doors and through the baying mob of reporters on the front steps.

All but alone in the station proper, Ackerman turned and said, "Alright, listen. Go to Purcell's. Search his office and find this ledger he's talking about. I'm going to look into Rudy Hoffman."

"Try and find that motel, too," Joe said. "Something that proves Purcell and David Richardson were there the night of the murders."

Ackerman stepped close and dropped his voice. "You page me when you have something, and don't tell anyone what you're doing. Be fast, but be *quiet*."

Laura

She had been asleep for a while—a couple of hours maybe, she wasn't sure. It was always hard to know at the farm. It was still dark when she woke, she knew that; and she hadn't moved one inch since collapsing on top of the sheets, she knew that too. The fading echo of a dream still working its way out of her head. Something to do with metal, with blood.

Lying there, trying to work out what had woken her, she heard it. A soft panting, like a dog, only too high-pitched, and as her vision focused she saw the outline of a man standing at the end of her bed, standing there watching her. She drew back into the mattress.

"Rudy?" she said.

The man stepped toward her, rounding the bed, and when his face fell into the moonlight she saw who it was, saw his ugly sneer and his yellowed teeth, and she saw it wasn't Rudy at all.

It was Mason.

Chapter Twenty-Six

It was late when Joe returned to the Purcell residence. A chill in the air that actually felt good after so many weeks of warmth. He stood in the driveway and looked across at the Richardson house. It was settled, he guessed. He couldn't think of it as anything other than that now. *The Richardson house.* Even now, in the dark, it seemed like his time there had been in another life.

No answer when he knocked, no car parked in the driveway. Joe wondered if Julie had gone to stay with a friend. The doors were bolted but a rear window was open. Securing her home clearly not as important as getting the hell out of it.

He quickly found Steve's office. It was small and sparsely decorated; a simple desk against one wall, some shelves and a map of the world pinned to another. It was the only room in the house that hadn't been ransacked. The guy had three drawers and just one of them was locked. Breaking in wasn't difficult.

He pulled out a bound notebook, stuffed with papers. Clicking on the desk lamp, he went through it. A list of names, dates, locations. Details of when David Richardson had met with this Anatoly Marchenko, perhaps.

Some of the entries had dollar amounts written next to them. Pretty hefty dollar amounts, too. Joe ran his eyes down the ledger and a name jumped out.

Sam Lemire.

Again and again he saw it, the politician's name appearing a half-dozen times on the first page alone.

Joe spent nearly an hour combing through the papers. When he was done, two things had become clear. The first was that Lemire was getting paid to the tune of twenty grand just about every other month. Dirty money, Joe figured, to look the other way; to help the cartel keep its foothold in Cooper.

The second thing that became apparent was that if Anatoly Marchenko was involved in the Richardson murders, Joe now had a solid way to get the cartel's attention.

He checked his watch; a little after one. With a bit of luck, Sam Lemire would be fast asleep.

It wasn't hard finding his address. The guy lived in one of those nice apartment blocks by the water. Wasn't a penthouse, but nothing in Cooper was. Nice view of the river, maybe. High enough for all the shit down below to lose focus. And Joe would be willing to bet this was just Lemire's hideaway in shabby little Cooper, his refuge for when he absolutely couldn't avoid visiting his district.

By now it was after two. Joe rode the elevator up. Banged on Lemire's door long enough to wake half the floor. The light behind the peephole went dark, and when the man eventually showed, he looked tired and pissed. Dressed in boxers and a T-shirt, his pristine hair ruffled from sleep.

"Detective Finch. What the hell are you doing here?"

Joe nodded into the apartment. "I think you should invite me in, Senator Lemire."

"Do you have any idea what time it is?"

"We can do this in the hallway if you want . . ." He trailed off, let his jacket fall away to show his holstered firearm. Lemire's eyes fell on it. One thing talking tough; another getting into a fight with an armed, agitated cop in front of your neighbors.

"I just want to ask you a couple questions," Joe said.

"About what?"

"Anatoly Marchenko."

If the gun didn't do it, the name did. Lemire backed up a little. Joe smiled and stepped inside.

A long hallway that opened into a decent-sized living room. Low sofas and big mirrors on the walls; lamps that bent over on stalks like palm trees. Hard to imagine a person actually living here.

"Fancy apartment," Joe said, wandering through it. "Always wondered what sort of place folks like you lived in."

"Folks like me?"

Joe grinned. "Yeah, you know. Politicians."

Lemire gave a forced smile. "I guess it's nice enough," he said. "An apartment's an apartment at the end of the day."

"Oh, sure. And I bet your pipes rattle when the guy upstairs takes a shit, too, just like mine."

The living room was dark, and Joe stared out the large window. Cooper sprawled below him. A darkness punctured by odd patches of piss-yellow streetlights. Behind him, he heard Lemire pad across the room, and a moment later those fancy lamps flickered to life. Cooper disappeared, and in its place he saw Lemire's reflection, watching. Cogs in his brain turning. Running an exit strategy on the fly.

"I get you a drink, detective?"

"Not while I'm on the job."

"So this isn't a social call, then."

Joe smiled and turned away. Tapped at the window. "You know, up here, Cooper doesn't look half bad. Almost looks like any other town."

"You were born here, right?" Lemire went over to a drinks cabinet in the corner of the room and started pouring himself a glass. Man had been asleep not five minutes ago. Booze for breakfast, interesting choice.

"Someone's been doing their homework."

"No homework. Just a feeling I had."

"Oh yeah—a feeling? What feeling is that?"

"That you're protective of this place. In a way most people might not be."

Joe shrugged. "Most people aren't from here."

"Exactly my point," Lemire said, raising his drink.

The man walked slowly over to the window, composure sliding smoothly into place. Joe could smell the whiskey as he approached.

"You're angry about the second attack," Lemire said. "I understand that. Believe me, I am too." He sank down into a large armchair, gestured at another. Joe stayed standing.

Lemire's hands moved excitedly as he set his well-oiled verbal machinery into motion.

"What's occurred in this town is an abomination, detective. Acts of sheer, unadulterated evil. And I think I speak for everyone when I say that justice must happen, and will happen, and once it *has* happened, we can then look ahead to bringing Cooper together, and allowing this town the chance to heal."

Joe stared at him. "You done?"

"Oh, I've barely gotten started," Lemire said, grinning. "I truly want to make this town a better place. Of all the people I've spoken with, I would think you'd appreciate that."

"Save that shit for your re-election. I didn't come here to listen to a campaign speech."

"I'm sorry that's what you think you're hearing. You have a vested interest in what happens in this town. I admire that. And that's what I'll say to Captain Harris in six hours' time when he asks me why I look so tired this morning." Lemire set his glass down on a small table and leaned back, his gaze heavy. "You have a bright future ahead of you, Joe."

Joe didn't say anything. He took three steps to cover the distance between them. Picked up Lemire's glass and fanned its contents across the picture window. The shadow-Cooper outside blurred, the streetlamps flaring. He tossed the glass onto the carpet. Stood towering over the man in the chair.

"Don't talk to me about any bright future, you hear me? As far as I'm concerned, Harris is just as dirty as you are."

Lemire's face darkened. He interlocked his fingers carefully. "I'm not sure what you think you know," he said. "But you want my advice? It's time to leave, detective. Go home and get some sleep. Perhaps we can chalk this up to a misunderstanding."

"I know you're on the payroll of the Marchenko cartel," Joe said. "I know David Richardson was working for him."

"Those are serious allegations."

"I want to set up a meeting. Tell Marchenko I want to see him."

"I have to confess, I don't know what you're talking about."

Joe reached down and grasped Lemire by his T-shirt. Stretched it out something awful as he hauled him to his feet.

"Playing dumb, Senator Lemire, would be a mistake." At this range, the man's breath reeked of expensive scotch. In spite of himself, Joe's mouth watered. "I'll tell you one thing I'm talking about: twenty grand, every other month. That'd add up in a hurry. What do they get in return?"

"You're treading on very thin ice. If I were you I'd—"

With a roar, Joe hurled him against the window. Lemire squealed as he crashed against the wet pane. The glass shuddered in its frame, and down below, shadow-Cooper seemed to flex itself excitedly. With effort, Lemire kept on his feet. He'd lost some of his polish.

Joe stepped up close. "I've got papers, Lemire. Names, dates, figures. Even if I can't prove it, there's enough there to cause a stink. Think you'll survive an investigation? How useful are you to Marchenko then?"

Lemire swallowed. "You think you've got it all figured out, don't you."

"Let's run through it together; you can tell me where I'm wrong. David Richardson was stealing from Anatoly Marchenko. A couple hundred grand. Marchenko found out and butchered his family in return."

"That's quite a theory. And the Taylors? Was that a cartel hit as well?"

"Why don't you help fill in the gaps."

Maybe surviving his encounter with the window had allowed some confidence to sink back into Lemire. Some anger, too. He measured Joe through narrowed eyes, then smiled. "Whatever got the Richardsons killed, it wasn't Anatoly Marchenko. David was stealing from him, sure, but he's a businessman, not a monster."

"Oh yeah? And what does his money buy him?"

"Police protection, a little real estate." His frankness making clear how little he viewed Joe as a threat. "He helps keep Cooper clean of the real gangbangers. He's a necessary evil."

"Save me the ends-justify-the-means bullshit. It's late and I'm tired. Politicians need help making this town safe? Build more fucking streetlamps. Put more police on the streets. We're being *overrun* out there."

"Everyone always wants more police. It's the easy way out—"

"You want an easy way out?" Joe pressed Lemire's back against the window. "How much pressure you think this glass will take?"

"You wouldn't."

"I'll leave Purcell's ledger on the coffee table." Joe grinned. "Maybe they'll chalk it up to a suicide."

"You're a thug, detective."

"And you sent bent cops into the Richardson house to search for Marchenko's stolen money once Forensics were done. Was it Fields? Next time tell him to replace the security seal on the front door. Now tell me where the money is."

Lemire stayed quiet.

Joe pounded his fist on the glass next to Lemire's head. It rattled again, Cooper shimmering below. "I'm not messing around here. Where's the cash, Lemire?"

"Look, I'm just a middleman—"

"Don't sell yourself short."

"Do you have any idea what Marchenko will do to you?"

"I'm looking to find out. Now cough it up, or I swear to God I'll shove the back of your head through this window."

Lemire finally nodded and Joe released him, took a step back.

The man pulled his T-shirt straight and fixed his hair. "You know I have to call him the minute you're gone," he said.

Joe smiled. "That's exactly what I'm hoping."

Laura

It was Mason's touch that did it. His rough, warm hand pressing over her mouth. In that moment, any pretense that she might still be dreaming vanished. Dreams couldn't get it right, not like that. Why did he have to go and touch her goddamned mouth?

"Shh," he said. "I take my hand away, you going to scream?"

She forced herself to be still, to hold his gaze in the dim light. He was sweating, she could see it gleaming on his forehead. Could feel his hand trembling on her lips. When he finally peeled his palm away he left the taste of salt and engine oil behind.

It wasn't until he reached over and switched on her bedside lamp that she got her first good look at him. His eyes were wide, his hair wild, messed up and greasy. And she could smell him, too; a ripeness, a sour scent, the sort that comes from sweating into your shirt for days on end. He grinned at her, and it was a terrible grin. A grin that said, *Finally, I've found you.*

She dug out her voice at last. "I thought you . . ."

"You thought I was dead?" Mason said, his words throaty and deep. "You wanted me dead, you should have cut me deeper."

He was swaying now, back and forth on the balls of his feet, fists clenching and unclenching in front of him, his tongue running over his lips like he was going to enjoy whatever came next.

"You shouldn't have come here," Laura said. "You have no idea what this place is."

Mason laughed. His upper lip peeled back when he did. She'd forgotten how ugly he could look when he laughed.

He reached down and grabbed her wrists, pulled her from the bed. "This place is nothing but a bunch of bums. Can't handle a real day's work. Now, you're coming back with me, you understand? You show me you're sorry and maybe I'll forget what you did to me." Another laugh, another lip peel. "But you're going to have to try real hard."

"I'm not leaving with you, Mason."

"Don't be silly, now."

"I'll scream, I swear I will—"

Crushing her wrists in one big hand, he slid the other around her throat. She winced, the skin still tender from last time. He squeezed; not tight enough to choke, but still, tight enough.

"Just try it," he hissed. "You made a fool out of me once. Won't be a second time, I promise you."

Then he was lurching toward the door, dragging her behind him with both hands. Her bare feet scrabbled on the wooden floor until she found her balance. He pulled her out into the long corridor. He was so loud, his heavy boots echoing around the cramped space. By the time they

193

reached the door to the fields she was sure he must have woken the whole house. But if he had, no one came.

His rusted SUV was parked outside. She knew once she was in there, it was all over. He would take her back and she would never escape him again. Mason would make sure of it. Already he'd dropped one hand to dig into his jeans pocket, searching for his keys.

She started to twist away, her feet sliding across the thick grass. "Mason, no . . ."

He kept moving forward, kept pulling her toward the car.

"Please, just leave me here."

Mason turned and slapped her hard across the face. Her neck twisted, pain crackling along her tendons. His meaty hands grabbed her shoulders and seemed to press her entire body inward.

"Now you listen to me," Mason snarled. "You're getting in that car and I'm driving you back. Understand? I'm here to take you home."

"She is home," said a low, drawling voice.

Mason looked up. "And who the fuck are you?" he asked.

"I'm Rudy," came the reply.

He was standing behind them, dressed in his white tank top and faded jeans. Tall and lean, muscles taut. In that moment, he was the greatest thing she'd ever seen.

If Mason was scared, he didn't show it. "Fuck off," he growled, his upper lip peeled back again. "This is nothing to do with whoever you are, or whatever hippie shit you're running here."

"Last chance," Rudy said.

"Or what?"

"Or I'll feed your corpse to the pigs and bury your teeth out in the fields."

194

That was the moment Mason should have backed off. Laura saw it—saw it come and go—and instead of leaving he reached behind him and pulled a gun from the waistband of his jeans.

He pointed it at Rudy. His arm shook a little. Might have been fear, more likely it was drink. Laura tried to duck away but Mason kept one arm on her, his hand gripping her elbow, his long nails digging into her skin.

"I'm serious now," Mason called out. His voice sounded off. He was straining to keep his nerves from showing. "You go back inside or I'll shoot."

Rudy's gaze shifted slightly, sliding to just over Mason's left shoulder.

"Now," Rudy said softly, and suddenly something was glinting in the moonlight, something metal, and with Kyle beneath it as he stepped out of the darkness by the SUV. The metal whistled as it swung through the air. Mason didn't have time to fully turn—even if he'd been sober he wouldn't have had time—before the tire iron connected with the side of his head.

There was a sickening crunch and Mason dropped the gun. It landed in the grass by Laura's feet. She dropped to the ground and grabbed it, and without thinking stuffed it into the folds of her shirt.

Kyle swung the tire iron again. Mason's legs shook and he crumpled. He fell to his knees, somehow staying upright even as blood gushed down the side of his face and over his front. Laura watched as Kyle lined up a third swing and let fly.

Afterward, Mason lay in the grass, his body convulsing as he set about dying. Kyle gave him a rough shake with his boot, and then, satisfied, he wandered back inside, tire iron dangling from his fist.

Rudy stayed for a little longer. It didn't seem like he'd moved an inch the entire time. Laura gazed at him, and in the darkness she wondered if he was staring back, if he'd seen her pick up the gun.

Mason lasted a while, lying there. Longer than she'd have expected. And as she sat and watched him gasp and moan, his body twitching, she wondered whether she was glad she hadn't killed him after all, or whether it would have been better if she had.

He looked up at her now, this broken man. *People act so tough*, she thought, *and yet they're so easily put down*. He reminded her of the rabbit Kyle had caught. The way its chest had risen and fallen, rapidly, over and over. The way its eyes had held her gaze. What was it she had told herself then? *Sometimes it was better to murder something than to let it live.* She reached out and stroked his matted hair. *They called it a mercy killing.*

She moved her hand down Mason's face and firmly placed it over his nose and mouth.

He struggled for a moment—a long moment, his back arching—but she kept her arm steady. When his eyes drifted off and his body went still, she took her hand away and sat back.

Movement in the nearby darkness; Rudy turning and walking back toward the house. He hadn't said a word the entire time. Hadn't told her to do it, hadn't told her to stop. She watched as he disappeared inside, lit up by the first dawn rays cresting the treeline.

With steady hands, Laura unwrapped the gun from her shirt and got to her feet. She watched the morning sun swell until she felt its warmth on her face. It was a new day, and she knew exactly how she would spend it.

Chapter Twenty-Seven

Joe spent the rest of the morning parked outside Cooper Memorial. Slept a little with his seat down. Restless sleep—the sort of sleep you wake up from feeling more tired than when you started. Visiting hours were at seven. He was at the front desk at five to.

The briefcase felt like a siren in his hands as he walked. Like it was bright yellow and screaming, like carrying it was the most guilty thing in the world. He'd counted the notes in the car— twelve blocks from Sam Lemire's apartment, and only after he was sure he wasn't being followed. A little over two hundred thousand, as promised. Thick wads of cash wrapped in elastic bands. Fresh stuff, too, hot off the press, no wrinkles or anything.

He'd known what he was going to do with it before he'd even told Lemire to hand it over. Since he'd seen the reams of numbers on Steve Purcell's ledger. Getting Marchenko's attention was only part of the solution.

Frank was alone when he got there. Same look on his stitched-up face he had every time Joe saw him. As though he'd just fallen asleep a couple of minutes before. As though he'd wake up at the slightest sound.

It had been weird at first. A strange urge to be quiet around him, to not disturb him. Two weeks in, Joe had clapped his hands three inches away from Frank's nose, just to be sure. He hadn't even flinched.

"Morning, buddy," Joe said now, moving over to the window and peering out. He could see his car in the parking lot, sitting alone. "Have I had a week."

He scanned the lot and the street beyond for a couple of moments longer, then collapsed slowly into a chair. Set the brief-case down by his feet. "If Cathy's been watching TV in here, you've probably heard about it already. Killer tried to attack another family, mom pulled a pistol and scared him off. She got lucky, but so did he. And now a guy's off to Lincoln who almost certainly isn't involved."

Sometimes Frank's eyes twitched as he lay there. The lids fluttering. Dreams, maybe, who knew. Joe looked at them now. They were still.

"Sometimes I think I'm starting to get in over my head a little, you know?" Joe murmured.

A voice from the doorway: "Ever thought about taking a vacation?"

Joe turned. Cathy was standing there, smiling sadly. She held a coffee in her hand, and she offered it up as she sat down across from him. He refused it.

"You look terrible, Joe."

"I feel terrible."

"I've already had two this morning. You'd be doing my blood pressure a favor."

Joe smiled and took the cup.

"I've been following the case on the news," Cathy said. "God, it's so awful."

"I know," Joe said, and took a drink. He closed his eyes. "You have no idea how nice it is to taste real, actual coffee right now."

Cathy laughed. "You should try their chicken salad. It's actually the real reason I keep coming back here." She leaned in, adding, "Don't tell Frank" in a whisper, giving her husband's leg a playful squeeze.

Joe smiled and shook his head.

"How are you guys getting on?" he asked.

"Oh, we're fine. He's still got another couple days to snap out of it." No desperation in her voice, just the truth. He knew Cathy had learned long ago to accept things as they were—not the way she'd like them to be.

"Cathy, listen . . ."

"We've put the house on the market," she said. "Not exactly a great time to sell, what with everything that's going on, but we should hopefully make enough to keep him going a little longer."

"Where are you going to go?"

"Oh, I've been meaning to downsize for a while now." Cathy smiled, the dark shadows under her eyes sinking deeper into her cheekbones. "What do I need all that space for?"

"You going to sell the timeshare in Martha's Vineyard?"

"Oh, sure. And the Ferrari, it's just so impractical. Do you have any idea how much gas that thing uses?"

They smiled, and Joe watched her as she stared at her sleeping husband, her hands cradled in her lap. His gaze slid over to the briefcase by his feet.

"What if I was to tell you that you could keep the Ferrari," he said. "If you wanted."

She looked up at him. "What?"

Joe lifted the case and laid it at the bottom of the bed. Took a breath and went for it. "There's just over two hundred thousand dollars in this briefcase. I want you to have it. Use it to cover Frank's medical bills. Use it for whatever you need."

Cathy's face froze. Her eyes on him, then back on the case.

"I know it sounds crazy," he said, "but trust me, this money needs to do some good."

"Joe, you can't afford—"

"Don't worry, it's not mine."

She shifted in her seat. "Then where did you get it from?"

"It doesn't matter."

"It matters to me."

"It's dirty, Cathy. Alright? But it's real. And that's all you can know. That's the only way I can give this to you."

He pushed the briefcase across the bed until she had to move her hands to take it. Her fingers froze when they touched it. There was a long silence. Joe waited, knew she would be running through it all in her mind. Knew if she didn't take it he wasn't sure what he was going to do.

At last she looked up at him. She had tears in her eyes. "I can't ever repay this . . ."

"I'd never ask you to."

He stood, reaching over to squeeze her hand. She squeezed back, numbly.

"Where are you going now?" she said.

Joe smiled. This hospital, he'd always thought of it as Nicky's. Even now, even after all this time. Like a piece of his brother had been left behind, baked into the walls of the place. The place he'd spent so long suffering in. The place he'd been brought to when he was cold. Now maybe it belonged to Frank, too. Now maybe his brother wouldn't be so alone anymore.

He thought about what was going to happen next. Maybe it had always been building to this. Maybe it would be nice to get it over with. He gave Cathy a farewell embrace.

"I'm going home," he said.

They were waiting for him outside his apartment. Three guys in sweatpants and leather jackets. It all seemed a bit like overkill.

Joe nodded at them as he approached. "Morning, gentlemen," he said. "I presume you're here on behalf of the man whose money I stole."

The lead man grinned. His teeth were rotten. "Mr. Marchenko would like to speak with you."

"Listen, I haven't been home all night. Can I go inside and let my dog out first? He's an old boy and he'll shit himself if he's left much longer. Last time he trampled it around the place. Took days to get the smell out of the carpet."

More smiles, more yellow teeth. The man gestured toward the apartment door.

Laura

Laura spent the morning in a daze. She went through the motions on autopilot—showering, dressing, making her bed. All of it viewed in snapshot glimpses, a strobe effect that seemed to pulse every time she closed her eyes. In between those moments she drifted, retreating into a dark tomb where the world was quiet, where she couldn't feel the icy water, couldn't feel the hard metal of the revolver in her pocket. She washed her palm three times and yet still she felt Mason's open mouth against it.

Avoiding breakfast once again, she stood in the spot where it had happened. Someone had moved Mason's SUV. Someone had moved Mason, too; just a dark patch of grass where his body had lain dying. She wondered where he'd been buried. She thought back to what Rudy had said about the pigs, and she wondered if he'd been buried at all.

Rudy made his announcement mid-morning. "I've finally decoded the message that God left for us." Said it with tears in his eyes, with just the right amount of tremble in his voice. "Tomorrow, we ascend this world."

People started crying then, started hugging each other and throwing their hands up toward the sky. "After all this time," they said, "we've been chosen."

Rudy stood in front of them and drank it in. He clasped his hands and smiled, his eyes roaming the room. They stopped when they reached Laura. His face didn't change but she knew what he was thinking. Ascension Day was tomorrow. Everyone knew that if the Devil was going to try anything, this was his last chance.

In the early afternoon, she huddled with Francine and Patrick by the small trees on the edge of the fallow ground. Of the three of them, Patrick was the most agitated. His face was red, his breathing labored. Francine reached over and took his hand.

Laura had told them both everything. Well, nearly everything. As far as they were concerned, Kyle had killed Mason. It was simpler that way.

"We have to leave," Patrick said, rocking his weight back and forth like he needed to go piss. "We have to leave before someone tells the police."

Laura shook her head. "No one is going to tell the police."

"But they might work it out, they might know he came here. Oh, God." He put his hand over his mouth. "I think I'm going to be sick."

Francine squeezed his hand. "Relax, Patrick, we'll work this out."

"Don't you get it? I've been inside once already, I can't go back there. I won't." He got to his feet and started pacing. "I'll die before I go back."

"No one's going to prison." Laura glared at them both. "And no one's *ascending* tomorrow, either. This whole place is going to explode in twenty-four hours when nothing happens. Rudy's got everyone wound up so tight they're just ready to crack."

"So let's go," Francine said. "Let's just grab our things and leave."

"It's not enough, not for me. I need to end this."

"What do you mean, *end this*?"

Laura reached into her pocket and pulled out Mason's revolver. Her friends shrank back. "Once Rudy is gone, this whole place will just tumble apart peaceably," she said. "Everyone here will be free."

Francine shook her head, her palms lifted between them like Laura might throw the gun at her. "That's murder you're talking about. *Cold-blooded* murder."

"It's for the greater good, Francine—"

"Oh, horse crap it is! Besides, people are already suspicious of you. How do you think they're going to react, seeing you walk into Rudy's room with a loaded gun?"

Patrick was leaning forward now, his hands on his knees. "I can't be caught with a weapon," he moaned. "I can't."

The man was *all* about staying out of prison. But there were all kinds of prisons, and Rudy's needed dealing with first. Laura was about to say as much but Francine cut her off again, her voice hard. "You put that away, you understand me? I don't want to see that thing anymore. Patrick's right: we just need to *leave*, as close to *now* as possible. Things are going to get ugly. I sure as hell know the best time to leave somewhere is *before* all that shit starts. So I say we wait until it's dark, when everyone's busy lighting their candles and praying, and we just slip away."

Patrick was nodding next to her, standing up straight and letting out a long breath. "Leaving gets my vote."

Laura glanced down at Mason's revolver in her hands. Thought about how she had planned to use it. Getting rid of Rudy would be a kindness to the world, she knew that. But maybe her friends were right. Maybe it *was* too dangerous.

She slid the gun back into her pocket and looked Francine and Patrick in the eyes. "Fine," she said. "We leave tonight. As early as we can make it work." Last thing she wanted was to get caught by Kyle's wild-eyed girls and their ilk—tonight of all nights, they'd jump at the chance to burn her at the stake.

Chapter Twenty-Eight

"Please," the man said, smiling, and nodded at the apartment door. Joe was dismayed to see they'd broken the lock.

Inside, he found another couple of men. They were standing by the windows. They were dressed in sweatpants and hoodies and had chunky handguns tucked into their waistbands. A man in a suit was stretched out on his sofa. The man from the photo. Anatoly Marchenko.

Leo was curled up asleep next to him. *Traitor*, Joe thought to himself.

"Good morning, detective," Marchenko said, rising from the sofa. He grinned, ran ringed fingers through thick black hair. "We have never met, but I believe we are already familiar with each other."

"Have you let my dog out?"

Marchenko stared at him. Then his grin widened further. "This old boy? My men took him out when we first arrived. He pissed all over someone's hydrangeas."

"That'll be the woman across the hall. She plays her music too loud anyway."

"Well then, you can consider it *payback*, perhaps." Marchenko looked down at the sleeping pug. "A wonderful creature you have here. Leo, yes? It is on his collar. Leo is a good boy, I think we both agree."

Right on cue, Leo rolled over on the sofa and let out a contented sigh. Marchenko laughed and scratched the dog's belly. Joe had to force himself not to leap across the room.

Marchenko spoke with what might have been a Russian accent. His mouth, when he smiled, corkscrewed up at one side; a faint scar ran across the edge of his lips toward his left eye. He must have caught Joe staring.

"You wonder about this?" he said, tracing its outline with a dirty nail. "Perhaps I got it in a knife fight, yes? Like in your American movies. Like Rambo."

His men jeered at that. Some of them chanting "Rambo Rambo Rambo" like a tribal cry. Joe shivered.

"Or maybe it was just a lucky strike," Marchenko continued, "from a man as I held his head below the water." He shrugged. "Do you know what the best motivator is, detective?"

Joe held his gaze and said nothing.

"It is *life*," Marchenko said. "A man will do anything for you, if he thinks doing it will let him live. A man will kill a stranger if he has to."

"Is that what you do? Ask men to kill strangers?"

Marchenko sniffed and rubbed at his face. He looked tired. "I know about you, Joe. I know about Frank. I know about Leo. I understand what it is like to care for something."

"From what I've seen, all you care about is money."

"Money, yes, money is important. But money is not everything. Family, detective, now *that* is important." He wandered over toward the kitchen. Joe was prodded along with him. "I have a son," Marchenko said. "His name is Demyan. One day he will take over from me—later than he would like, I am sure. And I have a dog too, a mongrel. Her name is Scout. Maybe she is how I got my scar, hmm?"

"Can we get to the point of all this? I really don't care about your scar."

Marchenko laughed. He opened Joe's fridge, started rifling through it. "Most people do," he said. "Most people are scared by it, of the story I tell about it. As though that story could happen to them."

"I'm not scared of your scar, Marchenko. I'm bored of it."

Joe forced the words out, ignoring the trembling in his legs. Told himself that if he ended up in the trunk of a car with a bullet in the back of his head, then maybe that wasn't the worst way to go. Wasn't worse than Frank, and maybe that's all you could really ask for. To die quick, and with a little dignity.

Marchenko turned back to him. "This is a very poorly stocked fridge, detective. I think there is something rotting in the salad drawer."

"I didn't get much sleep last night and I'm tired. How long is this going to take?"

"Your problem is that you jump to conclusions."

"I do?"

"Yes. You do not think about the simplest answers. You think I have something to do with the murders in Cooper. You come here and threaten me with it."

"Hey, I live here, remember? Feel free to piss off back to Omaha."

Marchenko smiled thinly. He picked out an apple from the fridge and closed the door. Leaned against it and took a bite. "What would you say if I told you I didn't have anything to do with these murders?"

"I'd say you're a liar. How many politicians do you pay to look the other way? How many farms do you own to store your product?"

"You don't think they get something out of this arrangement? You don't think this *town* gets something?"

"You mean organized crime running through its streets? What a win for Cooper."

"Detective, I *protect* Cooper. This town is very important to my business. It's in my interest to keep things steady."

"Everyone always thinks they're the hero of their own story."

Marchenko sighed. Tossed the half-eaten apple into the sink. "What is it you want, Joe? All this, stealing my money, interrupting my operations. You are trying to get my attention? Well, you have it. What are you going to do with it?"

"I want the truth, Marchenko. How did you know David Richardson?"

"He worked for me."

"What do you know about his death?"

"Nothing."

"Bullshit. He was stealing from you. Keeping notes on your racket. You're telling me you either didn't know or didn't care, and I don't think you're that stupid."

Marchenko said nothing for a moment. He stared at Joe—like he was disappointed, almost. He gave a lazy motion to his men and Joe felt hands grab his upper arms.

"You ask for the truth, detective, so here it is." Marchenko moved back toward the sofa. "The scar I got in a car accident when I was a boy. I don't know who attacked these families. I was aware that David was stealing from me and I allowed it, because a man that steals from me is not a man that will rat on me, and sometimes one is more important than the other. And finally, I know that last night you stole two hundred thousand dollars from me, which I had reclaimed once David no longer had need of it. You do not work for me, and I will not allow you the same freedoms that I allowed David. So here is how this will work. If I do not get my money back in full, I will drive you out to the scrapyard and I will place you—alive—into the trunk of a car and crush it into a cube. I promise you, detective, I will push the button myself."

Joe tensed his arms against the men who were holding him. He saw Leo, still sleeping through all of this around him. He thought about Frank, about Cathy. He thought about Lemire's fancy apartment and the dead family. "I don't have the money," he said at last. "And I wouldn't return it even if I did."

Marchenko glanced beyond him and nodded. His men forced Joe to his knees.

"You think you are clever?" Marchenko said. He sounded bored now. "You take my money, you give it away. But that much, it does not simply vanish. Not in a place like Cooper. I will have it back. I will have it back by the end of the day. Perhaps I should start with your old partner, hmm? With Frank. With his wife."

"You leave them alone," Joe growled. "They've got nothing to do with this."

"They do now, thanks to you. Unless, of course, you have other means of repaying me." Another nod to his men. Joe's left arm was forced out straight. Pressed against the sofa, within a foot or so of Leo. The dog snorted and rolled over. "Two hundred thousand to buy a police officer's loyalty," Marchenko said. "I wonder if that is a good deal."

"You've already got Lemire. Probably Harris, too. Hell, I'm sure half the station is on your payroll. What do you need me for?"

Marchenko shrugged. "You are someone who would cause me trouble, I think. And killing a detective, there are always questions."

"I became a cop to put people like you behind bars, Marchenko."

That corkscrew smile flashed once more. He waved a signal and one of his men picked up Joe's hand. Wrapped a fist around his pinkie finger.

"The things I do," Marchenko said, "I think I do more good for Cooper than others. More than you, perhaps."

Joe tensed as his finger was forced up and then back, with a sickening crunch. He cried out, half-falling forward. Hands held him in place. Marchenko reached down and stroked Leo affectionately as he nodded again. Joe felt his ring finger held tight. He closed his eyes as it was snapped backward.

He retched, a wave of nausea rolling over him. This time when he fell forward they let him land hard on his living-room floor. He pulled his broken hand under him, cradled it as he lay there.

Marchenko laughed. "I think we are going to work very well together, you and I. But for now, we will let you get some sleep. I hope you don't mind me saying that you look terrible, detective."

Chapter Twenty-Nine

By the time Marchenko and his men left, it was ten-thirty in the morning and Joe had been awake for nearly two days straight.

He tended to his broken fingers as best he could, taping them together to keep them straight. He took a couple of painkillers, managed to kick off one shoe before giving up and falling into a fitful sleep.

When he woke proper it was dark. The clock said nine-fifteen but it felt later, felt like it was three in the morning; he was out of sorts. An uncomfortable shower helped a little; painkillers helped more. He figured a visit to Stacey's would finish the job.

The walk was quiet, the streets bare. Yesterday's atmosphere had been drained overnight. There were remnants of it, if you knew where to look; the tissue paper caught in the breeze, the goblin mask lying face down in the gutter.

Inside the bar it was much the same as it was outside. A handful of drinkers. Barstool action heroes, the sorts of people who looked like they might relish the chance to go one-on-one with a murderer. All eyes on the television set—a newscast, running silent, but Joe could guess what it was saying. Footage of both homes, of Sam Lemire giving a statement on the station steps. Aerial shots of squad cars among the Halloween crowds. He felt eyes slide onto him as he made his way deep into the room. That uncomfortable feeling that everyone knew he was involved.

He took a corner booth and a bourbon. Extra glass of ice to numb his broken fingers. The news footage ran over him, he couldn't focus. He barely noticed the man ambling over to his table.

"Mind if I join you, detective?"

Father Brading was standing there, beer in hand. Joe scowled.

"I'm not in the talking mood, Father."

"Not in the drinking mood either, I think. Been nursing that glass since you got here."

Joe raised his bourbon and drained it, then turned back to the television.

The priest laughed. "Same again, I take it?"

"What?"

Father Brading motioned to the barman and sat down across from him. "It's on me," he said, smiling.

"Look, I don't want to offend you, but I'd really rather be left alone."

"It's alright, we don't have to talk. We can just watch the news together in silence."

Joe settled back. "Suit yourself," he muttered.

Their drinks arrived. A couple of quiet minutes passed. Then the priest said, "You don't like me very much, do you?"

"I thought you said we didn't have to talk."

"Oh, come now, it's the same news report that's been running all day."

Joe sighed and set his glass down.

"What I can't work out is whether it's priests in general or me personally."

"Alright," Joe said, turning to look at him. "You want to do this? Fine. I *don't* like you. I don't like the way you hang around crime scenes—"

"Praying for the victims, detective."

"I don't like the way people are around you. Or that we held a press conference in your church."

"Ah, so it's me personally, then," Father Brading said, still smiling. He finished his beer, swapped it for the fresh bottle. "I'll try not to take offense."

"Oh for Christ's . . ." Joe glared at the priest. "I don't know shit about you, Father. My problem is with everything else."

"The church?"

"That's part of it, sure. You see that guy?" Joe pointed to the barman. "He's convinced he can't be hurt, on account of him having some kind of magical protection tattooed on his chest. That's belief for you, Father. And it makes my skin crawl."

The priest spent a moment thinking this over, then said, "So it's the *people* you despise."

"People are idiots," Joe said, waving his good hand through the air. "They do what they want, they're just looking for a way to do it guilt-free. A tattoo, a couple of Hail Marys, a sense of purpose, whatever. And I'm not even talking about that idiot bartender. I'm talking about the people who write the damn rule book to begin with."

"Like that man from the legislature."

"All of them." Joe jabbed his finger down on the table. "They take what they want and they leave us the bones. Protected, through it all, by some twisted internal conviction that what they're doing is right. Belief like that? It's strangling this town, Father."

He sat back, sniffed. Ran a hand across his forehead.

Across from him, Father Brading continued to smile.

"For what it's worth, I agree with you," Brading said.

"You do?"

"People have said or done things for centuries in the name of the Lord. Terrible things. If it annoys *you*, imagine how much it annoys *me*."

Joe stared at him for a moment, then let out a laugh.

"You really go to crime scenes to pray for the victims?" he asked.

"Sure."

"Well, you're a nicer guy than me."

Father Brading shrugged. "I struggle, same as everyone."

"I doubt everyone would have taken in someone in need."

"Who, young Ethan?" The priest finished his second beer. "That was nothing. I always figured what's the point in the church having an empty house when there are people without."

"Listen, I didn't mean to tear into you."

"I know," Father Brading said, glancing at the newscast. "But don't be so hard on others. Or yourself. Who among us hasn't acted in the way you described? We all at times do something we know is wrong, yet tell ourselves it's right."

Joe sighed. In that moment, all he could hear was the sound of Sarah Miller's taillight as he'd smashed it. Had he done it because it had felt right, or because he just wanted to take his anger out on something? Did it even matter?

"What happened to your fingers?" the priest asked.

Joe glanced at them. Moved his hand to his lap. "Caught them in a car door."

Father Brading nodded. "Accidents will happen," he said. "You need to be more careful."

"I'll keep that in mind."

"If you're ever struggling, detective, I find that talking helps."

The priest smiled warmly as he pulled on his coat. Then he shuffled off, dropping a couple of bills onto the bar as he left.

Joe sat for a while after that, still staring at the television, still taking none of it in. Maybe some of the stuff Father Brading had said hit home. He knew what Frank would say; would tell him to stop feeling so goddamn sorry for himself and fix things. Would tell him it could be worse—he could be sleeping his life away in a rundown hospital.

He suddenly thought of Holly Williams. All alone, walking into that cold water one last time. Yeah, it could be a lot worse.

Chapter Thirty

Sarah wasn't happy to see him.

At least, it didn't look that way, what with her standing holding her purse like she was expecting the delivery boy, dressed in sweatpants with tinfoil twisted through her hair.

"Detective," she said, moving her head back slightly as she said it. "This is a surprise."

"Yeah, sorry to drop in on you like this."

"I'm guessing you don't happen to work nights delivering for China Palace."

Joe smiled. "No, I do not. You mind if I come in?"

She looked over his shoulder, then glanced behind her. He wondered if she had someone with her. A guy, maybe. He spread his hands wide. He saw her eyes go to his bandaged fingers.

"I'll be gone before the food arrives," he said. "I promise."

"What's this about? Is it something to do with your case?"

"Please, I just got something to say, and the longer it goes on the less likely I am to say it. You want me to say it on your porch, that's fine."

Sarah stared at him, then stepped back. "Come on," she said.

Joe tipped his head then stepped inside. Her home was small, the front door opening right into the living room. A television was on in the corner, some half-muted gameshow. He was just happy to see she wasn't watching the news. On the sofa was Ethan, bundled up under some blankets.

"Poor guy's got a fever," Sarah said softly. She wandered over and ran a hand through his hair. "I swear, these late summers. Everyone goes around in shorts and sleeps with their windows open."

"I don't think many windows will be open tonight."

"No, I guess not," she said. "Can I get you anything? Glass of water?"

"Why, I look like I need it?"

She shrugged. "Didn't mean anything by it. But yeah, I can tell you've been drinking."

"Had a couple over at Stacey's."

"Should I know her?"

He laughed. "The bar. Pretty shitty, although I guess most of the bars around here are."

"Detective . . ."

"You know, I had a drink with your friend, Father Brading."

"I wouldn't exactly call him my friend. I work for the guy."

"He pays you to look after Ethan?"

"Course he does. Or don't you think being a caregiver is a full-time job?"

"Listen—"

"Is this what you came to ask me?"

Joe sighed. He glanced around the place, the damp flicker of a jaundiced streetlamp spilling through the window. Thing made the whole street look ill. And even though he couldn't see it, he knew it was parked there. The yellow Ford with the smashed taillight.

"See, ah, here's the thing . . ."

Sarah held up a hand. "Shit. Sorry. My scalp is burning. I need to go rinse this off before I go bald."

"Changing your look?"

"Hiding my greys. I'll be two minutes. If the food arrives, get it for me? Money's on the table there."

Joe nodded as she darted off down the cramped hallway and into one of the rooms. A few moments later he heard the sound of running water.

There was a sudden noise from the TV; a laugh track turned too high. A buzzer sounded and the gameshow's scoreboard lit up red. Amber hues flooded the kid's face. And just like that, Joe was back there on that road. Lying flat on the asphalt as Frank rolled on the ground, clutching his face. The roar of the shotgun still ringing in his ears.

Another flash of golden light, another round of cheers.

He started pacing. Around the room, his eyes roaming. He didn't know what he was looking for; didn't matter, probably nothing. His broken fingers throbbed. He needed something to take his mind off it all. What he got was an old photo album, stacked lengthways on top of other books in a cabinet. He pulled it out and started flicking through it.

The pages were half-filled. Photos of Sarah and Ethan, mostly. Fairground rides and school trips. The usual crap. He turned the page. Ethan dressed as a pirate. Turned the page. Ethan behind the wheel of a tractor. Turned the page.

Stopped.

Frowning, he bent his neck to get a closer look. It was a photo of Sarah and Ethan in this very living room. Might have been when they first moved in, by the look of the place; boxes were stacked, every wall bare. They were standing by the living-room window. Ethan was smiling timidly. In his right hand he held a small stuffed bear.

The same bear as the ones from the Richardson house.

"Everything alright?"

Joe glanced up and saw Sarah standing in the doorway, towel-drying her hair. She nodded at the photo album. "Having a snoop, are you?"

He didn't answer. Slid the photo out of the plastic frame and held it up.

"When was this taken?" he asked her.

"What?"

"This photo. When was it taken?"

Sarah took a step forward, frowning at the picture. The towel was still in her hands. "I don't know. Move-in day, I think. Why?"

"This bear Ethan's holding. Where is it now?"

"I have no idea. Probably lost. I haven't seen that thing for months."

"Do you know where he got it?"

"He had it when I started looking after him. Now will you *please* tell me what this is about?"

But Joe barely heard her. He moved for the front door.

"Dammit, answer me, detective," she said. "Why are you so interested in Ethan? Is this . . . is this to do with what happened to him, out on the road?"

He paused, turned to look back. At her, at the sleeping kid.

Sarah stepped between them. "You were there, weren't you?" she said. "You were there when they found him."

Her voice sharpened painfully. Ethan stirred, sat up on the sofa. He stared at them both with heavy eyes.

Sarah went over to him, ran her hand through his hair. "It's okay, honey, we didn't mean to wake you. Go back to sleep."

Ethan's eyes focused for a moment on Joe's, and in that instant Joe knew he'd been right. There *was* something more going on here: the boy was connected. To the Richardson murders, to Frank's shooting. He was connected to it all.

220

Laura

They should have left already.

Laura knew it, they both knew it, had been waiting at the wooded edge of the fallow ground for nearly forty minutes now for Francine and her son, Arthur, to show up. She'd set a deadline of one hour.

"Something's gone wrong," Patrick said. He was in a bad way, bouncing from one foot to the other. "I should go and find them."

"Don't be stupid, Patrick. You'd just be asking to be seen."

"It's not a crime to be walking around the farm after dark, Laura. It's not *prison*."

"Dammit, just wait, alright? They'll be here soon. Twenty minutes before the hour's up. And keep still, for Christ's sake, you're driving me crazy."

Patrick glared at her and sat down against a large tree. Ten silent minutes crept past. Laura stared off at the small collection of farm buildings. What were she and Patrick going to do once they reached an hour? Would she leave without Francine? Patrick wouldn't, she was sure of that. And he was right, of course. If Francine didn't turn up it would be because something had happened. They couldn't just walk away from her.

Then, at last, Laura saw figures moving across the darkened fields. Francine hunched forward and moving quickly. Pulling Arthur behind her by the hand.

"There you are!" Patrick said, his voice breathy with relief. "We were worried you weren't going to show."

"And we were worried you'd be gone," Francine said. Her face was hot and sweaty, and she held Arthur close to her. "Just as we were leaving we saw Kyle and his"—she glanced at her son—"girlfriends out on the lawn, smoking weed. Everyone's dressed in these white robes I've never seen before and holding hands. We had to take the long way around to get here."

"I'm just glad you're here now," Laura said, smiling. "Come on, we've still got plenty of time."

"Should take us about an hour or so to find our way over to the main road," Patrick said. "Plenty of time to find a ride before sunrise. People will stop, seeing Arthur."

They'd discussed the best way to leave. Francine had wanted to take one of the cars. Laura and Patrick had convinced her otherwise. A missing car would arouse suspicion. Worse, if someone caught up with them before they reached the highway, there wasn't any place to hide a car on the open dirt road. Slipping away quietly through the woods was the best option.

Laura watched them as they wrestled bags onto their shoulders; their entire belongings packed away, everything they held dear. She looked back at the farm one last time. The scattered buildings doused in black under the shadows of the moon. She imagined Rudy, holding court in front of his white-robed, smoked-out disciples. Mason's revolver was still in her pocket. What she'd wanted to do with it rose in her, but she swallowed it down. Turned and joined her friends as they headed into the woods.

"What's everyone looking forward to, then?" Patrick asked. He nudged Arthur with his elbow. "You ever play a Nintendo before?"

Arthur shook his head.

"Well, neither have I," Patrick said with a grin. "We'll try it together, what do you say?"

"Biggest thing I'm looking forward to?" Francine said, striding through the thick undergrowth. "Diner pancakes. I swear, there is something about the way they make 'em, just covered in butter and maple syrup." She laughed. "I've been dreaming about them ever since—"

There was a metallic clank and Francine fell forward. Then she started screaming. Laura rushed to her, shouting her name. Pulled the undergrowth aside but already she could smell the blood, could see it glistening, splashed up on the weeds. One of Kyle's bear traps had clamped around Francine's right leg. Its metal jaws had crushed her shin bone.

Chapter Thirty-One

This time of night, the station was quiet. A bored woman on desk duty, barely a hello as Joe barreled past. He threw himself into his chair, fired up his computer. Ackerman was there before it had finished loading.

"Alright, now will you please tell me what's going on?" he demanded.

Joe pulled out the photo and held it up. Careful not to involve his broken fingers. His partner's eyes narrowed as he took it in.

"Where did you get this?"

"From the kid's foster mom."

"From that woman?"

"Her name's Sarah Miller. She was hired by Father Brading to look after the kid that social services handed over to the church."

"Same kid that was in the back of the car the night Frank got shot."

"Same kid. Social services named him Ethan. And when Ethan gets handed over to Sarah Miller, he's got this bear, see? She takes a photo of him holding it, doesn't know what it means."

"And that bear—"

"Same as the bears from the crime scene."

Ackerman collapsed into his seat. Tossed his hat on his desk, ran his hands through his hair. Joe gave him a moment as he finished logging into his computer.

"Where were you yesterday?" Ackerman asked.

Joe looked over. "What?"

"You heard me."

"Look, I know. I've been . . . occupied."

"That all I get?"

"It's better this way, believe me."

Ackerman stared at him. "Joe, if we're going to be partners—"

"But we're not, are we. Not after this is over. Hell, I'll be lucky if I'm still a goddamn detective after all this. Christ, can you imagine the headlines Gonzalez is going to write once this is done?"

"I'm serious here." Ackerman's face was stern, and he leaned forward to look Joe straight in the eye. "If you're in some kind of trouble, tell me. I can help."

"I don't want you involved."

"You don't get to make that decision. Now, if you want me to trust you on any of this, I need to know what we're dealing with."

"It's not as simple as that."

"It really is, Joe. I've been plenty patient—but I want to know what happened with that information Stephen Purcell gave you."

Joe paused. Then, in a rush, it all came out. "David Richardson was keeping a ledger. Tracking the product he moved for the Marchenko cartel. Money too, crazy sums from all over. Sam Lemire was getting twenty grand every couple months to smooth things over."

"Lemire, the state senator?"

"The one and only. So I decided to pay him a visit."

Ackerman's face fell. "Joe . . ."

"It was stupid, I know. He had the money David Richardson had been skimming. I took it back. Wanted to stir things up, see what would happen."

"And what happened?"

Joe held up his battered, bandaged fingers. "Marchenko and his men paid me a visit. Asked me to return the money, only I'd given it away already."

"You *what*?"

"I gave it to Frank. They're going to switch off his machines, Brian, I had to do something. This buys him a little more time."

"So what does this mean now?"

Joe shrugged. "Means Marchenko has something over me. Just as he does with Lemire, just as he does with the captain. So long as I work for the guy, he doesn't go after Frank's wife for the cash."

They sat in silence for a few moments. Then Ackerman said, "Why didn't you come to me for help with all this?"

Joe considered keeping his answer to himself. Then figured what was the point holding any of it back now. "Honestly, I thought you might be in on it too. I was so messed up, I wasn't sure who to trust."

Ackerman rubbed at his face. "I need coffee."

"Look, I'm sorry. I know I messed up."

"You're damn right you did."

"Tell me about the forensics on the second house."

"What, you don't read the papers?"

"You heard about my day. I only caught a minute of the TV news."

"Well, you missed a Gonzalez special. Some kind of Halloween pun."

"Brian . . ."

"I told you, I need coffee. Gimme a minute to process all this."

Joe watched his partner wander off, tapping a cigarette out as he went. When he came back, Joe was searching through police reports. Ackerman sat a Styrofoam cup of dark sludge on the desk. Joe picked it up, burned his fingers, and winced. Took a drink and winced again.

"Alright, so what's the story with the second house?"

Ackerman sank into his chair. Blew out a long stream of smoke. "I'm still waiting on Bob's report. My guess is the killer's plan was to break in, kill Patricia Taylor, then wait for her husband and kids to get home."

"What about the motel the night of the Richardson murders?"

"The Rainbow Inn Motel and Bar," Ackerman announced. "For all your illicit hookup and drug dealing needs. Real classy place. Guy who runs it charges by the hour. He identified two individuals matching Purcell and Richardson's descriptions the night of the murders. Says they booked adjoining rooms."

"Wholesome arrangement. And Rudy Hoffman?"

Ackerman took a gulp of coffee and screwed his face up. "Last known address of Rudy Hoffman is the house he shared with Patricia Taylor over in Wichita. Looks like he lived there for a short while after she left with the kids, then dropped off the grid."

"You lost him that quick?"

"Give me a break, Joe, I've done a hell of a lot in a day. And by myself, too." He pointed his coffee cup at the screen. "So, what's your theory here? Kid from the back seat was connected with the killers somehow?"

"Or at least crossed paths with them, yeah."

"What was the driver's name again? Colder?"

"Colfer. James Colfer. Might not have been him, but *someone* gave the kid that bear before Frank and I pulled his car over."

"How'd you know it's the same bear? Thing could be a dime a dozen, sold in some flea market somewhere."

Joe shot him a look. "Those things are handmade. Not from some factory. I'm telling you, it's a connection."

Ackerman drained his coffee. "So what, keep digging on the driver?"

"Keep digging on the driver." Joe tapped his screen. "This is my report from the night Frank was shot. Maybe I missed something."

"Car belong to Colfer?"

"No, it was registered to Gordon Scott. He crossed paths with Colfer inside, they both served time in Triple-C-L."

"Triple-C-L?"

"Sorry, Lincoln Community Corrections Center. Robbery and arson."

"They sound nice. You ever speak with Scott?"

"Never found him."

Ackerman leaned back, his chair squeaking. Thinking. "When were they inside?"

"Ninety-one."

"Patricia Taylor said Hoffman used to visit prisons, convince people to join his group when they got out."

Joe snatched up his notebook, started flipping through it. "So she did."

"Get on the phone with Lincoln. Ask them to fax over their visitor logs. If Hoffman visited Colfer, he would have had to put his address down."

It took nearly thirty minutes for Lincoln Community Corrections Center to send over the information. Joe stood by the fax machine and pulled each page as it came through. Ackerman watched him as he read.

"Well?"

Joe looked up, triumphant. "Colfer only had a handful of visitors, but our man Hoffman showed up six times, right up to the day he was released."

"He leave an address?"

"Yeah, somewhere along the back edge of MacFarlane's place. I always figured it was just an access road for farm equipment. There must be a second knot of buildings down there."

Ackerman reached for his car keys, tossed them to Joe. "Well then," he said, sliding on his hat, "why don't we go for a drive?"

Laura

Patrick carried Francine back through the trees and across the fallow ground to the farm buildings. At first, she howled with every step. The bear trap was old and heavy, and Laura struggled to keep it steady. After a while, however, Francine's screams ebbed away to long, slow sobs.

Little Arthur had run on ahead to alert the others, and by the time they neared the farm a small group were rushing out to meet them. They were all dressed in white, just like Francine had said. Crazies, waiting for the End Times.

Kyle, of course, was at the front. He held a shotgun in both hands, his eyes bulging a little when he saw Francine. "What the hell—"

"Help us, Kyle!" Patrick barked.

Kyle nodded, tossed his weapon to another follower and scooped Francine up. Patrick kept hold of the trap, and the two of them carried her quickly across the clearing and into the dining hall.

Left suddenly alone, Laura gazed at the others. They stared at her. Their faces filled with suspicion, white robes rippling in the cool breeze. *The Devil sends people to sway others.* For a horrible moment, Laura thought they might just fall on her. Tear her to pieces.

Behind her lay the open fields and the river, and beyond that the dirt road that led back to the highway. If she took off now, she might have a chance.

Only, that would mean leaving Francine. The person who had actually come for her when she'd needed help. What kind of person would she be if she abandoned her now?

Laura slid her hand behind her, to the waistband of her jeans. The reassuring heft of Mason's revolver was still there. Francine had convinced her not to use it, and look how that had turned out.

She pushed forward. Tensed herself for a fight, but the crowd of people simply moved aside, whispering to each other as she passed. Her T-shirt was pulled down over the handgun. Its handle within easy reach.

There was blood in the corridor. Great droplets and smears of it on the floor and along the walls. Laura followed it toward the dining hall. Toward the guttural howls that echoed from within.

The lights here were off, but the corridor wasn't dark. Followers lined it, standing in silence. They held candles, and in the flickering light their faces seemed to shift and warp, the shadows of their features dancing with the flames.

Laura strode past them. No one spoke, and maybe that was worse. Maybe she would have preferred people to shout at her, to call her out like Kyle had done that first night. At least that might have covered up the sound of whatever was happening to Francine behind the door.

As she neared it, however, two figures stepped out and blocked her way. It was Kyle's girls, Katherine and Louise, and they held their candles in front of them as though they were warding away evil.

"Rudy said no one is to go in," Louise told her. "Especially not *you*."

Laura glared at them. "What's he doing in there?"

"He's healing her."

For a moment, Laura didn't react. Then she pulled Mason's revolver and pointed it at Louise's chest. "Get out of my way," she said.

Louise didn't flinch. Instead, the corners of her mouth twitched upward in a terrible smile. "Go ahead," she said softly. "I'm not scared of death."

Behind her, Laura heard the others moving to close off her exit. Holding the gun, her arm was so tense it had started to ache fiercely.

Francine let out another howl. Katherine jumped slightly at it, her candle wavering in her hands. Laura swung her aim downward and pulled the trigger.

The shot blew apart most of Louise's left foot. The woman screamed and fell against the wall. "You fucking bitch!" she cried, staring down at her missing toes. "You shot me, you fucking *bitch!*"

Laura turned, moving the gun in a wide arc. The rest of the group scattered. Katherine shrank away, bending down to help her sobbing friend as Laura pushed past them.

Inside the dining room, Francine was stretched out across the long table. One mangled leg was still in the jaws of the bear trap. Rudy stood over her, his eyes shut, his lips moving silently. The place was lit by candles, dozens of them scattered around the room. As she got closer, Laura could see that someone had tied a gag around Francine's mouth. Kyle, probably, who now stood in the corner of the room, next to Patrick. His shotgun was leaning against the wall.

If any of them had heard the gunfire, none reacted to it. She reached for the light switch and Rudy's voice rang out: "Don't touch that."

Her hand froze. That voice still striking something inside her. An urge to obey.

"I need her to be still," Rudy said. "Kyle, tie her down."

Kyle came forward. Laura looked over at Patrick and he stared back, his face pale.

She raised the revolver once more. "You leave her be, Kyle," she said, and he stopped. "We need to phone for help. She needs to get to a hospital."

Rudy didn't even bother looking up as he spoke. "We are not bringing any more outsiders to the farm," he said, and he turned to a small leather pouch on the table. He unrolled it. Surgical tools glinted in the flames.

"I mean it, Rudy. Get away from her."

"I can save her, Laura."

"If you don't step back, I'll shoot you."

Rudy laughed lightly. "Perhaps you will," he said. "Perhaps the Devil sent you after all." He reached for the tools.

Laura took a breath and pulled the trigger.

The gun clicked empty. She pulled it again, pulled it a third time. Knocking the barrel open, she saw with disbelief that Mason had only loaded it with a single bullet. A bullet she had wasted already.

Rudy finally turned to look at her. He smiled that dreamy, maddening smile. "These things happen for a reason, Laura," he said. "Why don't you take a seat next to Patrick? I'm about to perform a miracle."

"Kyle," she begged. "Don't let him do this."

"Do what, Laura?" Kyle said, his face set. "Fix a mess you caused? *Again?* Just what the hell were you all doing out there anyhow?"

"Enough, both of you," Rudy said quietly. "I need to focus."

Laura tossed the gun. Scanned the room for anything she could use. Kyle was lashing rope across Francine's chest and hips, tying her securely to the table. She'd stopped moaning now. She lay there, gazing at Laura. Her eyes wide with fear.

Rudy selected what looked like some sort of chisel. He raised it, both arms held high like Francine was a sacrifice to the gods, and then in one swift motion he stabbed downward, into the trap.

He leaned his weight against it, slowly prizing the jaws apart, panting with the effort. Francine strained but the ropes held her tight. When the trap had opened far enough, Kyle plunged his hands between the metal teeth and pulled Francine free.

With the pressure gone, blood started spurting from the wound. Rudy clamped his hands over it but it sprayed through his fingers. Francine was still now, her leg a mashed pulp of bone and flesh. Her foot hung at an angle, her exposed shin bone glinting in the candlelight.

Rudy pulled off his belt and tied it above the wound. The blood slowed. He turned to his kit and lifted out a hacksaw.

Chapter Thirty-Two

"How far to go?" Ackerman asked.

They had finally turned off the main highway a couple of miles back. The car lurched about on the uneven road as they drove deeper into the fields.

"Not far now, I don't think," Joe said, hunched forward. "Another couple of minutes."

"I'm starting to wonder if charging in like this is the best idea," Ackerman muttered.

"What's the matter, leaving the big city made you soft?"

"I just think if this *is* where Rudy Hoffman is hiding out with a bunch of his friends, maybe it wouldn't have been the worst thing in the world to call for backup."

"You trust who Harris would send us?"

"Christ, you make it sound like the whole station's against us."

"Relax," Joe said, pointing. "Look, we're here."

Laura

A monstrous explosion rang out in the dining hall. Laura's gaze snapped upward as glass shattered above her. Patrick was standing there, Kyle's shotgun in hand, a shocked expression on his face. He'd blasted a hole in one of the skylights.

"Hey!" Kyle bellowed, marching over. "Give that here, right—"

Patrick fired again, this time squarely into Kyle's chest. Kyle flew backward and skidded to a sprawling stop halfway across the room.

Everything went still. Then Rudy dropped the hacksaw and rushed over. Patrick swung the shotgun toward him, let off a third shot but it went wild, and then Rudy was on him, grabbing the barrel and wrenching it from his hands.

Laura ran to Francine on the table, but it was obvious she was too late. Francine's face was slack, her eyes empty. The floor was drenched in her blood. She reached down and grasped her friend's hand. Then she looked slowly back at Rudy, who was hunched over Patrick as he cowered on the floor.

"You killed her," she said.

Rudy turned. Blood was splashed down his front and his pale face was like that of some supernatural creature. His hair messy, his teeth glinting in the soft light as he spoke.

"What did you say?"

"I said you killed her."

Disgust flooded through her. The events of the last few weeks sitting high in her chest, too high to push back down again, so high she could just about taste them. Rushing through her like vomit, like that night with Mason, the night in the kitchen, the night she'd tried to murder him with the kitchen knife.

"I think I must be confused," Rudy spat. "After everything I gave you? Shelter, protection. You left. You *left*, remember? And you came back and I welcomed you, Laura—with open arms I welcomed you. And when your ignorant townie husband came for you, I was there. I was the one who took care of you. And now you . . . you turn against me—worse, you turn *others* against me, like I'm the one causing all of this. But it's *you*, Laura. *It's always been you.*"

Laura turned and started for the door. She heard Rudy's footsteps closing the gap. Her hand brushed the door handle and then his fingers were in her hair. Twisting, pulling. Her head snapped back and she cried out as her arms windmilled, knocking a small table over. She landed hard on the floor and watched a candle roll into a bundle of curtains. The cheap fabric caught fire in an instant.

And then Rudy was on top of her. In the blaze of the flames his blood-soaked face seemed more terrifying than ever. His long hair fell forward onto her and his hands slid around her throat.

"You've ruined *everything*," he said.

Laura closed her eyes.

Chapter Thirty-Three

Joe brought the car to a skidding halt. The headlights lit up a wide, fallow field, and beyond that a group of wooden buildings—a long outbuilding flanked by a smaller structure, and beyond them a crooked-looking farmhouse. He killed the engine and they climbed out. Clicked on flashlights, pulled their weapons. Better to approach on foot with everything ahead of them than to drive into the barnyard, exposed to fire on all sides.

The field and the buildings beyond were utterly still. They moved slowly across the ground, flashlights aimed forward. All Joe could hear was the crunch of their footsteps on the dried-out weeds, and the cool wind rustling.

In front of them, the buildings were backlit by the moon. Ackerman pointed to the first, long building, and moved toward its door.

"Should we knock?" Joe asked.

Ackerman swung his flashlight beam over the structure. The rotten joists, the blackened walls. "Just to hear the echo?" he said. "This place feels abandoned as all hell."

Standing there before it, Joe shivered. He stepped up and tried the door's handle and it swung open easily. They pointed their flashlights inside.

It was empty. No, it was burnt out. Joe followed scorch marks as they danced along the walls. The fire hadn't got everything, but there wasn't much left. A couple chairs, an old kitchen unit. A long dining-room table. A hole in the skylight that had let in the rain.

Wordlessly, they checked the second building. It was a dormitory of some kind. Similarly abandoned, the rooms empty. While Ackerman moved down the corridor, Joe checked one of the little rooms and wondered what sort of person had stayed here. He opened the bedside cabinet and found a Bible. Flicked it open. *Property of Lisa Reynolds* it read in the top corner, in neat, slanted writing.

"Joe!"

He dropped the book and hurried back outside. Ackerman was crouched by the edge of the field.

"You find something?" Joe said.

Ackerman stood. Motioned with his flashlight.

Joe followed the beam, saw wooden crosses in the dirt. "*Kyle* and *Francine*," he read out loud. "What the hell happened here?"

"Whatever it was, it wasn't all that recent," Ackerman said.

Joe scanned the small cemetery. A third grave stood off to one side. He walked closer, bent down to read the name.

"Shit," he said.

Laura

The fire was spreading now. Fast, up the curtains and along the floor, scurrying across peeling wallpaper. The smoke was thick and black. It stung Laura's eyes as Rudy tightened his grip on her throat.

After everything, she thought to herself. *It ends the same.*

She gave up clawing at his hands and scratched at the floor until her fingers brushed something long and thin, something metallic.

The chisel.

She gripped it like a knife, and when she drew it back Rudy's eyes went to it and widened, and he turned, lifting one hand from her throat to protect himself as she drove it into him. The chisel popped clean through his palm and kept on going. Rudy screamed as she buried its tip into his neck.

He fell away, clutching at it. Pulled it out but that only made it worse. His face went white, his body flopping to the floor beside her.

Coughing—from the fire or from Rudy, she didn't know—she got to her feet. People were in the room now, shouting. She could hear them through the thickening smoke.

"Patrick!" she shouted, stepping over Rudy's still-twitching body. "Patrick, answer me!"

She stumbled forward to where she'd seen him last. Stumbled over the table, a horrifying glimpse of Francine's lifeless eyes, and then she saw Kyle lying on his back with a hole in his chest. Something glittered beside him. His keys. She fell on them.

Then Patrick was shouting her name. His voice high-pitched and panicking. She ran to him, her throat burning and her eyes streaming. She grabbed his shoulders. Shook him hard.

He blinked rapidly, clutched her arms.

"Come on, we have to go," Laura said. She reached for Kyle's shotgun and pressed it into his hands. "Take this."

Together they managed to make it outside. Into the cool air where they collapsed, retching.

"Where's Rudy?" someone shouted. "Where is he?"

A young girl grabbed at Laura's shirt. "Is Kyle in there?" she asked. "Is he still in there?" Her voice was frantic, and it took Laura a moment to realize it was Katherine. For a second, she actually felt sorry for her.

For a second.

"Get away from me," Laura coughed, pushing the girl back.

She manhandled Patrick away from the crowd, away from the heat and the light, and into the darkness by the field.

"You need to get Arthur," she told him. "You need to get him away from here, you understand me? Take the shotgun, go get him, and *run*."

Patrick shook his head, confused. "What?"

"People are going to come," she said, gripping his shoulders. "There are going to be questions. Arthur doesn't deserve any of this, and neither do you."

"Aren't you coming with us?"

"Go to the Essex Motel, in Cooper. I'll find you there in a couple days." She picked through Kyle's keys, slid off the one for his car. "Take his Buick and go."

Finally, he nodded. He looked down at the shotgun in his hands. "I killed him," he said. "I killed him and . . . and she's dead."

"Listen to me, Patrick. You *saved* me. You understand? You saved *me*."

Patrick smiled at that. "My name's not Patrick," he said softly. "It's James. James Colfer. Patrick's what he gave me."

Laura squeezed his arm. "All right then. James. Now please, you have to go. I'll see you soon."

He slung the shotgun over his shoulder and embraced her. It seemed to surprise him almost as much as it did her. Then he was gone, his face red as he ran toward the dormitory in search of Arthur.

She waited until he reappeared with the boy, pulling him across the field toward the cars. Everyone was outside now. People hauling water from the nearby river in buckets, trying to douse the flames. Others were sitting cross-legged just back from the heat, praying and holding hands. All of them dressed in those stupid white robes.

The sound of an engine starting was almost lost in the noise of the fire. She turned and saw Arthur staring at her from the back seat, and she held up her hand as they passed. The last she saw of the car was its taillights, red eyes winking at her as they drifted off toward the highway.

She glanced down at the rest of Kyle's keys. One of them stood out from the rest. A chunky thing for a fancy lock. The name *Emily* written on masking tape around the head.

Laura frowned. Then she remembered what Katherine had told her. That he had a girl in town. That he'd gotten her pregnant. She closed her fist around the key.

Chapter Thirty-Four

The third grave read *Rudy.* Someone had etched it into the wood with care. More care than the other two. Joe clicked off his flashlight.

"I guess we finally found him," he muttered.

"Alright, let's break it down," Ackerman said, taking off his hat and scratching his scalp. "We know James Colfer came here after prison. Let's say he stayed here a while. Got hooked up with the boy somehow. Then he leaves . . ."

". . . runs into me and Frank on the highway."

"Maybe he left the night this happened." Ackerman gestured to the burnt buildings. "Maybe Colfer had something to do with these graves."

Joe grunted. "He sure did look scared the night we met him. Maybe he thought we knew about whatever had gone down here. Had come to toss his ass back inside."

The two men stood in silence a moment longer. That overwhelming feeling that the pieces were there, if only they could line them up. Around them, the abandoned fields seemed to rise up on all sides. Long grass bending in the chill wind, the rustle of the weeds and the gentle creak of rotten beams. Joe wondered about the people that chose to live in a place like this.

Ackerman sighed. "I'm too tired for this right now. Let's go home, get a couple hours' sleep. Think about our next step in the morning."

He headed back to the car. Joe stayed a little longer, his eyes still on Rudy's grave. *You didn't kill the Richardsons*, he thought to himself. He clicked off his flashlight and followed his partner. *But who put you in that grave?*

Chapter Thirty-Five

Sarah sat on the sofa and stroked the kid's hair. He felt cooler now, his fever broken. She hadn't eaten much of her takeout. Hadn't really had the appetite. Her mind elsewhere; on the cop, mainly, on his face when he'd pulled that photo out of the album. That damned photo. How could she have been so stupid?

She quietly got up and went over to the album. Went through it to see what else she might have missed. Took out a couple more pictures just to be safe. Then she went into the boy's bedroom. Opened his toy chest and found the stuffed bear. She ran her fingers over it, remembering.

Remembering drifting through the dark Richardson house to Emily's bedroom. The look in the girl's eyes when they fluttered open to find her looming over her. Three hours she'd waited in the cornfield, watching for the last of the lights to click off, Kyle's keys and a bag of poisoned treats in her pocket. The dog slept in the laundry room and the fourth step creaked on the way upstairs. Knowledge she'd gained from earlier trips to the house when everyone was away.

Remembering the sound little Jacob had made when his head had popped. She hadn't enjoyed that, but she'd had no choice. She'd never had a choice, not really. A hard truth, but sometimes it was better to murder something than to let it live: Kyle couldn't be allowed to spread his poison through the world. Any offspring of his would surely only grow up to be as sick and twisted as their father. What she'd done, it was a mercy killing.

Remembering the pause in David Richardson's step when he'd come home and found his family dead. She'd enjoyed that more. The way he'd started for her, his hands outstretched like he wanted to rip her apart. Course, that had only lasted a moment. Funny how easy a man was to control when you had a gun in his face. People acted like they cared about each other, but all anyone really cared about was survival.

Remembering the drive across town with the gun pointed at the back of his head. He had a surprisingly delicate neck, like a little boy's. He'd been her chauffeur; she'd sat in the back and everything. Now that, she'd *really* enjoyed. It had helped her to relax, knowing that the hard part was over. The rest was simple: a hefty dose of Ambien, crushed up in some water. A promise that it would only send him to sleep.

The knife from his kitchen counter had glinted in the light of the moon before she slid it home. It winked out then. Her hands had trembled a little—not from fear—and she'd nicked the skin a couple of times. But in the end the blade had done its job. No mistakes this time.

Not like with Mason.

And not like on Halloween, with Rudy's children. She'd rushed that one. Never expected his ex to be home, much less pull a gun on her. Lucky she hadn't gotten herself shot. She'd have to give it some time before trying again.

Sarah went into the bathroom and emptied the garbage can into the sink. Tossed the photos inside. The bear, too. And finally she took from her pocket the note Francine had left her, unfolded it and read it again, read it for the hundredth time. *Everything will be alright.* She ran her thumb over the words and thought of her and Patrick, and smiled, and placed the note into the trash. She poured a shot of vodka over everything and dropped a lit match in after it, and as it all burned away she poured another shot for herself.

Chapter Thirty-Six

Of course, Joe didn't sleep the last few hours left before dawn. Couldn't. Didn't even bother trying. He was too wired, his mind running through too many possibilities.

Instead he sat at his kitchen table, Leo asleep by his feet, and drank an entire pot of coffee as he worked his way through the mental churn. The kid in the car, driven by a guy from a burnt-out farm on the edge of an enormous, empty field. Nothing left behind but graves.

In the end, he dozed a little. Hunched over the table, waking with Leo licking his bare feet. His fingers throbbed. His back ached.

Driving to the station, he found himself going past the church. He stared at Sarah's house. Part of him wanted to go back and apologize for last night. Most of him didn't. He waited for the light to change and tore away.

Ackerman was already at his desk. Joe fell into the seat opposite.

"You get much sleep?" Ackerman asked.

"Not really."

"Yeah, me neither. My brain's turned to fog."

"You want some coffee?"

"God no, that stuff is poison. Besides, I've drunk about a gallon of it already this morning."

Joe turned and glanced up at the captain's office. Behind the mottled glass he could see two shadows moving; Harris was pacing again. He wondered who else was in there with him. What they were discussing, who they were watching.

"You want to get out of here?" Joe said.

Ackerman followed his gaze. "Worried about the captain?"

"Aren't you?"

"Where we going?"

"Right now, I'd be more comfortable talking in that damn diner than in here."

"Fine by me. I could do with some breakfast. Let me just check in with Bob before we go, see how he's getting on with his report." Ackerman rolled to his feet and ambled off to the basement.

Joe yawned and rubbed at his eyes. Pulled out his notebook and flicked through it idly. His eyes caught on a page, was still mulling it over when Ackerman returned.

"Forensics are done on the backpack," his partner said, holding up a report. "Nothing much, but listen to this. That mystery man Patricia Taylor shot at? He was a she."

"What?"

Ackerman dropped the report on his desk. Pointed to a page. "She left some hair behind on one of the backpack's straps. Bob says he found traces of dye on it."

"Hair dye?" Joe was only half-listening, still staring at his notebook.

"Blonde, right out of a bottle," Ackerman said. "Hey, you hearing me?"

"The name on the Bible," Joe said.

"What's that?"

"At the farm. I found a Bible in one of the rooms. Someone had written their name in the inside cover. *Property of Lisa Reynolds.* Maybe she was there the night it happened."

Ackerman nodded. "Worth trying to find her." He glanced up at the captain's office. "I'd rather not shout her name too loud, though."

"Harris will see any APB we issue."

"Then we'll need someone outside the force to help track her down." Ackerman grabbed his jacket. "Maybe someone who distrusts this place as much as we do."

Joe stared at him. "Oh, no."

"Come on, there's a payphone on the corner. You can call him there."

"And say what?"

"Tell him breakfast's on us. Greedy bastard won't be able to resist."

It didn't matter that a chill had settled itself over Cooper. Daniel Gonzalez still sweated.

"Well, isn't this cozy," he said, staring at them both across the table. "Boy was I surprised to get a call from you two."

"What's the matter?" Joe said. "Not happy with your front-page exclusive last time?"

Ackerman leaned in. "I seem to remember some pretty early questions at the press conference."

"Nice photos, too," Joe added.

"You destroyed a full roll of film, remember that?" Gonzalez glared at Joe. "You have any idea the shots I lost?"

"Relax, Daniel. How about another exclusive to smooth things over?"

Gonzalez tapped out a cigarette on his arm. Ackerman gave him a light, lit up one of his own.

"What did I tell you boys about the *Tribune*?" Gonzalez said. "You cops, you think you can just use us whenever it suits. Makes me sick to my stomach."

"You don't feel well?" Joe said. "I'll cancel your food."

"You think a stack of pancakes is all it takes to buy my paper?"

"Please. I can buy your paper for fifty cents, and trust me, I'd be better off tossing the money straight down the goddamn toilet—"

"*Alright*," said Ackerman, banging his palm on the table. A couple of nearby diners jumped. "Gentlemen, do we really have to do this every time? Now, Daniel, we have a proposition for you. If you're interested, we'll talk details. If not, then we'll leave you to enjoy your breakfast."

"You still paying if I tell you to get lost?"

Ackerman paused, swallowed whatever remark was working its way up. "Sure."

Gonzalez sat back and mulled it over. Fake mulled though, like the fat prick hadn't made up his mind already. Even if he hated it, the guy wasn't going to miss an opportunity to listen to two cops ask for his help.

"Fine, get on with it."

Ackerman gave his partner a nod. Joe cleared his throat.

"Our investigation has turned up a name. A woman that we're trying to locate."

"Don't you have people for that? I mean, aren't *you* the people for that?" Gonzalez frowned. "Isn't that what cops *do*?"

"This is a little delicate," Joe said. "We don't want to involve the department on this one."

Gonzalez was silent. He stared at Joe, and for the first time Joe got the impression the reporter was actually thinking it through. After a couple of moments, Gonzalez said, "You don't want to involve the department?"

"That's right."

"You mean you don't want your captain to know what you're up to."

Joe nodded.

"What is this, some kind of police corruption?"

Joe shifted his weight. "Any of this leaves this table, Daniel, I swear to Christ—"

"Oh, calm down, detective." They sure had his attention now. "How do I know *you're* not the dirty cops, huh?"

Ackerman said, "If we were dirty, we wouldn't be asking a reporter to look into it, would we."

"Jesus, you guys *are* desperate."

"You interested or not?"

"Why come to me?"

"Because no one has a bigger hard-on for Cooper PD than you do, Daniel. And right now, that makes you just about the least likely person to be in cahoots with them."

Gonzalez grinned. "I haven't heard someone use the word *cahoots* in a long while."

"Interested. Yes or no."

"Alright, keep going."

There was a clatter from the kitchen and the door swung open. A waitress appeared and started laying plates down on the table. Ackerman fell silent, glanced over at Joe, and Joe could tell he was glad of the interruption. A couple of moments to catch your breath—Gonzalez had a way of burrowing under your skin, of making you trip yourself up.

Stack of pancakes with bacon and eggs for the reporter, couple of refills for the detectives. Joe's stomach rumbled. He and Ackerman still hadn't eaten breakfast yet, on his insistence. Sitting with Gonzalez was one thing, eating was another. The sickly smell of maple syrup hit him hard. Made him think of his mother's baking, of Nicky. His broken fingers burned.

"You sure you boys don't want anything?" Gonzalez asked around a mouthful of pancakes.

Joe grimaced. "We already ate."

"I guess the good cops start early. So, who's this woman you want me to find?"

"Her name's Lisa Reynolds. She spent time in some kind of commune over on MacFarlane's land. Place is a burnt-out wreck now though, probably hasn't lived there for a while."

"That it?"

"We can give you a couple of other names, too. Known associates, people who stayed at the farm with her."

"Uh-huh." Gonzalez was already halfway through his stack. He speared chunks of food with his right hand, scribbled down notes with his left. Leaned back and picked up a piece of crispy bacon with pudgy fingers. "Lisa her birth name—or could it be, I don't know, Melissa or whatever?"

Joe shrugged. "That's literally everything we have."

"Who is she?"

"She's maybe connected to the Richardson murders and the attack on the Taylors. *Maybe*. Honestly, we're still working out how."

"Fine. So let's say I track her down. What then?"

Joe glanced at Ackerman, who said, "You let us know where she is."

"Uh-huh. What are you two going to be doing in the meantime?"

"We're following the forensics on the second house, first and foremost. And Daniel—"

"I know, I know, your little side investigation stays very hush-hush."

Ackerman let out a sigh and nodded. Lifted up his coffee and just about drained it in one go.

Gonzalez picked at something in his teeth. "And now we come to the most important question."

"What's in it for Daniel Gonzalez," Joe said.

"Hey, I don't work for free."

"You find her, you get to burn a bunch of dirty cops once this is all over. You get first interview with her. Another exclusive. And trust me, it'll be worth it."

The reporter picked up a napkin and wiped grease off his fingers, mopped at his brow. Then he grinned and stuck out his hand. Joe stared at it and got to his feet.

"You find anything, you call me," he said.

"What about my breakfast?"

Ackerman pulled out his wallet, muttering.

Gonzalez said, "You ever wonder why diners always market their pancakes so aggressively? I mean, look at this menu. All this 'classic' business, like you're buying a vintage car. Pancakes sell themselves, you know?"

Joe slowly gazed over at his partner. Ackerman was glaring at the reporter as he tossed a couple of bills onto the table. "Just eat your damn pancakes," he growled, grabbing his hat. He looked over at Joe. "Not another word."

They were on their way out when Joe's pager beeped. A number he didn't recognize. He turned to Ackerman. "I'll meet you at the car."

His partner nodded and headed out. Joe motioned to the young kid behind the counter, got him to bring around the phone.

"No long-distance," the kid said.

Joe ignored him and dialed. A woman's voice answered.

"This is Detective Finch," he said. "I help you with something?"

"It's Sarah Miller. I hope you don't mind, I asked the station to page you my number."

Joe grimaced. Pressed the receiver into his ear. "Look, about last night—"

"Can we meet?"

Outside, Ackerman was waiting by the car. Joe could see him through the glass doors. He was lighting another smoke while he watched his partner talk.

Joe said, "Sure, but now's not a good time."

"How about tonight?"

"Tonight's fine. Where?"

"That bar you mentioned. Stacey's. Nine o'clock."

"What about Ethan?"

"I'll get a sitter. It'd be good to clear the air, I think."

"Yeah, I agree."

"See you then, detective."

Joe hung up the phone and headed to the car.

"You still hungry?" Ackerman asked.

"Starved."

"You ever tried a klobasnek?"

"Is that the one where she straddles you in an airplane toilet?"

"It's a classic Texan breakfast, Joe. Think of it like a hot dog in a warm donut."

"Oh, so I was close."

Ackerman rolled his eyes as he pulled away from the curb. "Come on, there's a bakery near here that'll just about manage it if you ask them nice. Be good to go over everything one more time."

Chapter Thirty-Seven

The diggers broke ground on MacFarlane's land just before noon. The exhumations of Rudy and his two friends would likely take the rest of the day. Ackerman went to keep watch.

Joe knew it might take a while before they got a positive ID on the three corpses. A fair chance that the people who buried them weren't too educated in preserving remains. All that time in the hot ground, fingerprints were probably rotted to hell.

Dental records would be the next step. A process that could take a couple of days, if they got a hit on anything. Again, Joe worried about the type of person who joined a commune like this. You only got dental records if you ever visited a dentist.

Last chance would be DNA, and that would be weeks. Too long to help them stop another attack.

Joe leaned back against his sofa. The floor around him was carpeted in crime-scene photos, statements, forensic reports. He'd been staring at the documents for hours now. Waiting for something to jump out at him. Waiting, he was ashamed to admit, for Gonzalez to call.

Leo was curled up on the sofa. Asleep by his head. Joe reached back and gave the dog a scratch under his ear. Leo groaned and rolled over slowly.

A quiet dinner, scrambled eggs on toast. His cupboards were practically bare. Marchenko had been right about that, at least.

He was nervous about meeting Sarah Miller, he realized. Mainly because he'd convinced himself already that he was going to tell her the truth. That Ethan had been in the car the night Frank got shot, that he'd been keeping an eye on him ever since. On her, too. That he'd been the one to break her taillight. A reason to pull her over, to see the boy up close. His certainty that the kid knew more than he let on.

He took Leo outside. A quick stop in the shared yard out back. Watched the old dog stand in his favorite spot and bark at a crow. Someone from upstairs slid open a window and shouted at him to be quiet. Leo didn't pay them any mind. By the time Joe left his apartment, the pug was already snoozing, curled up on Joe's sofa.

Stacey's was much the same as it had been all week. Quiet. Joe got there early, ordered a beer and took a seat in the corner. When Sarah arrived, she gave him a thin smile.

"Thanks for meeting me," she said.

"Thanks for calling. I've got some stuff I need to say."

"Same here."

"You want a drink?"

"In a minute." Sarah looked around as she sat down. "So this is the famous Stacey's."

Joe tilted his beer at the room. "This is it. It's normally a littler busier."

"I like the privacy."

"Well, then I should probably warn you. Last couple times I've been here, I've spotted Father Brading nursing a drink."

"Don't worry about him tonight. He's keeping an eye on Ethan."

"Does he know you're meeting me?"

"He's my employer, not my dad, detective."

"Jesus, and you're not my captain. Call me Joe."

She gave what seemed to be a genuine smile. "Alright, Joe. I'm going to get a drink. What are you having?"

"A beer, if you're buying."

"You sure I can't tempt you into something a little more exotic?"

"Like what?"

"How about a Last Word? Gin, green chartreuse, maraschino liqueur, and fresh lime. It's something I used to drink."

"Considering I understood about half those ingredients, good luck getting the barman here to make that for you. But sure, I'll give it a try."

Joe watched Sarah as she ordered. Steering the tattooed bartender to the correct bottles. His gaze drifted around the bar. The same bored faces staring at the same muted TV channels. He thought about what he was going to say to Sarah. He'd brought her photograph back—after making copies, of course—and he placed it on the table now.

Looking back, she was still at the bar. Leaning over the drinks. Inspecting them, maybe. Joe finished his beer, and when he put the bottle down she was on her way over.

The cocktails were green and fizzing slightly. Joe picked his up and gave it a precursory sniff.

"It's not quite the same recipe, but it's close enough," Sarah said.

"It looks radioactive."

"I'll warn you, it's strong."

"It's not going to kill me, is it?"

"The lime looked a little rotten, but I think you'll be alright." Her gaze fell on the photo. She reached over and took it back. Smoothed it out. "Thank you for bringing this."

"Listen, I'm sorry for last night. Going through your things like that, taking the photograph without explaining why."

Sarah played with her glass. "I appreciate that. But I'd appreciate an answer to my earlier question as well."

"What question is that?"

"Were you there the night they found Ethan?"

Joe paused. "I was there," he said.

"Were you ever planning on telling me?"

"Honestly? Probably not, no."

Sarah nodded. Joe took a drink. It was sour, the alcohol strong enough to make him wince.

"Jesus, where did you find this?" he asked, clearing his throat.

"My ex-husband."

"I can see why you left him."

"Tell me about the night it happened," she said.

Joe did. Frank and the coin toss, the red taillights in the dark.

"Tell me about the man who was driving," she said.

He took another drink. He could feel it starting to loosen him up. "James Colfer. An ex-con. He was running from something," Joe said. "Guy was scared out of his mind."

For a moment, he thought he saw sadness in her expression.

"And you think this James Colfer was involved in these murders?"

Joe tried to pick his words carefully. "I think there's a lot we still don't understand about these murders."

"Like what?"

"Like, with the Richardsons . . . Why take the father across town to kill him? Why take the risk?"

"At your press conference you said it was a suicide. You said he was a suspect in what happened to his family."

Joe shook his head. Took another drink. "Between us, I don't believe that. Do I think he killed himself? Sure, that's what the evidence says. But David Richardson was a victim, just like the rest of his family."

Sarah watched him for a moment. "Do you want to hear my theory?" she asked.

"Absolutely."

"I think whoever killed that family did it to make a point."

"Yeah? What point?"

"That power doesn't always rest with men. That it can be taken away from them. By a woman, by anyone."

Joe frowned. He was finding it hard to follow what she was saying. "I don't . . ."

"I think whoever killed that family waited until David Richardson was out, then unlocked the front door and let themselves in. I think they poisoned the dog, I think they butchered the family in their beds. Then they stuck around for him to return home, and to realize just how easy it is to lose everything."

"Then why not kill him in the home?"

"Because it's about *dominance*, Joe. It's not enough to take a man's family away, you need to show that you control every aspect of him. That his fate is entirely within your hands."

Joe leaned back in his chair. His head was starting to spin. He glanced down at his half-drunk cocktail. "Jesus, this is strong."

"Don't fall asleep on me yet, detective. We're not done talking."

Her face swam a little in front of him. He said, "Alright. So this grand theory of yours. Why target the Richardsons? Why target the Taylors?"

"Easy. A personal connection to the killer. Have you ever thought that maybe she's doing the world a favor?"

"*She?*"

Sarah's eyes narrowed. "It doesn't even enter your headspace that it could be a woman, does it? You're so close-minded, detective."

"I told you, call me Joe . . ."

His words drifted away, adrenaline tremors running through his hands. He tried to slide them into his lap. The green cocktail still sat in front of him. Still fizzing.

"What's in this . . . ?" he managed, before starting to slump in his seat.

Sarah stood up, smiling sweetly. "Oh my, Joe. I think someone's had a little too much to drink." She came around the table and pulled his arm across her shoulders. "Come on, let's get you home."

Chapter Thirty-Eight

Joe floated in and out of consciousness. Snatches of lucidity. Staggering out of the bar and into the cold night was one. Being bundled into the back of a car was another. A time jump and he was outside his apartment building, a woman helping him inside.

He couldn't find his keys. Tried to pat himself down but his hands were moving slow. Too slow to work right. He motioned at the mat and that woman was there again, peeling it back. Picking up his spare.

Then they were by his sofa. He collapsed onto it. His eyelids felt heavy but his heart was racing. He couldn't breathe properly and now the woman was leaning over him. Reaching into her purse. Something that glinted, something metal.

"You should have stayed away from us," the woman said.

And then there was barking: Leo on his chest, snarling, spittle flying. The woman had backed away. Joe tried to sit up but he couldn't. The world around him fading out. Someone banging on his door, a voice shouting at Leo to shut up. The woman from across the hall. The woman with the hydrangeas.

And now the other woman, the first woman, the woman with the blade, was leaving, the door thrown open and slamming, and Leo finally stopped barking and started whining instead, like he was afraid, and he pressed himself into Joe's side and his warmth was wonderful and then Joe was gone.

Chapter Thirty-Nine

Joe woke the next morning on the sofa. Leo was on top of him, his face buried in Joe's armpit. He had a sour taste in his mouth. Rolling to his feet, the room swayed. A headache so bad he could barely feel his broken fingers. He clutched at his temples and winced. How much had he drunk last night?

He leaned over his sink, the cold water running. He dunked his head under the tap. Flashes of the night before. Nothing in sequence, nothing that made any sense. He remembered arriving at Stacey's. Remembered Sarah Miller arriving. Had he told her about Ethan, about her taillight?

It was after nine. He tried his machine, a missed call from Cathy. Her voice barely audible. He rang her back as he waited for the shower to heat up. When she answered she was crying.

"It's Frank," she said.

"What about him? Cathy? What about Frank?"

Cathy sobbed for another ten seconds straight before she was able to answer.

"He's dead, Joe. He's dead."

◆ ◆ ◆

Joe pulled up to Cooper Memorial twenty minutes after getting off the call. Twenty minutes of running to the car, sitting in traffic. Might as well have been twenty hours. Sure as hell felt like it. His head ached, a pressure that painkillers couldn't relieve.

He found Cathy in the room, in her chair. Frank was there too. Tucked up in bed like he always was, lying on his back with his eyes shut, only this time it was different. Before, he was only sleeping.

In a lot of ways, this last time was a lot like the first time. He sat with Cathy, amongst the dead and the dying, and she wept on his shoulder and Joe wept too. Five months had passed since the night Frank was shot. Five months of a life being put on hold, and then this.

"What happened?" he asked.

"He just . . . gave up," Cathy said quietly, as though Frank could still hear her. "Doctors think he might have developed some kind of pneumonia, but I don't know. He didn't look like he had pneumonia, Joe. Didn't feel hot, wasn't breathing any different. I think . . . I think he'd just had enough."

Joe stared at his friend, finally freed from the feeding tubes and monitors. Where had Joe been, he wondered, while Frank was dying?

Cathy made it sound like Frank had chosen to go. Like the guy had lain on his back for months and finally decided *now's the time*. And sure, that was a hell of a nicer way to think of it. Nicer than the idea of some blended hospital food working its way down the wrong tube and kick-starting a bacterial infection in your chest. See, Joe knew this stuff, had spent weeks cornering the doctors when Frank had first slipped into his coma.

So yeah, he got why Cathy would want to think like that. Only, why would Frank have waited this long? Christ, if the tables were turned and it was *him* on that bed, Joe would've pulled his own plug a long time ago. Probably around the time they strapped that first adult diaper to his ass. Screw getting some male nurse in rubber gloves changing that every other day.

He got up and stood by the window. Looked out at the view. Probably a blessing the guy never got to see it. "What happens now?"

"I have no idea," Cathy said.

"If you need help with anything . . ."

"I know."

He nodded, wiped at his eyes. "It's all such a waste."

"Listen, there's something I need to give you."

Joe turned around. Cathy was over by Frank's bedside cabinet. She hauled out the briefcase and placed it gently at the foot of the bed.

"I want you to have this back," she said.

"What?"

"I don't know where you got this from, but I figure you probably got yourself in some trouble because of it."

"What trouble?"

"I can see it, Joe. I can see it in your face. In your eyes. You don't think I got good at reading people's faces, looking at Frank's for five months? How'd you break those fingers, anyhow?"

"Cathy, listen—"

"No, you listen. It was a nice thing you did here. Offering Frank that extra time? It was real nice. And you ask me, maybe he didn't want it. Maybe he didn't want you getting in whatever sort of trouble you're in because of him."

"Oh, so now *Frank* can read people's faces, too?"

Cathy smiled sadly. "You know he'd be saying the same thing if he was awake."

"If he was awake he wouldn't need the money."

"He's dead, Joe, he still doesn't."

She said it with a sharp edge. He clammed up. Stared at the briefcase and knew what she was saying made sense. He could give it back to Lemire, use it to get himself out from under all this. He glanced down at his bandaged fingers.

"How's the case going?" she asked.

"You been watching the news?"

"Snippets, here and there."

"For a minute I thought we were close. Now I don't know."

"Those poor families," she said. "I just can't imagine who would do something like that. What is wrong with some people?"

"Isn't that the question of the day."

"Well, I hope you catch him." Cathy sniffed. "I hope the bastard gets a firing squad."

"I'm not sure they've shot anyone in a while now."

"You know what I mean. Whoever he is—as far as I'm concerned, he shouldn't be allowed to live."

Joe thought of Bob's report on the bag. Of the hair sample he'd found. "Actually, we think it might be . . ."

He trailed off, frowned. Cathy looked over at him.

"You alright?"

Traces of hair dye. Ackerman's voice: *Blonde, right out of a bottle.* An image: Sarah Miller answering the door with tin foil in her hair. And nestled among them all: a green cocktail, fizzing slightly.

He got to his feet.

Cathy leaned forward. "Joe, what's wrong?"

"I need to get to the station." His gaze fell to the bag. "You really think Frank chose to go out on his own terms?"

"I have to."

"You said he did it for me. To let me have the money. Only I think you're looking at it all wrong—I think he did it for you."

"What?"

"Keep the money," Joe said. "Keep it and get the hell out of Cooper. Use it to start fresh, whatever."

"I can't do that."

"Why? Cathy, you've given up everything for Frank. Let him give you something back in return."

She stared at him, then back down at the briefcase. Joe knew she wouldn't take it. Not unless he forced her to. That was just how she was. She'd want it—deep down, she'd be begging for it—but her pride or her guilt or whatever wouldn't let her keep it.

So he made her decision for her. Walked over to the bed and said his final goodbye, then embraced Cathy tight, leaving before she had a chance to say no.

Chapter Forty

Joe drove slow along Elm Drive, parked around the corner. No sign of the yellow Ford.

He sat outside her home. Not long—a couple of minutes maybe. That was the thing about bad ideas. You left them a while and they started to rot. He wrapped his hand in a chamois from his car and used it to smash in her bedroom window. Climbed inside, that bad idea turning putrid.

Ignoring it. Moving to her dresser, her closet. In the bathroom he opened the cabinet above the sink. Found a grey residue in the trash can. Gritty between his fingers. Ash, maybe. A set of drawers under the window. He finally got lucky with the second one.

A hairbrush.

He collected a sample. Carefully, using toilet paper to avoid contamination. Then he slid it into his pocket and left.

Ackerman was at his desk. Reading paperwork, a half-eaten bagel in one hand. He looked up as Joe approached.

"Everything alright?" he asked.

"Just fine."

"Where've you been?"

"Nowhere. That Bob's report?"

"Yeah. You look like shit, by the way."

"Show me the page about the hair dye."

"What?"

Joe snatched the report from Ackerman's hands and flicked through it. His partner watched him, chewing on his late breakfast. After a couple of moments, Joe flattened the paper on the desk and tapped it.

"She's a brunette but dyes it blonde."

"Yeah?"

"Christ, she was right in front of us this whole time."

"Who was?"

Joe fell back into his chair. "It's Sarah Miller, Brian."

"Ethan's foster mom?"

"Think about it. She's connected to all this. Somehow, she is. That kid, the teddy bear, it's all connected, and she's part of it. How long ago you think that farmstead burned down?"

Ackerman set his bagel aside. "Alright, slow down now, partner. What're you thinking?"

"I'm thinking that's where it started. The kid and the bears. I'd bet your breakfast that's where she came from as well."

"I'd bet it too, it's a terrible bagel."

"I'm serious here."

"I can tell."

"What does anyone know about her?" Joe asked.

"You talked to the priest?"

Joe shook his head. "Father Brading took her in to help look after that kid. He's a goddamn charity, more interested in doing God's work than running background checks." He leaned forward. "She's new in town. She looks after a kid who has items from murder scenes. She dyes her hair."

Ackerman lifted his hat, scratched at his head, his face screwed up in thought. "I think you're reaching."

"I'm not, I'm telling you—"

"You want to bring her in based on what? Fact she dyes her hair? So does half the town."

"It's more than a hunch. I think she spiked my drink last night."

"You met her for a *drink?*"

Joe reached into his pocket. "I've got a hair sample I want Bob to run."

Ackerman raised his hands. "Easy now. Whose hair sample? Sarah Miller's?"

"I just took it from her bathroom."

"You get a warrant for that?"

"Course not."

"Then it's inadmissible."

"What if it's a match, Brian?"

"Doesn't matter. It's *inadmissible.*"

Joe waved his hand through the air. "Let's cross that particular bridge when we get to it, alright?" He got up and headed for the stairs.

Ackerman fell into step beside him. "And you talk about Lemire and Harris breaking the rules."

"This is different."

"Bullshit it's different."

"You ever hear of the greater good?"

"I'm sure that's what they tell themselves at night, too."

Joe stopped and turned on his partner. "Enough. If I'm wrong, then you don't have to worry, because this is all baseless and I'm clutching at straws. Only reason you're worried is you think there's a chance I'm right."

"I'm worried because I don't want to see you going down this path. I've seen too many good cops get lost down it."

"You really think I'm a good cop?"

"Oh, screw you."

"Let's just see what Bob says. Then we'll revisit this conversation."

Ackerman glared at him. "We *will* revisit this, Joe. I promise you that."

Chapter Forty-One

It was closer to lunch by the time Joe got any breakfast. Even though he hadn't eaten for over twelve hours, he wasn't hungry. He sat on the bank of the reservoir, ass in the dirt, and chewed on a pastry that tasted of nothing.

He'd left the hair sample with Bob. Asked him to check it on the side, as a favor. A blood sample for the tox boys too, but Bob had warned that might take a couple of days. The hair he could do today. Joe left strict instructions for him to page as soon as he'd had the chance to look it over. *Priority one*, Joe had called it as he handed it over. Like he was some bullshit army general. *This intel is priority one, soldier.*

It was the first time he'd been back to the lake since the day they'd found David Richardson at its shore. Just over a week had passed, and it felt like Cooper had undergone some sort of change in that time. A metamorphosis. Course, he'd always known it could do that. Anyone who grew up here did. Right now the water was clear blue and inviting, but it wasn't always. At times it seemed like the reservoir was filled with oil. Thick, nauseous stuff that made you wonder how you could ever have swum in it.

And it wasn't just the water. It was the people, the birds, the weeds that grew along the sides of the streets. Cooper was always shifting, adjusting itself, rolling over in an attempt to go back to sleep. Sometimes it threw up something nice—a warm night and a naked girl—but mostly it threw up something worse. Dead children, human ugliness. He thought of Holly Williams again, a woman who had plagued his thoughts ever since the start of this case. Thought of her sitting in Kansas City like he was now, staring out at the dark water. Her thoughts churning. Loading her pockets with nearby rocks. He picked up a handful of them, weighing them in his palm. He wondered how many it would have taken to keep her under. What was it Steve Purcell had said to him? *Life's little quirks.*

Only in Cooper, Steve.

He tossed the remainder of his breakfast into the brown paper bag by his feet. Picked up the coffee and took a long drink. The gentle breeze rolled over his bare arms, rippled across the water's surface. He kept thinking about last night. Flickers of memory coming through like strobe lighting. Someone helping him into his apartment. Someone banging on the door. A cocktail, bright green. She'd called it a Last Word.

He wondered what Cathy was doing. Packing, maybe. He wondered about the money, too, pictured it still in its briefcase, tucked away at the bottom of her closet or slid under the bed. Two hundred grand wasn't a fortune, but it was a lot, certainly enough to buy her some time. And maybe time was the most important thing right now. Time to get out of here, time to work out what she wanted to do. Time to get her life back on track, to buy back a little of all that time she'd lost sitting next to Frank.

He knew he could never leave this place. No matter how much money someone gave him, no matter if it was a million dollars. This town was in his blood. It fed him and it poisoned him, and he lived off it and grew sicker and stronger every day. Cooper changed, and he along with it.

The sun was just cresting its peak when Bob paged. Joe dropped his empty cup in the bag and headed back to his car. Ten minutes later he was at a payphone.

"I ran your hair through a comparison microscope," Bob said. He always did like to show off. "It allows me to view both hairs at a microscopic level simultaneously."

"Sounds great. What did you find?"

"I can't definitively say that they're the same, Joe."

"Uh-huh. What *can* you say?"

Bob let out a breath. "I can say that the unknown hair exhibits certain characteristics that are similar to the known hair. Now, it's not enough for an absolute identification, but I would be extremely surprised to find two different individuals whose hair shares the same microscopic features."

Joe squeezed the receiver. "Thanks, Bob."

"If you want to be conclusive, I'd recommend a DNA analysis. It'll take about six weeks or so. I can try and put a rush on it—"

"No, that's fine," Joe said. "There's no time for that."

Bob paused. "I don't know where you got this sample from, Joe, and frankly I'm not interested. My job is just to analyze what's in front of me."

"Well, I appreciate that."

"Just don't mess up whatever chain of custody you've got going on, alright? You keep that clean, and you'll be fine." The man paused, then added, "I hope you know what you're doing, detective."

Joe hung up and headed for his car, Bob's words ringing in his ears. Seemed like he was getting told that a lot these days. It sure was nice to see people so worried about him.

Chapter Forty-Two

Joe pulled up sharply outside her house. This time, the yellow Ford was parked on the street. Wouldn't have mattered if it wasn't. He'd have waited.

His pager buzzed—fourth time in the last half hour. Same number, too. Station really wanted to get hold of him. Joe could guess why. He should have told Bob to keep his findings to himself.

He pulled his .38, checked it over. They drilled it into you during basic training: *Never pull your firearm unless you are prepared to kill someone.* Too many movies showed the cop going for the leg shot. *Aim for the chest*, they'd been taught. Hardest part to miss; most likely to lead to death. Before this case, only other time he'd ever pulled it had been five months ago, on that long stretch of highway. And he sure as shit hadn't been thinking about going for the leg shot then. He slid it back into his holster. Sure as shit wasn't thinking about it now, either.

He popped open his door. Got two steps when Ackerman pulled in ahead of him, dust flying. The guy leapt from his car and ran over, one hand on his hat.

"You need to come with me," Ackerman barked. "Captain knows about the hair sample."

"I figured. He send you to bring me in?"

"I came on my own. He doesn't know you're here."

"I'm not waiting for Harris to find his integrity, Brian. Purcell's innocent. She'll prove it, even if I—"

"What? Beat it out of her? You going to drag her out of her house and take her in?"

"If I have to."

"Harris is pissed, Joe. No way he doesn't know you spoke with Marchenko. He's not going to have your back on this one and you know it. We don't do this right, he'll bury us."

"So what's your grand plan?"

"Gonzalez called. He tracked down Lisa Reynolds."

Joe took half a step back. When he spoke, it was almost a whisper. "Where?"

"Someplace over in Scottsbluff. Let's go pick her up, right now, you and me. Present a case so watertight Harris *has* to back it. Hell, let the *Tribune* publish if he doesn't, Lemire and his fancy suit be damned."

Joe ran the numbers in his head. Scottsbluff was nearly three hours away. It was time he didn't want to lose, but maybe Ackerman was right. Last thing he wanted was for this to get tossed by some public defender six months from now. Or worse, to end up in the trunk of a car on its way to the scrapyard on his captain's orders.

So he went with Ackerman. Kept his eyes on Sarah's house as they swung a U-turn and headed back across town. A heavy feeling inside him that she was slipping away, and that no matter what they did next, it was the wrong move.

Chapter Forty-Three

Gonzalez sat in the back seat with the window down the whole way to Scottsbluff, on account of his overheating. He spoke nonstop and cracked pistachio nuts, coughing every time he swallowed too many. Joe watched him in the wing mirror and counted down the mile markers.

"It's easy to look at me and think, *There's someone who hates his town*," Gonzalez said to no one in particular. "But it's actually the opposite. I love my town. Cooper's not perfect, don't get me wrong. It's got issues, same as any other place. And that's exactly why I'm such a perfectionist. Because if I don't try and hold Cooper to account, lift it up to a higher standard, then who will?"

Joe closed his eyes and prayed that Ackerman would drive faster.

Gonzalez coughed again. A wet, hacking sound that made Joe's skin crawl. The reporter tossed another handful of pistachio shells out the window. "You know, people say the temperature has started to drop, but I really don't feel it," he said, running a sleeve over his forehead.

He'd traced Lisa Reynolds to an auto shop using an old PI that the *Tribune* paid a couple hundred dollars a month in beer money. Guy was a retired cop, but Joe wasn't too worried about him. Far as the PI was concerned, he was just doing his usual bit for Gonzalez.

"When we get there," Ackerman said to the back seat, "you let us do the talking, alright?"

"Now, Brian," said Gonzalez, leaning forward between them both, "I seem to recall we had an arrangement. Or are you planning on reneging on this one as well? There's always another story I can write here, remember."

"You can write whatever story you want."

"You promised I could interview her."

"So long as she wants to speak with you, sure."

Gonzalez nodded and sat back. There were a few blessed moments of silence, and then the rustle and crunch started up again.

"You think you can give it a rest with the nuts?" Joe said, turning in his seat. "You sound like a goddamn circus elephant."

"I have low blood sugar, detective. You want to take me to the hospital instead?"

"Oh, happily."

Gonzalez rolled his eyes. "You're a broken record, you know that? Maybe if you didn't spend so much of your time focusing on people like me and tried to actually catch whoever killed those families, we'd all be able to get on with our lives."

"If you think I'm going to spend this drive being lectured by a—"

"Jesus!" Ackerman yelled, pounding his fist on the horn. "I have had it with you two! Now both of you keep your mouths shut until we get there." He reached over and flicked on the radio. Country music. Gonzalez started to protest and Ackerman turned it up louder.

Joe let his head fall back against his seat. He closed his eyes. It was going to be a long drive.

◆ ◆ ◆

The auto shop stood in a small industrial park. Shuttered buildings scattered around a near-empty parking lot. Place looked half-deserted. Joe wondered if this wasn't a colossal waste of their time.

"Simpson Auto," Gonzalez said, reading the faded sign that hung above the shop. "This is the place."

"Alright, come on," Ackerman said, killing the engine. "Now, remember, we're out of our jurisdiction here. So we need to play this gently. We push her too hard and we've got nothing."

"Or worse," said Joe, "Harris gets a phone call from some angry police lieutenant."

Gonzalez leaned forward. "You boys didn't phone the local PD? This really is off the books."

"You think we'd have asked you for your help otherwise?"

"Well, *excuse me* for trying to help, detective."

"I give up," Ackerman muttered, climbing out.

Inside, the place was quiet. A couple of cars raised up on lifts; the radio playing in one corner.

"Hello?" Ackerman called out. "Anyone home?"

A burly man in oily overalls emerged from behind a car. He wiped his hands on a dirty rag and stared at them. "Can I help you?"

"We're looking for Lisa Reynolds," Ackerman said, flashing his badge. "Just need to ask her a couple questions. She in today?"

The man tossed the rag onto a bench. "What's all this about?"

"I'd rather discuss the matter with Ms. Reynolds."

"She's my employee."

"And it's her business, all the same."

Joe glanced between them. Ackerman held his ground, an amiable smile plastered on his face. The man eventually grunted and jerked his head. "This way."

The three of them followed him through a short corridor and into a back office. A blonde-haired wisp of a woman was sitting behind a desk, scribbling in a ledger. She looked up when they entered.

"Lisa? These policemen would like to have a word with you," the man said. "Won't tell me why."

If Joe had to put a word to it, he'd probably have said that Lisa looked a little scared to see them. Course, not many were ever thrilled to see a couple of detectives roll up to their place of work. He watched her eyes dart.

"You want me to tell them to leave?" the man said, putting his hands on his hips. Acting tough, maybe a protective thing.

Lisa shook her head. "No, it's fine. Thanks though."

"You need me, just give me a yell."

"Thanks, Ryan."

The man nodded and left. Gave them all a narrowed glare as he did.

A silence settled itself on the small room. Even with Ryan gone, four people packed the place pretty tight. Joe stood awkwardly against one wall.

"Thanks for taking the time to speak with us," Ackerman said. "I'm Detective Ackerman, this is my partner, Detective Finch."

"And who's he?" Lisa asked, looking at the third man.

"This is Daniel Gonzalez," Ackerman said. "He's a reporter, and he'd like to sit in on our chat if you're agreeable."

"Is . . . is that normal?"

Joe smiled, said, "Not at all. Personally, I'd ask him to leave."

Gonzalez pushed forward. "Now, listen, you want your story to be told proper—"

"I don't think I want him here."

Joe turned to Gonzalez. "You heard her. Go wait in the car."

"But we had—"

"Car. Now." Joe stepped toward him and the reporter shrank back. Glowering, he scurried out of the room.

Ackerman perched on the edge of a seat piled with papers. "I get the impression you know why we're here."

Lisa had been playing with her pen the entire time, but she put it down now. Placed her hands flat on the desk. "I might have an idea, yeah."

"It got anything to do with your time at MacFarlane's Farm?"

Joe watched her sink into herself a little. Relief. Some shit, it was a physical weight on you.

"I always figured this day would come," she said. "What do you want to know?"

Joe pulled out his notebook. "Tell us about the farm," he said.

When it came down to it, she didn't want to talk. Not at first. Joe got it: three people dead and a building on fire. He wouldn't have wanted to talk to the cops about it either.

"We're not interested in whatever you did," Ackerman said, trying his best to relax her. "Or whatever you think you should have reported at the time, alright? We just need to know what happened."

Lisa glanced at the doorway one last time and nodded. When she started, her voice was slow, faltering. But it got easier. She told them about the community, about the long season she'd spent there. She told them about living off the land and hunting animals for dinner. About the freedom they'd got by unhooking themselves from the rest of society.

"It was a nice place," she said, her eyes cast down. "That's what I thought when I was there."

"And after you left?" Joe asked.

"Part of me is still there," she said. "I think it might always be there."

Ackerman said softly, "Tell us about Rudy."

Lisa smiled and leaned back. "Rudy was . . . complicated. He had this way about him, like he would explain something in such a manner that you would listen, and afterward you would wonder how you could ever have thought it was anything different. Like he could tell you to jump off a roof and you'd ask yourself, 'Why didn't *I* think of that?'" She shook her head. "*That* was Rudy."

When she spoke about Rudy, it was like how people speak about an old lover. Wistful, a little sad. Like all you ever had was good times. She told them about how she'd met Rudy on her first day at the farm. How it had seemed to her and all the others like it was going to be the start of some great adventure.

Ackerman glanced at his notebook. "Who's Kyle?"

Lisa's face flushed slightly at the name. "Kyle . . . We met Kyle in town, he brought us to the farm."

"*We?*"

"Me and Dianne. But . . ."

Ackerman waited patiently.

She let out a sigh. "They give you these new names when you join, alright? Like, you're leaving every part of your old life behind. When I was there, I wasn't Lisa Reynolds anymore. I was Katherine. Dianne was Louise. It . . . it sounds stupid when you say it out loud."

"What was Kyle's real name?"

Lisa shrugged. "I didn't know anyone else's."

"You said Kyle brought you to the farm," Joe said. "From Cooper?"

"Yeah. Me and Dianne, we were just passing through, looking for work. We met him in a bar."

"What was he like?"

"He was the guy that all the girls had a crush on. You know—tall, blond, broad-shouldered. Like a quarterback or something."

"Were you involved with him?"

"Me and Kyle? No. I mean, sure, we had fun sometimes. We'd drive into town, go to the movies. Park by the lake and get drunk, fool around." She went quiet. "He had a serious girl in Cooper, though."

Ackerman leaned forward. "Who?"

"Said her name was Emily. People said she was having his kid, but you never know with people. They like to talk."

Joe thought of Emily Richardson, of four-month-old Jacob. Wondered if Sarah had targeted them because of Kyle. To spite him maybe, even though the guy was already dead.

"What about Francine?" Ackerman asked.

"She was another girl at the farm. She had a kid, Arthur. She was nice, kind of a mother figure, I guess. A lot of the girls didn't like her, thought she was trying to ruin their vibe or whatever."

"We went out there, my partner and I," Ackerman said. "Place has seen better days."

"That would be the fire," Lisa said.

Joe flipped to a new page. "I think you better tell us about that."

And she did. Spoke for nearly a half hour about it, no stopping. Like she'd pulled the plug in a bathtub filled with everything she'd been carrying around, and now it came out in a rush. *The accident*, she kept calling it. *Francine had an accident in the fields*. Her leg. Lots of bleeding.

"What was she doing in the fields?" Ackerman asked.

"Leaving," Lisa said. "Trying to."

She told them how Rudy had tried to save Francine—Kyle, too. She told them she didn't know what had happened in the dining hall, but there had been screams and gunshots, and then when they'd finally gotten inside the place was on fire.

"There was so much smoke," she said quietly. "You couldn't tell who was there and who was safe. We didn't know who was dead until we'd managed to put the fire out."

Joe reached into his pocket and pulled out a bunch of photos. Slid one face up across the desk. It was the photo of Ethan he'd copied from Sarah's album.

"That kid you mentioned," he said. "Francine's son. Arthur. This him?"

"That's him."

"You know anything about the teddy bear he's holding?"

"Sure. We used to make them. Made a lot of stuff like that. Sold them to raise money."

He showed her the second photo. James Colfer's mugshot. "What about this guy?"

Lisa stared at it for a while. Joe saw tears prickle at the edges of her eyes. "That's Patrick," she said. "He disappeared the night of the fire. Arthur, too. Do you know what happened to them?"

"James—Patrick—he's dead," Joe said. "Got himself shot the night he left." He decided not to tell her who had done the shooting.

"Oh God," she said. "What about Arthur?"

"Kid's being looked after by the church. Got a new caregiver." He slid over a third photo. Sarah Miller. "This woman."

There was an icy silence as Lisa looked at the picture. "That's Laura," she said. "She had a bad time at the farm."

"Oh yeah? Why's that?"

"Some people . . . I guess they just have a way about them. Like, everything they ever do, you just know is going to end bad. I don't mean she brought it on herself—"

"Brought what on herself?"

"She was there, the night it all happened. She was in the dining hall, with Rudy and Kyle and Francine and Patrick. And all I know is that after the flames died down, Rudy, Kyle, and Francine were dead, and Laura and Patrick were gone. Now, you tell me Patrick died later that night? So that means Laura is the only one left. If you want to know what happened, only she can tell you."

Chapter Forty-Four

Joe and Ackerman half-ran back through the auto shop toward the car.

"We got Sarah Miller and the kid, at the farm," Joe said, flicking through his notebook. "Same place the bears from the crime scenes were made. We know she's involved in at least three deaths up there. Off the record, we can place her at the second house. Brian—"

"I know, I know," Ackerman said. "It's enough. Let's bring her in."

Gonzalez was waiting for them at the car. He was holding his bag of pistachio nuts. Raised his arms wide when he saw them.

"I just want to make myself clear—" he started.

Joe grabbed the bag of nuts and tossed them. "Get in the car," he growled. "And if you say one more word I will fucking shoot you, understand?"

Gonzalez looked over at Ackerman. "You hear that, detective?"

Ackerman climbed in and started her up. "All I hear is the sound of someone walking to the nearest train station."

The reporter threw himself into the back of the car. Joe gave his partner an impressed side-glance as he buckled up. Grabbed the radio out of instinct before tossing it back on its holder. This far out, they wouldn't reach Cooper PD Dispatch. The car revved loudly and they left the curb with a screech.

Ackerman said, "Something wrong?"

"Just feel like this is taking too long."

"You want to stop at a payphone? Get unis to bring her in?"

Joe shook his head. "I get Dispatch involved, word gets out. Without us pressing, Harris and Lemire might let her go. She'll vanish."

Ackerman reached into the footwell and tossed the blue light on the dash. It was getting dark now, and the twirling bulb lit up the quiet highway in a never-ending loop. The car roared as he pressed his foot down. "Let's see if we can't shave some time off that drive," he said.

◆ ◆ ◆

In the end they made the trip in a little over two hours. When they got close enough for their radio to work, Joe called it in and requested his warrant. *By the book*, as Ackerman would say. Nothing she could later use to get out of her arrest. No forgotten Mirandas, no inadmissible evidence. Besides, once they had her they could control things. Present a case so watertight even Harris would have to see it.

They pulled up outside her house just as a couple of cruisers rolled into view. Lights on but silent, as requested. Last thing they wanted was to scare her off.

Joe turned to Gonzalez. "Stay here."

Climbing out, he checked his firearm. Waited as Ackerman did the same. They headed toward the front door as uniformed officers joined them.

Ackerman got there first. Knocked loudly. "Sarah Miller!" he bellowed. "Cooper PD. Open up!"

A couple of moments passed. Nothing. Ackerman glanced at one of the officers and jerked his head. Stepped back as the man moved forward clutching a Halligan bar; slid one end into the doorjamb and levered the lock clean off. The door swung inward.

Joe pushed inside. "Sarah Miller!" He reached for the light switch and flicked it on. Stopped.

The place was empty.

Not just of people, but of everything. Bare shelves where he'd seen books just eight hours ago. Pictures gone from the walls, plants from the windowsills. She'd even taken the television set.

"No," Joe whispered. "No, no, no . . ."

He moved through the room and into the hallway, Ackerman and the officers swarming behind him. Everywhere was the same. Traces of her: a piece of clothing, an empty shampoo bottle. And there, in the corner of her bedroom, a stuffed bear. Joe stared at it.

"She's gone," he said quietly.

A flash bloomed, flooding the room with a crackle of light. Joe turned. Gonzalez was lowering his camera. He was across the hall but Joe crossed it in three strides, knocking the reporter backward and pinning him against the wall.

"You piece of shit, I'm going to *end* you," he snarled, snatching the camera from him. "You hear me? Get the hell out of here."

He threw Gonzalez with a squeal toward the front door.

"I need my camera!" the man protested.

"Allow me," Joe said, and stamped on the camera until it had cracked and shattered.

Gonzalez roared, his face reddening. "This is suppression!" he shouted. "This is censorship!"

Joe took one step toward him and the man backed up, turned, and marched for the exit. His cries of "police brutality" could be heard all the way to the street. Joe stared after him, his anger fading. He could only imagine what tomorrow's headlines were going to say.

Chapter Forty-Five

Father Brading didn't know where she'd gone either. Last time he'd seen her was at yesterday's mass. "She helped collect the hymn books after we were done," he said, giving that off-distance stare someone gives when they can't quite believe how easily they've been fucked. "I had no idea she was planning to leave."

"Neither did we, Father," Ackerman said.

Outside the church, Joe paced around in a tight little circle. A habit he'd picked up from the captain.

"You alright?" Ackerman asked him.

Joe stopped and glared at him.

Ackerman nodded. "Stupid question, I know."

"She was right here, Brian. She was *right here*."

"We'll get her."

"Will we? Because she did a pretty good job of living under our noses already. You ask me? She's a hundred miles away and counting."

His pager buzzed. He glanced at the number.

"Harris?" his partner asked.

"Paged me three times now. He's going to be pissed."

Ackerman grunted. "Guy's been pissed since day one on this case. What's another screw-up for the collection."

Joe stared at his pager. "I should have called ahead from Scottsbluff. Should have stuck her in the bullpen while we came back. Took our chances she'd get turned loose. At least then it wouldn't have been on my head."

"Hey, it's not on your head. We handled it together, remember? Made decisions the best we could."

For a moment Joe didn't say anything. Then he looked at his partner and said, "This would never have happened if you hadn't stopped me bringing her in this morning."

"What?"

"At least then it would have been on Harris and Lemire if she'd got away. Now it's on *me*."

Ackerman started to speak but an officer shouted at them both, "Detectives! I've got Captain Harris on the radio. He wants to speak with you."

Both men turned and glared at him. The officer shrank back slightly.

"I'll talk to him," Joe said.

"No, I will," Ackerman said, sighing. "I'm lead. Let him take it out on me." He glanced back with a sad smile as he slid on his hat. "Don't worry, I'm sure there'll be plenty left over."

It was dark when Joe arrived home. He let the car shudder into silence and sat for a while, staring into the night. The street stretched out ahead of him, deserted and badly lit. A road he knew well, and yet tonight it might have led him somewhere completely different.

He'd never seen Cooper like this before. The desolation, the emptiness. In a way it was comforting to know it could still surprise you. For it to show you a face you didn't realize it had.

Walking to his apartment door, the November chill crawled across his skin. It was going to be a cold month. A harsh course correction from their late summer.

Inside, he kicked off his shoes and dumped his jacket. Emptied his pockets on the coffee table and collapsed on the sofa. He was so tired. His body ached all over, his broken fingers throbbed like they might burst. A weariness that had moved in and paid up to the end of the month.

His mind drifted. Back to Sarah Miller's house, her bare house. The captain had been pissed. Joe had listened to him ranting at Ackerman from her front door. Whole damn unit could hear him. Squawking through the car radio, Ackerman barely paying attention. It didn't really matter anyway. Lemire would spin it, sell it to the papers as a win. *Serial killer driven out of town.* It would be messy, but it would be enough; his next term was secured. Harris's too, no doubt. Wasn't that the point of being in the pocket of men like Anatoly Marchenko?

Joe rocked to his feet with a groan, his back popping. Pulling at his shirt, he stretched as he padded out of the living room. Patted the punching bag affectionately as he passed by. A lifetime since he'd felt energized enough to actually use the thing.

"Leo!" he called as he moved into the kitchen. "Come on, pal, dinner time."

He opened the fridge, peered inside. It wasn't like he was really that hungry anyhow.

Leo's dog food took up most of the cupboards. He grabbed a bag, poured a scoop into Leo's bowl. Caught a whiff of himself on the way down. Sniffing at his shirt, he winced. Dinner could wait until breakfast. He needed a shower and then some sleep.

The answering-machine light didn't catch his attention until his second trip past it. Red light flashing soft in the dark. He hit the button as he pulled off his shirt. A shrill beep and the sound of tape rewinding. A heavy clunk, and then: "Hello, Joe."

He froze. Sarah Miller's voice filled his apartment. He turned, slowly, and stared at the machine.

"By the time you get this message, I'm sure you'll have realized that I've gone. Long gone. Unless I miscalculated, of course." She laughed gently down the line. "Maybe I'm sitting in a jail cell right now, orange jumpsuit, the whole nine yards. Wouldn't *that* be embarrassing?"

Joe patted his pockets for his notebook. Force of habit. It was in his jacket, on the sofa.

"Anyway, I just wanted to say goodbye. I'm sure you'll get some shit for all this. You really did make a mess of everything in the end, didn't you? But do you see now? This is what I wanted to show people. Not you, not in particular. People like you. The so-called protectors. The leaders and the fathers and the policemen . . . We look to them to shield us from the truth of the world—because the truth is that it's an awful place out there, Joe. You know that, you've seen it now."

She was rambling, her voice getting faster, more excited.

"And what do people do when they get a little bit of power? When we ask them to look after us? They *abuse* it. They twist it, they take it for themselves. They don't give a shit about us. And don't tell me I'm wrong. There is nothing worse in this world than a powerful man. And there is nothing they fear more than a powerful woman. And that's what I am. I'm the balance. I showed you—these protectors? They're all phony. They can't protect their families, they can't protect themselves. They can't even protect their fucking *dogs*."

Joe's chest tightened. He turned, moved through the apartment. "Leo?" he shouted. Behind him, Sarah's voice continued, ranting still, her words lost. "Leo!"

He found him then. A small bundle lying on the floor, tucked away in the corner of the living room. He was on his side. Curled tight into a ball, his eyes closed.

"Leo . . ."

Joe reached out and touched him. The dog was cold, his fur already hardening. He pulled Leo toward him, ran his hand through his bristly hair. Shook him gently, held his face, and when that didn't work he hugged him close to his chest. He could feel the chill spread across his rib cage. A physical pain. "Come on, pal, it's alright, it's going to be alright."

He sat there for a long while. Hunched forward, cradling Leo's little body. Sarah's voice finally clicked off into silence. Leo's fur was wet now, tears were still rolling down Joe's face, and still he kept on sitting, murmuring about how it was going to be alright, over and over, like he couldn't stop, like if he just kept on saying it maybe it would come true.

Chapter Forty-Six

It rained the day they buried Frank.

Joe stood under an umbrella. They all did. Wasn't a big turn-out—funny, the people who forgot about you when you dropped off the earth for five months. Most of the mourners were patrol officers. Guys that had known him—probably some who'd just wanted the morning off. Father Brading stood at the grave and read words Joe couldn't hear. Might have been because he didn't want to hear them. It was hard to listen to someone talk about God and His wisdom when the person speaking had paid a murderer to look after a child.

It had rained the day he'd buried Leo, too. Only then, he'd not had an umbrella. Hadn't been wearing a fresh suit, either, top button done up and everything. He'd buried Leo in the backyard. In his favorite spot. Dug the hole himself, the ground soft from the rain. Small mercies and all that.

He'd stared into the shallow pit and he'd wanted to say something, some words that might be considered impressive, but after a half hour he was drenched and the words still weren't coming. He buried Leo with his favorite brown duck. Packed it into the cardboard box next to him.

That had been nearly a week ago. He'd spent most of the time since feeling sorry for himself. Pushing paper around his desk at the station; sitting numb on his sofa at home. All that time to think. Memories resurfacing, ones he didn't want to relive but couldn't bring himself to push away. Papering over one pain with another just didn't seem to make much sense anymore. So now, when he blinked, he didn't see the Richardsons, didn't see Holly Williams slipping under the dark water. Now he saw Nicky, he saw his mother.

Which was maybe how he'd found himself taking a personal day and driving the eight hours to Minneapolis. Didn't even really know why he was doing it until he was, and even then he couldn't be sure. Joe hadn't thought about visiting his father since the day William Finch had walked out on him. Maybe this case had stirred up shit he couldn't put back in the box. Maybe he had to work through it, somehow.

His father lived in an apartment block in a busy neighborhood. Place couldn't have been more different from Cooper. It was a true city. More lights, more noise, more people. The perfect place to blend into the background if you wanted to.

Which was exactly what William Finch had done. Worked a simple nine-to-five in a pharmacy, kept his past to himself, lived a solitary life. Standing there, watching from across the shop floor as William served a customer, Joe wondered if his father had found some kind of peace in fading away.

Their eyes had met over the customer's shoulder. His father's hands suddenly shaking hard enough to drop the bottle of pills he'd been holding.

His father had always said that what his mom did took strength, but to Joe, all she'd done was leave. He'd hated her for it—hated him for defending her. Then later, when his father vanished, he'd hated him for that, too.

But time had given Joe a perspective he wished he'd had sooner. His mom had left him, sure, but she'd also left his father. Dealing with the fallout, all that paperwork. Emotional, financial. For his faults, William Finch had sheltered Joe from it.

"I go on break in fifteen," his father had said to him. Quietly, like he couldn't quite catch his breath. Or maybe he just didn't want people to hear. "There's a coffee shop across the street. We could talk."

"Sure," Joe had said. "That'd be nice."

◆ ◆ ◆

And it had been. Driving home after, he'd wondered if maybe they'd gotten some closure from it. That's what everybody wanted, right, with stuff like this? Might be he'd managed to get himself a little. Or at least the beginnings of it, the first steps toward it. Too much time had passed to hope for any real relationship, they both knew that. There was no point getting tearful over that loss. It had died long ago.

Today at Frank's burial was similar. Removed. The way he'd gone out, everyone had likely done their grieving for him already. Months ago, probably. They'd spent their anguished nights and they'd sat by his bedside. In some ways, today was almost a relief.

Afterward, he stood next to Cathy as the small crowd filed out of the cemetery.

"I'm leaving," she said.

"When?"

"Soon as this is over."

"Good," he said.

He hugged her, wished her well. Told her he hoped he never saw her again. She smiled at that. When he turned to leave, he found Ackerman standing there.

"Can we talk?" his partner asked.

"Later."

"Joe—"

"I'm tired, Brian. I haven't slept much the last week."

"I know it's not how either of us wanted this to end—"

"I don't want to hear it. Not today." Joe glared at him. "Far as I'm concerned, Leo's dead because I didn't act. But I've learned my lesson, for what it's worth."

"What lesson?"

Joe pulled his collar up. "I'll never wait again. If I can put someone away, I'll do it. If I have to plant evidence, I'll do it. Whatever it takes to keep this town safe."

Ackerman didn't say anything for a long while. Then he nodded and left.

Joe was just about at his car when a shadow fell across his path. He turned and saw a man dressed in sweatpants and a hoodie standing there. A stony face he recognized, his broken fingers twitching. The man gestured across the street to a parked sedan.

"Mr. Marchenko would like you to come with us," he said.

"Do we really have to do this today?"

The man shrugged. "I'm sure Mr. Marchenko can find other ways of retrieving his money." He looked past Joe's shoulder. Joe turned and saw Cathy, standing by Frank's grave.

"Alright, fine."

As he followed the man to the black car, he felt the eyes of the crowd on him. Ackerman, watching from behind his windshield.

Harris at the cemetery gates. Inside the sedan, Anatoly Marchenko greeted him with a corkscrew smile and gestured to the seat next to him.

"Please, detective, come in out of the rain. We have much to discuss."

Epilogue

The bar here is quiet.

It's a comfortable quiet. It's not deserted, and that's the distinction. Stacey's was deserted. Stacey's was near dead, especially at the end. Numbers on a Friday night so low they made you wonder how many weeks the place had left.

This place is different. A quiet like it's *supposed* to be quiet. Mood lighting and table service and piano music from little speakers buried in the walls. Joe doesn't need to go piss, but he knows if he did there'd be a neat pile of those one-time-use linen towels and a wicker basket to dump them in when you were done drying.

He sits at the bar. Unwraps his scarf. A bartender in a goddamn vest asks him how his day's going.

"Pretty good," he says. "The last couple months have been rough, but things are looking better today."

"Well, I am glad to hear that," she says, and of course she doesn't mean it but she sounds like maybe she does and that's enough for Joe.

"This is a nice place," he says. "You should see the bars I usually drink at."

"Oh yeah?"

"This sort of place wouldn't last two seconds where I'm from."

The bartender smiles. "And where's that?"

"Ah, you wouldn't know it," Joe says. "It's a smudge of a town about three states over."

"Well, I sure hope it's warmer than here. We're not used to all this snow."

He orders a beer. Some local stuff he's never heard of before. The bartender pours it in a fancy glass with curved sides. It's not really his thing but he tells her it's nice and he drinks it all the same.

"So, what brings you all the way out to Kentucky?" she asks him.

"Business," Joe says.

He stays at the bar for a while. Until he's tapped out a cigarette and smoked the whole thing. Until he's sure. It's important to be sure, he knows this. Been a couple of times he'd been sure before, thought he'd been sure. It was hard, sometimes, to take the time.

But he takes it now. Then steps into the hallway leading to the john and places a call on the payphone.

Back at the bar, he pulls out his notebook, flicks through it. Finds the list. Lists of cities, of towns. Lists of street names and apartment numbers. Each of them with a line scored through.

He finishes his beer, pulls his pen from his breast pocket, and circles *Louisville*.

"You know what?" he says as the bartender passes by. "I think I'd like a cocktail."

"Well, sure thing. What can I get you?"

He lists the ingredients. Gin, green chartreuse, maraschino liqueur, fresh lime. He stumbles on some of the pronunciations and they laugh together. It is a foreign sound.

Joe watches her as she mixes the drink. When it goes green, something slithers in his stomach. He reaches into his back pocket and pulls out his wallet. A photo of Leo as a puppy falls onto the bar. He puts it back.

"There you are," she says, and slides the drink across to him. "How does that look?"

"It looks perfect," Joe says. "How much do I owe you?"

"Oh, it's all on a tab, you can pay when you're leaving."

"I'm leaving now."

The bartender looks confused. "What about your drink?"

There's a commotion outside. Cars pulling up, doors slamming. Through the frosted windows of the bar, Joe can see cruiser lights spinning red and blue.

"It's not for me," Joe says. He points to the corner of the room. "You see that redhead over there? In the black dress?"

"Yeah?"

"Tell her Joe Finch owed her a drink."

The bartender is halfway there when the officers walk in, but they come in quiet. Not the kind of place you're in a hurry to make a fuss in. Joe barely sees them. His eyes are on the redhead. He wonders when she'll know. When she'll be sure, like he was sure. When she sees the drink, maybe. The bright green bringing it all back. Or maybe when the bartender delivers the message. When she hears his name again.

At first he had planned to stay and watch it happen. A part of him needed to see it, to witness her being led away. To a waiting patrol car, to a prison cell. Wanted to look her in the eyes, one last time.

But now the moment is here, and all Joe wants to do is leave.

He is moving already. Past the officers, their voices raised now and their handguns drawn, pushing open the door into the cold, pulling his scarf close to ward off the snow. Behind him he leaves chaos. The jumble of squad cars parked haphazardly across the wide street, dumped so quickly that they block traffic. People lean on their horns, they stare through frozen windows at the woman with the red hair, and Joe is surprised to find he doesn't wonder what they see. He leaves it all behind and he moves forward, to home, to Cooper.

ACKNOWLEDGMENTS

Writing this second book was a very different experience to the first. With *Welcome to Cooper*, I'd spent years working on it, producing countless drafts and refusing to share it with anyone until it was (in my eyes, at least) close to perfect. I had none of that luxury with *Follow Me to the Edge*. Second albums are always difficult—less time, more pressure to hit a certain quality. There's no way it would have been completed without the help of others.

First up—my editor at Thomas and Mercer, Victoria Pepe. You've been absolutely fantastic to work with (on both books!), really supportive, and I'm so grateful for all your help. Same goes to Dolly and the rest of the team. I never expected a publishing company to be so kind and welcoming.

The return of David Downing and his developmental editing know-how was something I was so glad of. Your ability to improve my writing and your grace in letting me take all the credit is astonishing, and I hope we continue to work together.

Thanks to my agent, Jamie, for continuing to help me navigate this new world and all your support.

Huge thanks again to Sophie and Emma for all the work you guys have done on the publicity front. Seeing my ugly mug in magazines in my local Tesco's is pretty cool, I have to admit.

Gemma and Sadie—thanks again for your amazing work fixing my wonky timelines, British-isms and generally making sure everything fits together. Knowing you guys will help smooth over the joins between drafts is so reassuring.

Marco—cheers for being my beta reader again, and for your invaluable feedback.

Thanks once again to my wife, Lucy, for letting me bounce ideas off her and for reading countless pages for her thoughts. And finally, thanks to our son, Sami, for being the coolest little guy around, but mainly for staying asleep for the last three hours to let me finish this edit.

ABOUT THE AUTHOR

Tariq is a solicitor based in Edinburgh, where he also runs WriteGear, a company that sells high-quality notebooks for writers, and co-hosts WriteGear's podcast *Page One*. He had no formal writing training or consultation prior to writing his first thriller, *Welcome to Cooper*. This is his second novel.